ALSO BY CAT DEVON

The Entity Within
Sleeping with the Entity
Love Your Entity

Tall, Dark and Immortal

Cat Devon

St. Martin's Paperbacks

This is a work of fiction. All of the characters, organizations, and events portrayed in this novel are either products of the author's imagination or are used fictitiously.

TALL, DARK AND IMMORTAL

Copyright © 2015 by Cathie L. Baumgardner.

All rights reserved.

For information address St. Martin's Press, 175 Fifth Avenue, New York, NY 10010.

ISBN: 978-1-250-05915-4

Printed in the United States of America

St. Martin's Paperbacks edition / September 2015

St. Martin's Paperbacks are published by St. Martin's Press, 175 Fifth Avenue, New York, NY 10010.

10 9 8 7 6 5 4 3 2 1

To my forever friends who are the guardian angels in my life—De, JK and FK, Susan, Jimmie, Margaret, Suzette, Alison and Donna. I love you guys! And to all my readers—I am so grateful for your support!

Chapter One

"Something is wrong." Keira Turner put her hands palm down on Chicago Police Detective Alex Sanchez's desk and leaned forward. "There's been a series of thefts at area blood banks and hospitals that aren't being investigated by the authorities. I want to know what you're going to do about it."

"The first thing I'm going to do is ask you to take your hands off my desk," Alex said.

She straightened and rearranged her messenger bag across her body. As a reporter, she approached her stories with passion and intensity. For personal reasons, this one hit her particularly hard, which was why she was standing in front of this particular Chicago detective and glaring at him. Her ten-year-old godchild, Benji, had a rare condition that required him to get frequent blood transfusions. The threat of a depleted blood supply was a matter of extreme concern for Keira. But that wasn't the only reason she was here.

She'd rushed right over to the police station from the trendy press luncheon regarding the city's upcoming Taste of Chicago event she'd been required by her editor to attend. Glancing down at her favorite red skirt and cheerful floral top, she wished she'd worn something less feminine and more kick-ass. But she hadn't wanted to take the time to change clothes before confronting Alex Sanchez. Instead, she pulled out her tough-as-nails attitude to deal with him. "That's it? I tell you that there's been a series of thefts that no one seems to be investigating and you do *nada*?"

"If that's a reference to my Latino heritage—" Alex began.

She cut him off, leaning closer again to murmur, "It's not. It's a reference to your *vampire* heritage."

That got his attention. His dark eyes met hers. "Shut up." His words were all the more threatening since they were spoken so quietly and intensely. His smile was equally dangerous. "Leave," he said. "Go home right now and don't come back."

"No way." She stood her ground. It was too late to turn and run at this point anyway. She was here on a mission and if she failed, things could get very bad for a lot of innocent people, including Benji.

Alex stood. She refused to be intimidated, but it was difficult not to be shaking in her size eight ballet flats. He was darkly sexy with his black hair tumbling over his forehead. No buzz cut for this guy. He had classic features with standout cheekbones. In his black jeans and black shirt, he didn't look like any of the other Chicago detectives that she'd spoken to over the past few days. But then he was a vampire.

She still found that fact hard to believe, but believe it she did. The past twenty-four hours had changed everything.

Yesterday at this time she'd been walking into the bank and opening a safe-deposit box with the key she'd

found among her recently deceased mother's posses-
sions. While still mourning her loss, Keira was going
through her mom's things in an attempt to clear up her
estate. As an only child with no other close relatives,
Keira was left with the task of getting things in order and
slowly clearing out her mother's condo. Her mother was
killed by a drunk driver, and going through her house
and everything she'd held dear prevented Keira from
focusing on the huge hole in her heart. She refused to
fall apart; there was just too much to do.

She wasn't sure what she expected to find in that safe-
deposit box—perhaps birth certificates and other important papers, that sort of thing. That kind of stuff was
in there, it turned out, along with an antique-looking
journal and a letter from her grandfather who'd died a
year ago.

She'd gathered everything up and taken it all home
to look over.

Keira went through the diary in a state of disbelief.
The handwritten text dated back to the days right before the Great Chicago Fire in 1871 and ended with his
death a year ago. She'd thought he was an accountant,
so surely what he'd written was mere fantasy and not
reality.

But he addressed her assumptions in his letter to her.
She had already memorized parts of it.

> *Listen, kiddo, I know you're finding this all hard to*
> *believe. I would if I were in your shoes. But it's*
> *the truth. Evil does exist. Vampires do exist. Check*
> *the records I have left. You can also verify the*
> *newspaper clippings in this journal. You'll find*
> *that my birth certificate dates back to 1841. I'm*
> *a vampire hunter and as such I have extreme*

*longevity. The fact that you're reading this now
means my time on this earth is done. Your mother
knows nothing of any of this. I slipped my journal
into her safe-deposit box without her being aware
of it. Seek out vampire Alex Sanchez in the Chicago Police Department. Trouble is coming . . .*

"Let's talk. In here," Alex said, interrupting her
thoughts as he opened the door to an interrogation room.

Keira paused. She'd done what her grandfather re-
quested. She'd researched on her own and reached the
conclusion that it was possible vampires did exist. So
here she was, mere inches away from one. The reason
she was here was twofold: both for Benji and the blood
thefts, as well as for the contents of her grandfather's
journal. She'd been up most of the night skimming the
journal's many pages and hadn't thought things through
regarding her plan of action with Alex.

To fight or to flee? She'd always been a fighter. So she
stayed and walked into the room.

"Take a seat," Alex said.

"I'd rather stand." She kept her back to the wall and
stayed near the door should she need to make a quick
exit. Who was she kidding? Like she could run from a
vampire if he wanted to stop her.

Keira had been accused of being an adrenaline junkie
in the past. She blamed that trait for her willingness to
have a private conversation with a vampire.

According to her grandfather's journal, vampires
came in various shapes and ages. Some were darkly attractive like Alex, who was even sexier than the hot
guys on a Telemundo telenovela. Others were completely
nondescript. All possessed the ability to move at freaky-

fast hyper speed. She had a snowball's chance in hell of escaping unless Alex chose to let her go.

Alex leaned his hip against the table and tossed down a yellow legal pad. "So tell me, what's your interest in this case?"

"Really?" she challenged him. "That's the first thing you're going to ask me? Not about my vampire comment?"

He remained calm. "What's your name?"

"Keira Turner."

He wrote her name on the legal pad. She noted that he was a leftie. He had artistic hands that had her wondering what it would feel like to have them on her body. That freaked her out, making her fiddle nervously with the ring on her right middle finger. The evil eye ring had been a gift on her sixteenth birthday from her grandfather after he'd taken a trip to Turkey. The red stones were rubies and the white ones, diamonds.

Her grandfather had told her that the ring would provide protection and good luck. At the time she'd asked if that meant she'd get into Northwestern as her number one college choice. Now she wondered if the ring could help save her from unfriendly vampires. As if there were friendly ones.

Alex wasn't looking very friendly at the moment. Not that he went all feral and bared his fangs at her or anything. Indeed, he had an edgy surface charm that belied the fact that he was a vampire. She still wasn't sure why her grandfather had insisted she see Alex, but his notes had indicated that it was imperative she do so.

"And your interest in this case is . . . ?" he was saying.

"You're really going to stand there and pretend this is just another case? I don't believe you," she said.

"Yet you believe I'm a vampire." His eyes glowed with anger.

"Because you *are* a vampire," she said with absolute certainty.

Alex looked at the fiery woman in front of him. He didn't have time for this shit. He had a heavy caseload as well as the issue of the stolen blood. The human officials in the police department weren't placing the latter very high on their priority list.

And now this woman walked into his police station. He could sense the rapid beat of her heart, yet she showed no other signs of fear. She couldn't be compelled or she would have left when he'd ordered her to do so. He knew from experience that humans who couldn't be compelled weren't ever completely human.

She wasn't a vampire. He inhaled deeply and analyzed her scent. Lemons. She smelled like lemons. Her dark hair barely brushed her shoulders, and her big brown eyes were much lighter than his. She was tall, curvy, and wearing a flowery top with a flirty red skirt and flats. He preferred heels on his women. Very high heels. Despite the fact that it was midsummer, her skin was pale and luminescent. So even though she wasn't one, she looked more like a vampire than he did.

"Your address?" he asked.

She bit her bottom lip. Her mouth was highlighted with a lush red lipstick that glistened in the fluorescent overhead lighting.

The flash of her white teeth nipping her own flesh made his vamp senses spring to life. Just looking at her made him go hard. He hadn't expected such an intense reaction. But there was something about her that called to him on some deep level.

Being a detective meant that Alex had to deal with more humans than the rest of his clan. Her accusation that he was a vampire was a first for him. So was his response to her. Sure, he'd seen sexier women, but this one spiked his interest. She was different . . . not in a good way but in a guaranteed-trouble kind of way.

"What's your interest in this case?" he repeated.

"I'm a reporter with *ReadIt*." She held out her press credential.

He reached for it. Their fingers touched and he felt the reverberations throughout his body. He could sense her heart rate speeding into the stratosphere.

The photo on her ID didn't do her justice. He was familiar with the online news blog. She didn't look like a force to be reckoned with but she sure acted like one.

"Are you going to address the elephant in the room?" she demanded.

Alex deliberately looked around. "I don't see any elephants."

"You know what I mean."

"I'm not a mind reader."

"No, you're a vampire."

"So you've said. And you've reached that outrageous conclusion because of a series of robberies at blood banks?"

"No."

Getting answers out of her was like pulling teeth.

"Are you denying you're a vampire?" she said.

"Are you interviewing me as a reporter? Because that's not how this works. I ask the questions and you answer them," he told her.

"Why?" she countered.

"Because I'm a cop. That's what I do." It wasn't the only thing he did. There were times when he threw the police policy and procedures manual out the window and took things into his own hands. Justice was too blind sometimes. But Alex had excellent vision.

"As a cop, you should be solving crimes like these robberies," she said.

"Have you contacted the robbery division?" he countered.

"Of course I have. They brushed me off just like you are doing right now. Well, not exactly like you, given the fact that you have powers they don't. You tried to compel me a few minutes ago. It didn't work."

"You have a vivid imagination," he drawled.

"I have proof," she said.

"I doubt that."

"My grandfather was Horace Turner. He died a year ago."

"Is that supposed to mean something to me?"

"You might know him by his other name. The Executioner."

Alex was careful not to show any reaction. Hell, yes, he knew The Executioner. He was a vampire hunter extraordinaire, the stuff legends were made of. No one had been able to pin down his identity. He'd died mysteriously last year—or so rumor had it. Even then, no name had ever been attributed to him other than The Executioner.

"He was a hunter," she said. "Have you heard of him?

Alex kept his expression blank and his mouth shut. The sins of the grandfather shouldn't be the sins of the granddaughter . . . unless she, too, was a hunter?

"I'm a reporter—" she began.

"Doing a story about vampires and blood banks?" he interrupted her to demand.

"No. Well yes, sort of. Maybe I should start at the beginning."

"That would be a good idea. But keep it short." Alex tapped his watch. "I don't have all day."

"You have eternity."

"I'm a cop," he said. "I have other cases to work on."

"Fine. There has been a sudden rash of robberies from area blood banks and hospitals. Or to be more specific, robberies in certain areas of Chicago. The Gold Coast and an area northwest of there."

She was referring to Vamptown although she didn't know it. The Gold Coast was a well-known section of the city bounded by Lake Shore Drive and North Avenue. Back in the day, millionaires built their mansions there. The area was still inhabited by some of Chicago's wealthiest citizens and deadliest vampires.

But Vamptown, an area northwest of there, remained entirely beneath the human radar. You wouldn't find it on Google Maps or anywhere else. The vampires who resided there liked it that way. They existed within one of the biggest cities in America yet no humans knew they were there.

Keira was speaking again. "Several of the locations had surveillance cameras, but the strange thing was that nothing showed up."

"You're saying the surveillance was tampered with?" Alex said.

"Vampires can't be filmed."

Alex sighed. "So we're back to that, are we? Vampire lore? Really?"

"Yes, really."

"The cameras might have been tampered with *because someone on the inside with access to them* messed with them," he said. "A human, not a vampire."

"I realize it's not proof. I'm just saying that it's one of a number of things that are very suspicious," she said.

"What else do you have?"

"Why steal blood?"

"To get attention," he said. "Which is why we aren't promoting this in the press. There have only been three robberies and one attempted robbery."

The attempted incident had taken place in Vamptown last night. Damon Thornheart, the head of security for Vamptown, had heightened the security level because of the earlier thefts.

Alex agreed with Damon's early assessment that the Gold Coast vampires were probably responsible. But they had no proof. And now they had this reporter nosing around. Even more disturbing was the fact that she was The Executioner's granddaughter.

Before Alex could devise a plan to deal with her, the door to the interrogation room swung open and Lawrence Lynch, leader of the Gold Coast vampires, stood there. Tall, but not at tall as Alex, he was the embodiment of wealth, power, and entitlement.

"You may leave now," Lynch told the police officer he'd compelled to take him to Alex. The vampire's courtesy was at odds with his ruthless manner.

"It appears we have a situation," Lynch continued before eyeing Keira. "What have we here? A little snack before lunch?"

"She was just leaving," Alex said curtly before tilting his head toward the exit.

"Without you introducing us? But that would be so rude." He smiled at Keira. "I'm Lawrence Lynch. And you are?"

"Just leaving," she said to Alex's relief.

The instant she was gone, Lynch said, "What was that about?"

"Nothing." Alex got right down to business. He had no time or desire to exchange pleasantries. "I assume you're here because of the blood thefts?"

"Naturally."

"There's nothing natural about this. Stealing blood is a direct breach of the truce between our clans," Alex said.

"I'm aware of that fact. I'm also aware of the probability that you think we are behind the incidents."

"Are you saying you aren't?"

Lynch flicked a tiny bit of lint from his Italian-tailored jacket sleeve. "I'm saying that you should consider us innocent until proven guilty."

"That's mortal law," Alex said. "Not vampire law."

"Because vampires are never innocent," Lynch said. "True enough. But we aren't responsible."

"Did I say you were?"

"Not yet. I thought I'd stop you before you did."

"So the only reason you stopped by was to tell me that the Gold Coast vamps have nothing to do with the recent thefts?" Alex said.

"I didn't say that."

Alex balled his hands into fists out of frustration. "No, you didn't. Why are you here?"

"I'd hate to see a turf war break out over this."

"Then stop the thefts," Alex told him.

"How do I know that the Vamptown clan isn't behind them? After all, you have a busy funeral home in your territory . . . or do you prefer the term *neighborhood*?"

Alex shrugged. "Either one works for me."

"Your clan could just as easily be responsible for these troubles."

"We aren't."

"Your unwillingness to share your secrets about being able to tolerate sunlight has been a thorn in our side for decades," Lynch said.

"You seem to be doing okay."

Lynch shrugged. "It's cloudy today."

"Is that what this is about?" Alex demanded. "Your envy over our ability to tolerate sunlight better than you can?"

"No. I'm merely pointing out that it would be a bad move on your part to start trouble with us over this blood issue."

"Message received," Alex said curtly. "The same goes for you and your clan."

"You'll learn soon enough that you aren't as special as you think," Lynch said cryptically. And then he was gone.

Lynch's departure at vamp speed guaranteed that no human would see him.

"What was that about?" Keira asked the minute Alex crossed the threshold of the interrogation room.

"Get back in here." He tugged her into the room once more. "What kind of stunt are you pulling, strolling in here and making wild accusations? Are you writing some tabloid story or something?"

"*ReadIt* is not a tabloid. We do the stories others refuse to cover."

"Like vampire stories?" he mocked her.

"No, not like vampire stories."

"Why did you come here?" he demanded.

"I told you. There have been several robberies from—"

Alex interrupted her. "I know all that. I don't know what your connection is other than your claim about being interested in the story as a reporter."

"Action needs to be taken," she said. "So what's next?"

"What's next is that you go home and leave this to the professionals," Alex said.

"To the professional vampires, you mean?" she countered.

Alex had to figure a way to shut her up The fact that she knew he was a vampire made her a danger to his Vamptown clan. It would be so much easier if he could just compel her, but since he couldn't he would have to come up with another plan. He could lock her up somewhere and throw away the key, but then he'd have to give her food or she'd die. Death wasn't an option; she was annoying, but that didn't warrant a death sentence. He had to figure out what was going on with this Keira Turner, this vampire hunter's next of kin. And he couldn't do that here. It was too risky given the number of people at the police station. He had to get her someplace alone, where she couldn't tell others that he was a vampire. And he had to do it fast.

"Let's go." He took her by the arm and hustled her out of the building to the fenced-in parking area in the back. The day might be cloudy but the air was thick with humidity and heat, more heat than usual even though it was early July.

"Where are we going?" she demanded.

"To your place."

"I don't usually invite strange men to my apartment," she mocked him. "But then you aren't a man. You're a vampire."

"Okay, I'll bite," he said.

"I hope not," she muttered, fingering her ring nervously.

"What makes you think I'm a vampire?"

"The facts."

"As imagined by your grandfather, right?" He headed for his black Camaro, stopping long enough to open the door for her.

His chivalrous action was noted by her. "Thanks," she said automatically before hesitating. "I am not getting in that car with you. My apartment is only a few blocks away. We can walk unless sunlight bothers you?" she asked as the clouds parted.

"Does it bother you?" he countered. "You're paler than I am."

"Blame that on my Irish ancestors."

"Or your witch ancestors." He slammed his car door shut and took her by the arm again.

"Don't be ridiculous. I don't have any witch ancestors and my apartment is the other direction," she said as he headed off at a brisk pace, leaving the parking area and heading around the corner.

"I know a shortcut," he said.

Once again, she stopped in her tracks. "I don't do shortcuts."

"Tough shit," he growled. "Let's go."

She wisely didn't argue this time. Pissing off a vampire was not a wise move. He hoped she made that realization, but she didn't stay silent for long. "Why are we going to my apartment?"

"Privacy."

"To do what?" she demanded suspiciously.

He tugged her away from a texting pedestrian who nearly rammed into her. "Idiot," he growled.

"I don't think this is a good idea," Keira said.

"Too late now. We're at your apartment building."

"I can refuse to go in."

"You could," he agreed. "But then you'd never get what you came to me for."

"Which is?"

"Answers."

She stared at him intently for a long time. He let her. He could sense what she was thinking, wondering if it was safe to trust him. It wasn't, of course, but he couldn't let her know that. He wouldn't kill her. But he could make her life very difficult if she didn't cooperate.

"Okay," she finally said and unlocked the door to the building. The tiny foyer held mailboxes for the three apartments inside. The door from the foyer into the hallway and stairs had a security system requiring a code to be entered.

Her apartment was on the third floor. He would have expected her to live in one of the many high-rises instead of this throwback building located between a Starbucks and a twenty-four-hour Korean market. She seemed pretty upscale in that flirty red skirt of hers that he was finding more attractive by the minute. And those shoes of hers, while not heels, did draw attention to the sexy length of her legs. Definitely not struggling-writer attire. He expected her apartment to be upscale as well, but instead it had a trendy boho vibe.

She opened the door and stumbled back. Upended chairs and a broken coffee table rested on piles of books, papers, and mutilated pillows disgorging their feathers. Drawers from her bedroom had been dumped out and strewn all over. A silky black bra hung from a lamp shade, which was itself tilting drunkenly to one side.

"Messy much?" he drawled as he automatically shoved her behind him while he surveyed the room. He didn't sense anyone there—human or otherwise.

"I am a very tidy person," she shot back. "Someone broke in here and did this."

She seemed more angry than scared, which some might find heroic but Alex found problematic. She was strong, yes, but he had hoped to use fear to make her compliant.

"What are you doing?" he said as she took out her cell phone.

"Calling the police."

He took the phone from her. "I *am* the police, remember?"

She glared at him. "Did you do this? Trash my place?"

"I've been with you since you walked into the police department. Do you think I can be in two places at the same time?"

"You weren't with me the entire time. I left you with that other guy . . . Lynch. Lawrence Lynch. Was he a vampire, too? Did vampires do this?"

"You really do need to stop blaming vampires for everything that goes wrong. Clearly whoever broke in here was looking for something. They left valuables like your TV. What about your computer?"

She patted the large messenger bag hanging across her body. "It's in here."

Alex was getting a bad feeling about this. "This wasn't a normal robbery."

"What are they after?"

"You."

Chapter Two

Alex's words chilled Keira. Her grandfather had warned her in his note that trouble was coming. She hadn't taken his words as seriously as she should have. She thought he'd been speaking figuratively.

Obviously not, if someone had trashed her place and Alex was saying they were after her. Had they come after her because she went to see the vampire cop? And who were "they"? The thieves who'd stolen the blood? What did they want from her?

The sight of her home torn up so badly made her feel sick to her stomach but she kept up her tough attitude in front of Alex, just as she was hiding her fear now that he'd told her vampires were after her. Well, he hadn't said they were vampires, just that they weren't regular, whatever that meant. She took it to mean the worst.

Kind of like the state of her apartment. A giant mess. She bent over to pick up the framed photo of her mother, the glass shattered, and nearly jumped out of her skin at the feel of Alex's fingers on the bare small of her back.

"What's this?" he said.

"A tattoo." She instantly straightened and tugged down her floral top. "I'm sure you've seen them before."

"Not like that."

"It's a symbol of protection."

"It's a very elaborate variation of the Eye of Horus and it's quite unique in the way it's depicted."

"How do you know?"

He shrugged. "A good friend is a body artist and owns his own tattoo parlor."

"Is he a vampire, too?"

Alex rolled his eyes at her.

"It's a logical question," she said.

"Nothing about this is logical."

"Shouldn't you be contacting the crime scene people to dust for fingerprints or something?" she said, setting her mother's photo beside the TV.

"That's not necessary. I already have an idea who did this."

"You do? How?"

Instead of answering, Alex said, "Pack a bag. You're coming with me."

"No, I'm not."

"They'll be back," he told her. "Pack fast."

"I just told you, I'm not leaving."

"You do not want to be here when they return."

"What do they want with me?"

"Your grandfather had a lot of enemies."

"Vampire enemies," she said.

"Apparently."

"So you admit it."

"I don't have much choice," he replied.

"What makes you say that?"

"Them." He pointed to the pair of vampires on the

fire escape outside her living room window, their fangs showing. "Hold on."

"To what?"

"Me."

He took her in his arms and exited the building, moving at freaky-fast speed.

Keira hung on for dear life as neighboring buildings flashed by in a blur before her hair blew in her eyes, blocking her view. Her ears popped the way they did during takeoff on a flight. She had her arms around his neck and her hands clenched together as she heard what sounded like a door banging open. A moment later they were in a large room with brick walls. He set her on her feet, steadying her when her knees nearly buckled.

"Where are we?" she said unsteadily.

"Somewhere safe. For now."

"I was right. You are a vampire!"

"Don't go patting yourself on the back just yet," he told her. "We've got bigger problems."

"Those vampires outside my apartment?"

"No, the vampires at the door here."

Sure enough, there was a knock at the door. Alex opened it.

The vampire in the doorway had gray hair gathered back into a ponytail with a leather thong. He had a craggy face, wore a GOT BRAINS? T-shirt, and had a lot of tats, including those on the backs of his hands. If this guy was a vampire, he sure looked like the deceased comedian George Carlin.

"We've got trouble," the vampire said. "And she's standing right there." He pointed to Keira.

"Yeah, I know," Alex said. "Her grandfather was a vampire hunter."

"Not just any vampire hunter. The Executioner," the

still-unnamed vampire said. "I'm Pat Heller, by the way," he told her.

"I'm Keira Turner."

"I'd say it's nice to meet you but then I'd be lying," Pat said. "What's she doing here?"

"She knows about vampires and she can't be compelled to forget," Alex said.

"Of course she can't be compelled. She has hunter blood."

"She also has this." Alex moved closer and yanked up her floral top.

"Hey!" She yanked it back down.

"Did you see that?" Alex asked Pat.

"She has a protection tat."

"Not just any protection tat," Alex said. "It's the Eye of Horus. A very unique version of it. I've never seen anything like it. Have you?" Pat shook his head.

Keira closed her eyes and considered tapping her shoes together three times in order to leave this craziness and go back home where she was safe. But she was no Dorothy, this sure as hell wasn't Oz, and her home was no longer safe.

She opened her eyes and looked around. Why had her grandfather sent her to see Alex? Why had he sent her into a vampire's den . . . or loft as the case might be?

She'd spent most of the night reading his lengthy journal, some parts of which had been written in a language she didn't know. Latin perhaps? Parts had seemed to resemble small drawings or hieroglyphics.

She'd spent the morning at the Chicago Historical Society checking out the old files to confirm that the newspaper clippings were original. They were. The black-and-white photo in the October 9, 1871, *Chicago Tribune* of her grandfather standing beside the charred remains of city hall was real. He looked to be in his thirties at the time and had the same streak of white in his hair that he had later in life.

She'd always said he looked young for his age. Now she knew why. But she didn't know what it all meant. Maybe she should have figured that out before going to confront the vampire cop. "Ya think?" she muttered to herself.

But there was no turning back. She had to deal with the here and now. As if she didn't have enough to deal with given her mom's recent death. Did that have anything to do with all this? Had her mom's car accident been something else?

Why hadn't her grandfather told them, warned them of the danger involved with his line of work? She clenched her fists and confronted Alex once again.

"Did you kill my mother?" Her voice was thick with emotion.

"What are you talking about?" he said.

"She was killed in a car accident two months ago. They said it was a drunk driver but maybe not. Maybe it was a vampire who killed her."

"Remember what I told you about not blaming vampires for everything that goes wrong?"

"My mother's death is more than something that went wrong!" she shouted.

"Calm down," he told her. "Everything is going to be okay."

Keira couldn't believe he was saying that to her. But then she couldn't believe much of what was happening to her. Had she lost it? Was this a bizarre nightmare of some kind? "How do you figure everything will be okay?"

"You're alive, aren't you?"

"Am I?"

"What's that supposed to mean?" Alex said.

"Maybe you drugged me," she said. "Maybe none of this is real."

"Including your grandfather's journal? You read that before I met you."

Damn. He had a point. Okay, so this was real. At least part of it. Her grandfather was a vampire hunter. She'd have to get over it.

But Alex still hadn't answered her question about her mom. The memory of her mother's framed photograph with the shattered glass hit Keira hard. That picture had been taken on her mom's last birthday. She missed her so much.

Keira blinked back the tears. She couldn't cry in front of these vampires. She refused to show any sign of weakness they could possibly take advantage of and use against her.

"What is it with the girls you boys bring home?" Pat said. "Daniella asked Nick the same thing about her mom."

Keira's voice was shaky. "So you've killed other people's moms and blamed it on a car accident?"

"No!" Pat said angrily.

"My grandfather wrote that vampires are evil." Her voice was stronger now.

"Some are. So are some humans," Alex said with a hard edge to his voice. "We weren't responsible for your mother's car accident."

"Like you'd admit it if you were," she said.

"Why ask the question if you don't believe the answer?" Alex retorted.

"I don't know," she shot back. "This is all new territory for me."

"Me, too, muchacha," Alex said. "You're trouble."

"Then let me go," she said.

"You came to me. You started this. Remember that."

"And you're determined to punish me for that, right?" she said.

"Wrong." Alex shoved a hand through his already tousled dark hair.

"She's a security risk." This growled comment came from a newcomer. He was younger than Pat and much sexier. Everything about him was dark, from his inky-black hair to his deep-blue eyes.

"Damon," Alex began.

"You shouldn't have brought her here," Damon interrupted him.

"I didn't have a choice. Hostile vamps were after her. I couldn't let them take her," Alex said.

"Why not?" Damon demanded.

"Because of this." Keira lifted her top and pointed to the small of her back.

"So she's got a protection tat. Big deal," Damon said. "It would have protected her . . . maybe."

"Her grandfather was The Executioner," Alex said.

"Okay, that is a big deal," Damon said.

Keira was trying not to panic. She was now outnumbered three vampires to one reporter . . . her. She tried to turn the conversation away from her and back onto the blood thefts. "Does any of this have anything to do with the robberies from the area blood banks and hospitals?"

Damon said nothing.

"I suspect it does," Alex said. "And I suspect the Gold Coast clan is to blame. Lynch came to see me at the station."

"What did he want?" Damon said.

"To assure me the Gold Coast vamps weren't to blame for the troubles."

"Should she be listening to all this?" Damon demanded, jabbing his finger in Keira's direction.

"She's a part of the problem."

"I am not," Keira denied.

"You're the one who came looking for me," Alex reminded her yet again.

"For help stopping the blood bank robberies," she said.

"What is your interest in the robberies?" Damon said.

Alex answered for her. "She's a reporter."

Damon swore. So did Pat. Only Alex remained calm.

"I don't know which is worse. The fact that she's a hunter or the fact that she's a reporter," Damon said.

"I am not a hunter," she said.

"We only have your word for that," Pat replied.

"I had no idea vampires even existed until twenty-four hours ago. That's when I found my grandfather's journal . . ."

"Where is it?" Alex interrupted her.

She shook her head. "I'm not revealing that information at this time." She couldn't risk giving all her secrets away. If they knew everything, they might kill her.

"What was in the journal?" Alex said.

"Information about my grandfather's . . . uhm . . . activities."

"His vampire hunting activities? He could have been writing a book or making things up. Something had to make you believe. Something or someone."

"You made me believe," she told Alex.

Alex frowned. "How do you figure that?"

"Your name was next on my grandfather's hit list," Keira admitted.

Chapter Three

Keira eyed the trio of vampires cautiously. Damon had a smirk on his face while Pat was shaking his head. Only Alex refused to show any emotion at her words. That was strange. Of all of them, he was the one who should have been the most upset by her admission. Instead he appeared to be very calm.

"Who else was on the hit list?" Alex said.

"Just you."

"The last one on The Executioner's list," Pat said. "Why did he choose you, Alex?"

"I have no idea," Alex said. "So, intrepid girl reporter, why did he choose me?"

"I don't know. He didn't explain. Maybe it was your good looks and charm," she shot back, stung by his "girl reporter" comment.

"Yeah, maybe it was," Alex agreed with a mocking smile.

"I don't blame you for killing him," Damon told Alex before slapping him on the back. "You should have told us."

"What?" Alex looked confused then angry. "I didn't kill The Executioner."

That possibility hadn't occurred to Keira until now. Were the vampires determined to kill everyone in her family? She backed up as far away from them as possible.

Seeing her movement, Alex gave Damon a flinty look. "You're not helping."

Damon just shrugged.

Alex returned his attention to Keira. "So you came to see me believing I was a vampire. You didn't think that might be dangerous?"

"I didn't have a choice."

"Why not?"

"Because lives depend on figuring out why the blood is being stolen."

"You say lives depend on this. Whose life?" Alex demanded.

"My godson Benji for one. He has a rare blood disorder that requires him to get frequent blood transfusions. A shortage of his blood type creates a critical situation for him. He's only ten years old."

"What does that have to do with your grandfather? He couldn't have known about the robberies. They happened after his death," Alex said.

"Unless he's not really dead," Pat said.

Keira's eyes widened. "Is that possible?"

Alex didn't answer her question. Instead he said, "Or he somehow manipulated things so that the blood would be stolen after his death to start a vampire turf war. Maybe he planned that so we'd wipe each other out." His stare turned cold. "Are you part of his plan?"

Keira shook her head so fast she got dizzy. "No."

"Like she'd admit it if she was," Damon said, recit-

ing her own words back to her. "She can't be compelled,
but there are other ways to get her to talk."

Keira didn't like the way that sounded.

"Let me try first," Alex said.

Damon glanced at his watch. "You have ten minutes."

Pat left with him.

Keira backed up as Alex moved closer. "I . . . uh . . .
I'm . . . I'm telling the truth." She hated the fact that her
voice was shaking, but then she was being stalked by
an angry vampire. Any reasonable person would be
scared. Even an unreasonable person would realize that
they were in deep shit here. "I'm just a reporter."

Her knees almost buckled when he flashed his fangs
at her.

His eyes glowed for real now. "You're not just a reporter." His voice was harsh. "A mere reporter could be
compelled. You're The Executioner's granddaughter."

"I thought he was a tax accountant," she said as her
back hit the brick wall.

A second later he'd ripped her messenger bag over her
head and dumped its contents onto a large table.

"Hey!" she automatically protested before his snarl
shut her up. She inhaled a shaky breath; then the words
rushed out of her. "Never mind. Go ahead and check
things out. I don't have any weapons in there. No holy
water or crucifixes or stuff like that."

He held up a plastic container that made her blush.
"Tampons," she muttered. "And yes, those are condoms.
You can read the package. Or you can open it up to make
sure." Which he did before shooting her a look that made
her put her hands to her face. A second later she peeked
between her fingers and saw him opening her laptop
computer.

That did it. She had to draw a line in the sand some-where here. He wouldn't get very far trying to access information without her password.

She removed her hands from her face and put them on her hips, allowing her to inconspicuously wipe her damp palms on the cotton of her skirt. Glancing around, she searched for a way out. The windows were covered with dark wooden shutters.

The open floor plan didn't hide much. She didn't see any coffins or other vampire paraphernalia. She did see a huge bed in one corner . . . were those satin sheets? She avoided looking in that direction.

To her left was a tiny galley kitchen with a large high-end stainless-steel fridge. Was it packed full of stolen blood? Not that it was big enough to hold the large quantities that had been stolen.

To her right were a battered leather couch and two chairs. They looked like werewolves had attacked them. Maybe they had. A huge flat TV hung from the far brick wall along with a state-of-the-art media system.

"Give me your password," he ordered.

"No."

A millisecond later he was right in front of her, his hands on either side of her head, imprisoning her as his body pinned her to the wall. "Tell me."

His breath was warm on her cheek. She thought vampires were supposed to be cold. Alex was definitely hot.

She shook her head, but that only made his lips brush against her skin. She kept her own lips sealed, refusing to answer him. She wished her body's response to him could be equally defiant, but her hormones had other ideas.

Normally she wasn't the type to melt in a puddle when faced with raw sex appeal like Alex's. Not that she'd ever experienced the kind of charisma he radiated. It had to be a vampire thing. Too bad she couldn't be totally resistant to it the way she was to being compelled.

"Talk to me." He made the words sound part husky coax, part smoldering order.

She shivered. She wasn't cold. She was burning up. It was as if her body recognized him on some primal level. Even the tattoo on the small of her back seemed to heat up. She hoped that meant it was providing protection, but instead it seemed to throb in time with her heartbeat.

When he lowered his hand to her bare leg, she once again seriously regretted her wardrobe choice for this confrontation. She should never have gone to see him in a skirt. She should have put on jeans and multiple layers of leather . . . preferably with silver spikes.

"Answer me," he murmured against her skin.

His soft words frightened her as much as his earlier snarl had because her body was responding to him as if it had a will of its own. "What are you doing to me?" she whispered unsteadily.

"What does it feel like I'm doing?"

"Trying to scare or seduce the truth out of me. Maybe . . . maybe both." Her breathing was ragged as he licked her cheek near her ear. Was he tasting her to see if he wanted her as an appetizer?

Her grandfather's notes had claimed that vampires couldn't suck her blood because she was descended from a hunter. What if he was wrong? Maybe Alex didn't know he couldn't drain her blood. Maybe she should tell him, pronto.

"Hunter blood is not good for you," she said.

Couldn't you have put it more forcefully? she silently chastised herself. *You're a writer.* The phrase *not good for you* sounded so pitifully nerdy. She should have said hunter blood was toxic. Deadly.

Wait, vampires were immortal. Could her blood kill Alex? Her grandfather hadn't gone into details on the matter. That seemed to be a theme with him. She really should have done more research before marching into that police station and accusing Alex of being a vampire.

"I don't want your blood," he murmured. "I want your grandfather's journal."

Sure he did. And once he got it, he'd kill her . . . or do whatever it was that Damon had threatened her with. She might have been impetuous in her confrontation with Alex earlier, but she wasn't stupid.

She had no intention of giving him the journal, but she was all for using it as a way of getting out of the mess she was in at the moment.

"Let me go and I'll show you where it is," she lied.

He shifted his attention from the crook of her neck to her mouth. She nervously licked her lips. He looked at her as if he wanted to taste her. Was that sexual hunger or vampire hunger?

"You'll show me where it is, huh?" he said.

She nodded.

"Liar."

She was becoming increasingly pissed and tired of feeling like the victim here. Putting her hands on his shoulders, she shoved him away. "I've been up front with you. I told you I know you're a vampire. I could have played ignorant."

"You wanted to get my attention. Well, you've done that. Happy now?"

She wiggled in his hold. She'd only moved him a few inches. "Let me go!"

He continued to pin her in place. "Not gonna happen."

"I can't breathe," she gasped before pretending to faint, going limp in his arms.

Her move caught him by surprise, as she'd planned. When he readjusted his hold on her she kneed him in the groin.

"Shit!" He released her for a second.

Keira raced for the door, her only thought to get away. She was willing to leave her laptop and everything else behind at this point. Damn right that lives were at stake here—primarily her own. She couldn't help Benji if she was killed by angry vampires.

Reaching out her shaking hand, she yanked the door open only to find a woman standing there blocking her way.

"What the hell is going on here?" the female newcomer demanded.

Chapter Four

"I know you," Keira said. "You're the author S. J. Brennan."

"That's right. You can call me Sierra."

"This isn't a good time," Alex said, clamping a hand on Keira's shoulder.

Keira didn't know what to do. Would Alex hurt Sierra? She'd feel awful if something happened to one of her favorite authors. Hell, she'd feel awful if something happened to anyone else as a result of her actions.

None of this was going the way she'd planned. She'd thought that she and Alex would somehow be partner crime fighters and catch the bad-guy blood robbers. Or that he would use his superpowers to get the job done quickly. She hadn't anticipated that her apartment would be ransacked or that she would be snatched and whisked away to some secret location.

"Really, Alex?" Sierra said. "Not a good time? You're holding her hostage."

Keira was scrambling to catch up. Clearly Sierra knew Alex. Did she know what he was? And how did she know about him holding her hostage?

"You're frightening her," Sierra added.

"That was my intention before she attacked me," he said.

Sierra looked at Keira in surprise. "You attacked him?"

"I need to get out of here," Keira said.

"Sierra can't help you," Alex said.

"Well, I could but I'm not allowed to," Sierra said regretfully. "My loyalty is with the locals who live here. That doesn't mean I'm going to stand for you terrifying her, though, Alex." She shot him a reprimanding look before returning her attention to Keira. "You're Keira Turner, right? I follow your blog and your stuff on *ReadIt*. Your photo doesn't do you justice. I just loved your story about road rage. And before you ask, yes, I know Alex is a vampire."

"Stay out of this, Sierra," Alex ordered her.

"Pat and Damon sent me. Yeah, I know. They're vampires, too. Oh, I almost forgot." She reached into her tote. "I brought you a cupcake from Heavenly Cupcakes. I hope you like red velvet?" She pulled out a cardboard container.

Keira reached out as if to take it but instead dodged around Sierra before being stopped in her tracks by some sort of invisible wall. She hit it so hard she smashed her nose and saw stars.

Sierra said, "You could have warned her that there was—"

Alex cut her off. "The less she knows, the better."

Keira blinked the tears from her eyes before lifting her hand to her face.

"She's human. She doesn't heal the way vamps do," Sierra said, putting her arm around Keira and leading her to one of the battered leather chairs.

"She's not human," Alex said. "She's got hunter blood."

"She's the granddaughter of a hunter. Yes, Pat filled me in on the story," Sierra said.

"I can't believe you're okay living with vampires," Keira told Sierra.

"I know. I couldn't believe it at first, either," Sierra said. "I didn't have a clue. I'd come to Chicago to inherit a house from my great-uncle."

"Did Pat and Damon say why they wanted you to come up here?" Alex demanded.

"To stay with Keira while you go get an update from them."

"Don't try to leave," Alex warned Keira. "The place has a high-tech security system like the kind of invisible fences that keep your dog in your yard."

"I'm not some bitch you can lock up," Keira said, lifting her chin.

"Yeah, you are." With those words, Alex left.

Lawrence Lynch was not a happy vampire. He displayed his displeasure while sitting behind his elaborately gilded and carved Louis XIV desk in his penthouse headquarters by tapping a tungsten knife against his crystal glass of blood. Had he not been so distracted by his medical experiments, he would have realized faster that the human female at the police station with Sanchez was The Executioner's granddaughter.

"We sent a crew to search Keira Turner's apartment," Douglas Dimato told Lynch. As the director of operations, he'd been with the Gold Coast vampires since he was turned in Capone's time back in the 1920s. He'd worked as the mob's attorney for various kingpins before being attacked by Lynch and transformed into a vampire. "But they didn't find any journal."

"Did they find her?"

"They almost got her—"

"Almost?" Lynch interrupted. "Almost doesn't count in death and horseshoes."

Douglas frowned. "I'm not sure that's the actual quote."

Lynch banged his clenched fist on the desktop. "I don't care if it's the actual quote! Shut up and let me think."

Lynch had been immersed in his latest project to the point that he'd let the ball drop regarding following up on the search for The Executioner's journal. While he possessed other vampire hunter journals, they were nothing special. Chances were The Executioner's would be the same. But there was a slim possibility that the whispered rumors about it might be true. That it was more of a Hunter Manifesto with new ways to dispatch vampires not reported in other places. Still, all was not lost. Not yet.

Lynch took a deep breath before speaking. "Tell me exactly what happened. You sent two of your best vampires . . ."

"Actually I, uh, sent two new vampires—"

"Define *new*," Lynch interrupted.

Douglas shifted nervously. Lynch had not invited him to be seated so he stood there like a recalcitrant schoolboy in front of the headmaster. "They were eager to do the work."

"Define *new*," Lynch repeated.

"They were fledging mercenaries."

"Fledging mercenaries as in they hadn't eaten in days? That kind of fledging?"

Douglas nodded, beads of sweat appearing above his lip.

"You didn't consider the risk that they might drain Miss Turner of her blood?" Lynch inquired.

"They knew her blood would be toxic to them and I promised I'd give them plenty of fresh blood upon their return. I thought they could handle the job."

"You thought wrong," Lynch said before flicking the knife through the air and through Douglas's throat.

Douglas instantly disintegrated into a pile of dust.

"Time for a new director of operations," Lynch noted to himself before holding out his hand and compelling the knife to return to his desk, where he wiped it clean. The tungsten knife was a new addition to his arsenal, one he'd developed himself, giving him yet another way to destroy those who would not successfully complete their assignments. He had no tolerance for incompetence. No tolerance at all.

Damon was waiting for Alex in Vamptown's underground security center beneath the All Nighter Bar and Grill. Many of the buildings in the neighborhood had been built in the early 1900s, and most were connected with the tunnels used during Prohibition in the 1920s for those bootleggers transporting illegal alcohol. The tunnels came in handy for the vampire residents . . . as well as the resident witches.

"Zoe put a hex on the loft so the hunter can't leave," Damon said.

"I figured as much," Alex said. "I don't want Keira knowing we have witches here so I told her the security system was high-tech like those fences to keep dogs in their owners' yards."

"Did you put a collar on the bitch?"

"Damon, behave!" Zoe sternly reprimanded him as she entered the room filled with the latest cutting-edge computers and flat screens displaying neighborhood surveillance footage. Zoe was a breath of fresh air in the high-tech surroundings. She was also a witch and Damon's lover.

Damon glared at her. "What are you doing here?"

"I'm here to find out what's going on. I don't do hexes like that easily or readily. I did it because you asked me to but—"

"No buts." Damon put his hands on her shoulders, kissed her quickly, and turned her back toward the exit. "Now leave."

She escaped his hold. "Do not piss off the witch," she warned him with narrowed eyes.

"To answer your question, Damon, no, I did not put a collar on Keira," Alex said.

"Which is why he is a better man than you," Zoe said with a sniff.

"Better man but not a better vampire," Damon said. "He brought a hunter here to Vamptown . . ."

"A hunter's granddaughter," Alex corrected him. "Really Damon, you need to get your facts straight, bro." Turning to Zoe, he said, "Can't you do a locator spell to find The Executioner's journal or the missing batches of blood?"

"I wish I could. I tried, unsuccessfully," she said. "What's Keira's tie to the blood bank robberies? You don't think she's responsible for the attempted robbery at the Evergreen Funeral Home last night, do you?"

"It's too soon to tell. She has a godson who has some sort of blood disorder, and he needs blood transfusions," Alex said.

"Does he have a rare type?"

"Yes," Neville Rickerbacher said. The resident computer geek could hack databases at vampire speed. Neville had been turned by his own stockbroker in the 1980s when he'd accused him of being a bloodsucker. It turned out the guy was indeed a bloodsucking vampire.

Since then Neville had used his computer and stock market knowledge, along with his elite team, to make the money that kept Vamptown going. Despite his Midas touch, he insisted on wearing his glasses with duct tape holding the hinge together rather than spring for a newer pair. He was currently wearing a BYTE ME T-shirt with his jeans.

He pointed to the screens lining the wall. "Her godson is Benjamin aka Benji Goddard, son of Liz Goddard who is Keira's best friend." Photos of both appeared on the screen. "He's ten years old and has a rare medical condition I can't pronounce but basically it means he needs a lot of blood or he'll die. No vampire connection, though."

"So maybe Keira is stealing the blood herself for him and trying to make us suspicious of the Gold Coast vamps, and them of us. This could be some master plan her grandfather concocted." Alex said.

"I gave you ten minutes to get answers from her," Damon said. "What did you discover?"

That she has the kick of a mule, Alex thought to himself. Not that he'd admit he'd let his defenses down for a moment and she'd rewarded him by kneeing his nuts. Yes, vampires healed quickly, but damn that had stung— his body and his pride.

He wouldn't make the same mistake again. Keira might look all sweet with those root-beer-brown doe eyes of hers, but she was hell on wheels. He was glad she was wearing flats and not stilettos, which could have done some serious albeit temporary damage to his Sanchez family jewels.

"I was in the process of learning more when Sierra arrived and interrupted us," Alex said.

"That's it? That's all you've got?"

"She knows we can't bleed her. 'Hunter blood is not good for us,' as she put it," Alex said.

Zoe raised her hand. "Neither is witch blood. I'm just reminding you." She kissed Damon. "I'll be leaving now."

Once she'd departed, Alex spoke again. "I need more time to get Keira to turn over the journal."

"What makes you think that more time would make a difference?"

Alex just gave him a look.

Damon raised one dark eyebrow. "Really? She has a thing for Latino vampires?"

"I refuse to answer on the grounds I may incriminate myself," Alex said with mocking humility.

"Right," Damon said with equal mockery. "Since you're such a modest guy and all."

"Vampire. I'm a modest vampire."

Damon laughed. "Like hell you are. You're about as modest as I am."

"Which is not modest at all," Neville said before ducking his head and focusing on whatever he was typing on his keyboard.

"Right," Alex said.

"I could hook up some surveillance cameras in the loft," Neville said. "Maybe then we could get a better idea of what this hunter woman knows and how she plans on attacking us."

"Whoa, who said anything about her attacking us? And she's not a hunter," Alex said.

Neville pointed to one of the display screens where an infrared image of Keira appeared. While the loft didn't have surveillance cameras, every building had infrared imaging capabilities if required. "Look at her. She doesn't even compute on the scan to detect vampire, druid, and human blood. I'm clearly going to have to update the program to include hunter blood," Neville muttered before focusing intently on his multitude of high-tech tools. "I'll need some of her blood to do that."

"Didn't you hear me say that hunter blood isn't good for vampires?" Alex reminded him.

"Yeah," Neville said, "but I don't intend to drink it or anything. I just want Doc Boomer to work on testing it to figure out the particulates in it."

Doc Boomer ran the local Happy Times twenty-four-hour emergency dental clinic specializing in care for the area vampires. He got his nickname because of his booming voice. He had a medical as well as dental background.

"How do you suggest we do that?" Alex said.

"Doc Boomer could tell you how he'd decipher the blood work . . ."

Alex interrupted him. "I meant how do we get a sample of her blood? How toxic is hunter blood?"

"I would guess that hers has to be diluted by the fact that her parents were not hunters, just her grandfather," Neville said. "I say we compel a human phlebotomist to take the blood sample; then we can figure out how toxic it is. I can get a guy over there in twenty minutes."

"Do it," Damon said.

"Hold on," Alex said. "We go sending strangers with needles into the loft and she's going to freak out."

"She's already dealt with vampires today," Damon pointed out. "How freaked out can she get? And if she does then you can calm her down."

"Gee, thanks," Alex said.

"Traditionally the loft is one of the few places where we do not activate our cameras, but that can change," Neville said. "Nick didn't want us putting cameras in there, and since it is his place, and since he is a respected member of this community . . ."

"Who has to hear it from Zoe that we've got a hunter's granddaughter in our midst," Nick said as he strolled into the room. "And not just any hunter, but The Executioner."

Nick St. George was the owner of the All Nighter Bar and Grill as well as the head of the local business association. Vampires owned most of the area businesses, with the exception of Daniella Delaney, proprietor of Heavenly Cupcakes.

Nick preferred actions to words. He also preferred being with Daniella to being immortal. No one really talked about the link between Daniella and Nick or the clash with Miles, the deceased former head of the Gold Coast clan who'd had a centuries-old grudge against Nick. No one mentioned that much, or the fact that Nick could actually consume human food now.

No, Nick didn't talk much, but when he did, the residents of Vamptown paid attention.

"Alex was the next one on The Executioner's hit list," Damon said.

"Lucky you," Nick drawled before taking a seat. "I realize you two are the supposed security specialists—"

"Hey!" Damon protested. "What's with this 'supposed' shit?"

"But you report to me," Nick continued.

"I was just filling Damon in," Alex said. "Lynch came to see me at work about the thefts. He brought up the fact that Vamptown vamps can tolerate sunshine. Maybe they attempted to take the blood from the funeral home in the hope of figuring out how we do that."

"It has nothing to do with our food source," Damon said. "It's our tat."

"I know." Alex rubbed the back of his neck where the unique fleur-de-lis tattoo was located. "But they don't. That could be why they tried to get into the funeral home. I mean, why try to hit the place otherwise? Blood banks and hospitals make sense."

"We're lucky the alarm system scared them off," Damon said.

"Yeah, but the problem is that the vamp cams around the funeral home were all wiped clear," Neville said. "I'm working on trying to restore the image from before it went down, but so far no luck."

"That doesn't bode well," Alex said. "Those cameras belong to Vamptown, not the city of Chicago. They were designed to capture vampire images, which can be too fast for regular cameras. Could a human have messed with the cameras?"

Neville shrugged. "It is possible but not likely."

"So we're back to the Gold Coast clan being responsible for this," Alex said.

"Or The Executioner's granddaughter," Damon said.

"Don't worry." Alex's voice was grim. "If she is responsible, I'll take care of it."

"Are you willing to do whatever it takes?" Damon asked.

Alex's expression turned bleak. "I've done it before, haven't I?"

Nick placed his hand on Alex's arm. "Vamptown appreciates your service."

"They sure as hell better," Alex muttered darkly. He'd done more than his fair share to protect his clan.

Chapter Five

Keira eyed Sierra cautiously. The woman might write great paranormal ghost stories, but she lived with vampires. Alex had been gone for fifteen minutes. Keira should be glad for his absence. She wasn't. Not that she was relaxed. She wasn't. She should be trying to think of a way to escape. She wasn't. She did have a headache and a lot of questions. "Are you a vampire, too?"

"No way," Sierra said.

"Why can't you help me escape? Is it because they've compelled you?"

"I can't be compelled."

"Why not?"

"It's complicated."

"I can't be compelled, either," Keira said. "You and me, we've got that in common."

"I'm sorry I can't help you." Sierra sounded truly regretful. "But I can give you a cupcake." She held it up invitingly.

"Red velvet," Keira said bitterly. "Is this your version of the evil queen offering a poisoned apple to Snow White?"

"This cupcake is not poisoned. Look, I'll take a bite to prove it to you." She did so.

Keira still wasn't convinced.

Sierra sighed and set the rest of the cupcake on the large table that held Keira's laptop. "Maybe you'll want some later."

"Can I have my laptop?"

"You won't be able to use it."

"Then give it to me," Keira said.

Sierra handed it over.

Keira quickly opened it but the laptop was dead. The screen remained blank. Maybe the battery was dead, although she could have sworn she'd recharged it this morning. But then she had been rattled after reading her grandfather's journal last night. She couldn't trust her memory. She couldn't trust much at the moment.

She checked the contents of her messenger bag that Alex had strewn over the table. Nope, no sign of the cord needed to charge her computer. She must have left it in her apartment.

She blushed as Sierra eyed the box of condoms. "I bought them for a friend at the office," she muttered, stuffing them back in the messenger bag. "She's too embarrassed to buy them herself."

"You can order them online."

"She doesn't trust online stores. Not that any of this is anyone's business." Keira decided it was time to turn the tables on Sierra and ask her personal questions. "So are you and Alex a couple?"

"A couple?" Sierra laughed. "No."

"Right. Because that would be too weird, right?"

"Actually, no. I am in love with a vampire. Just not Alex. So if you want him—"

"I just met him."

"Vampire time is different from normal time. Things happen very quickly here. Relationships can develop very quickly. You'd think because they are immortal that it would be the opposite, that they'd take their time, but that hasn't been my experience."

"Yeah, well, I'm into normal time." Keira tapped her oversized watch to make her point. "As in, I've been held hostage here against my will for over two hours now."

"You'll be here a lot longer. So let's make the best of it," Sierra said. "How did you meet Alex? Did he arrest you or something?"

"Didn't your vampire friends tell you?"

Sierra shook her head. "Not the details, no."

"I went to see Alex at work because of the recent robberies of blood from blood banks and hospitals."

"Because he's a cop?"

"Because he's a vampire."

"How did you know that? Is it because of your grandfather's journal? And what gave you the courage to go see Alex, knowing he's a vampire?"

"It might not have been my smartest move," Keira readily admitted.

"It was a very ballsy and dangerous move. One that the heroine of my books might make but not me," Sierra said.

"I had my reasons."

"I heard about your godson. I'm sorry," Sierra said.

"Thanks." Keira was worried about Benji. He was such a good kid. It wasn't fair that he had to deal with needles and pain and illness. Despite all that, he still managed to keep a smile on his face.

"You worry too much, K," he'd tell her. His mom, Liz, had been Keira's closest friend since middle school.

When Liz found out she was pregnant, the father took off and had never been heard from again.

Benji's first words were *Momma* and then *K*. That was his nickname for Keira. "It will be okay, K," he'd say. "Don't be sad. Listen to your spidey senses."

Her spidey senses were telling her she was in deep shit here.

"You knew Alex was a vampire because your grandfather was a vampire hunter and he talked about that in his journal, right?" Sierra said. "You must have been surprised when you read that. Shocked, even."

"I was. Twenty-four hours ago I had no idea that vampires existed."

"That must be quite a journal."

It was, but Keira was not about to go into details. Sierra might seem nice, but she was aligned with the enemy. "How long did it take you to believe vampires are real?"

"A lot less than that," Sierra admitted. "But then I actually saw Ronan in action. He moved faster than humanly possible to save me from being crushed to death by a bookcase falling on me."

"I know about that freaky speed. Alex picked me up in my apartment to save me from vampires on the fire escape," Keira said.

"But you already knew he was a vampire before that. I didn't have a clue about Ronan. I didn't believe it until I saw his fangs. To be honest, even then I thought it was some kind of punk joke or something. But I was fairly quickly convinced."

"And Ronan is . . . ?"

"The vampire I love," Sierra readily replied.

"How many vampires are there here?"

"I don't know the exact count."

"That doesn't bother you?"

"Not knowing the vampire population? No, it doesn't bother me," Sierra said.

"I meant being surrounded by them."

"The tone of your voice is an indication that you don't approve. It's easy to judge when you don't know the facts."

"What facts?"

"Not all vampires are bad."

"Yeah, that's what Alex said."

"It's true."

"Forgive me if I'm not convinced," Keira said. "After all, they are keeping me here against my will. That can't continue, you know. People will be looking for me."

"Apparently you do have vampires looking for you."

"I meant humans. I have friends. They'll be worried about me when I don't show up."

"They'll be compelled with the information that you're fine."

"And you're okay with that?"

"It's not my call," Sierra said.

"My blood will be on your hands," Keira said.

"You're a hunter's granddaughter. Your blood is toxic to a vampire."

"They could still kill me like they killed my grandfather."

"If you thought Alex killed your grandfather, then why did you go to him?"

"I don't know he did it," Keira admitted.

"Alex put you here in relative isolation to protect you."

"Is that what he told you?"

"It's what Pat told me."

"And you trust him?"

"I do. I can't be compelled, so my trust has to be earned," she reminded Keira.

"Why can't you be compelled?"

"Like I said earlier, it's a complicated story."

"I have a lot of time on my hands."

"Why are you so interested?" Sierra countered. "Do you plan on writing a story about vampires?"

"Like anyone would believe me if I did."

"Some would. I should warn you that you won't be able to tell anyone in the outside world about any of this."

"The outside world?"

"We're a pretty tight-knit community here."

"Where is here?" Keira went to the windows, but they were covered by the locked shutters. "Are we in Romania or something?" The reference to Heavenly Cupcakes that Sierra had made earlier made Keira think they were still in Chicago, but she couldn't be sure.

"No, you haven't left the city."

"What's going on here?" a tall, tanned woman demanded from the doorway. She was super skinny and wore a tube top and mini skirt that looked like they'd been sprayed on her. "Sierra, you're supposed to be doing a chat with your street team in five minutes."

"I know, Tanya. I texted you that I plan on doing it later this evening."

"Who's that?" Tanya demanded pointing to Keira. "Is she some demented fan stalking you?"

"No."

Tanya eyed Keira suspiciously.

Keira eyed her right back. How had Tanya been able to enter the loft and get past Alex's security system? Unless . . . "Are you a vampire, too?" Keira asked.

A second later Tanya had her by the throat and flashed her fangs at Keira. Yep, definitely a vampire.

"Tanya, stop that!" Sierra said. "Keira is a friend of mine. Let her go."

Tanya released her reluctantly.

Keira stumbled backward. Why had she asked that? Another stupid move on her part. Did she have a death wish or something? Her fingers trembled as she rubbed her throat.

"What's going on?" Alex demanded, appearing out of nowhere. "What are you doing here, Tanya?"

"Protecting my favorite author," Tanya said.

"She doesn't need protecting," Alex said. "You can both leave now."

The instant they were gone Keira said, "They might not need protecting but I sure as hell do." Her voice was raspy from the hold Tanya had had on her throat.

"I know you need protecting. That's why you're here," Alex said.

"I'm not safe here. That vampire just tried to strangle me."

"Luckily you only mildly ticked Tanya off. Had she been really pissed she'd have torn your head off," Alex said.

"If that was meant to reassure me, it failed."

"I wasn't trying to reassure you. In fact, you're the one who has to reassure me."

"Why? Because you're afraid of me?"

"Brave words considering the trouble you're facing."

"Why were you next on my grandfather's hit list and why weren't you surprised?"

"Very little surprises me these days."

"I surprised you."

"Yeah, you did. That's not necessarily a good thing," he warned her. "I'm not real fond of surprises."

"So you weren't surprised that you were . . ."

"Your grandfather's next victim?"

"I have a hard time imagining a vampire as a victim," she said.

"I don't." He reached for her laptop.

"Hold on. What do you plan on doing with that?"

"It's already been done. Everything on it was copied wirelessly. Vampire Wi-Fi."

"But . . . you didn't have my password."

"Didn't need it."

"Then why did you bully me to get it?"

"To teach you a lesson."

"Yeah? And what lesson was that?"

He headed for the fridge . . . to the ice cube dispenser. Grabbing a towel from the counter, he wrapped it around the ice before bringing it to her.

"You could be getting a shiner," he said, placing the towel in her hand and then gently lifting her hand to just beneath her eye.

"Why were Sierra and Tanya able to get past your invisible security system and leave?"

"Because they aren't you."

"Lucky me," Keira muttered.

"Lucky you, indeed," Alex said.

"Sierra said I wouldn't be able to tell anyone else about you being vampires or where I am." Using her free hand, Keira pointed to the windows. "Am I really still in Chicago?"

"Yes, you're still in Chicago."

"Prove it. Let me see out the window."

"You're going to be the one proving you can be trusted, and that needs to be done before you see anything outside."

"What do you mean?"

"What I said. The others want a sample of your blood."

Keira's ears started ringing. "But it's toxic."

"They don't want to drink it. They want to analyze it."

"No way!" She wavered unsteadily.

"Sit down if you feel faint," Alex said. "I'm not falling for that act again."

Down she went.

Shit. Moving with vamp speed Alex caught her before she hit the floor. She wasn't faking this time. Lifting her in his arms, he carefully laid her on the couch.

Her face was so pale. He ran his fingertips along her cheek. Her skin was so smooth. He could hear the rapid beat of her racing heart. When she'd gone down he'd felt a panic in his gut along with a fierce need to care for her and shield her from danger. This went beyond his usual response as a cop.

Cupping her cheek with the palm of his hand, he tried to figure out what was going on here. Because his connection with her was nothing he'd ever experienced before.

He wanted to know more about her, what made her tick, if she could be trusted, if she felt the same attraction he did. She was sharp and observant. Not much slipped past her. She was fierce and not easily spooked. Had she really only come to see him because of the blood thefts? Or was there more to her story?

If this was what he thought it might be, then he was in deep shit.

It will happen one day, his sire Mitch had told him. *You might not know it at first sight but it won't take long for you to know.*

To know what? Alex had asked.

That you are experiencing The Longing. The woman who will inspire this emotion in you . . . she's not like you. But she's The One. In some way she will be your opposite. In others she will be your match. In all ways she will be your revelation. She'll change your afterlife for good . . . or for bad.

Alex swore under his breath. Had Mitch known that the woman he'd been talking about was a hunter's grand-daughter? Was that what that line about her being his opposite meant?

Was that why he'd been torn about taking her blood for testing? He stood by his decision that she should offer it willingly as proof that she was trustworthy. But looking at her now, so vulnerable and pale, made his protective instincts come to life with an intensity that surprised him. No one was sticking her. Not without her permission.

His hand still cupped her cheek. What kind of twisted karma was this? That The One for him was the one woman who could ruin him. Already he was going against Damon's wishes and putting his concern for Keira first.

Her eyes flickered open. She didn't say a word, just looked at him. Did she feel the same connection he did? Her brown eyes seemed to say so. She didn't pull away from his touch. Indeed, she seemed to nuzzle against his hand.

A moment later, realizing what she was doing, she moved his hand away. He twined his fingers with hers. Oh yeah, there was definitely a bond going on here.

Of all the women in the world, why did she have to be The One? He pulled his hand away and headed for the kitchen. He returned with a glass full of red liquid. "Drink this."

She eyed it suspiciously. "I am not drinking blood."

"Like we'd waste good blood on you. It's red wine." He took a sip. "A very nice burgundy."

Her eyes widened. "You only drink blood."

"Says who?"

"Everyone."

"I can drink several types of beverages. Most of them alcoholic." He held the wineglass out for her to take.

She refused to take it.

He shrugged. "Your loss." He took a healthy swig. "I probably need it more than you do."

"What does that mean?" She sat up and checked her arms for needle marks. "Did you take my blood?"

"No. I told you, you need to be willing to give a sample of your blood voluntarily. As a means of proving that you aren't a hunter, that you aren't part of some plan."

"How can my blood possibly prove that?"

She had him there. Only her actions could prove that. The blood would be analyzed and tested. He already knew from the heat sensors that she didn't have druid blood or vampire blood.

He tried to read her thoughts but couldn't pick up anything specific. To his surprise, she took the glass from him and sniffed its contents before expertly swirling it as if she were at a wine tasting in the Napa Valley. Then she darted her tongue out to daintily touch the liquid. "It is wine."

"I told you it was."

"Can all you vampires drink wine?"

"Not all, no."

"What makes you special?"

You do.

He didn't know yet how or why that she made him special, but he sure as hell planned on finding out.

"I've got to go," he said curtly. "Someone will be here shortly with your stuff."

"What stuff?" she asked.

But Alex was already gone.

Chapter Six

Keira blamed her light-headedness on a lack of food rather than a lack of courage. She hadn't eaten much at the press luncheon before going to see Alex. She'd just sampled a few of the buffet's bite-size selections.

The bottom line here was that she hadn't passed out because she was a wimp. She'd passed out because she needed sugar.

She eyed the cupcake on the table. Sierra had taken a bite and seemed fine. She'd seemed normal. But then she hung out with vampires on a daily basis. How normal was that?

Still, that didn't mean Sierra had handed Keira a poisoned cupcake. Okay . . . maybe not poisoned, but drugged in order to keep Keira quiet.

If that was the case, then why hadn't Sierra shown any symptoms? Would Sierra really risk taking a bite of something tainted? Doubtful.

Was it worth the risk? Keira's stomach growled an answer. She stood, holding on to the back of the couch as the room spun a bit around her.

She waited until her equilibrium returned before walking to the table. She took a dainty bite of the cupcake . . . just the cake. Mmmm. Yummm. Next she ate a hefty sample of the icing.

"Hey there," a jolly male voice greeted Keira as she turned with a mouthful of cream cheese icing. "How's it going? Great cupcake, huh? Not that I know from personal experience, but everyone says they love the red velvet cupcakes."

"Would you like a bite?" she automatically asked, then wondered what made her offer it to a complete stranger.

"A bite?" He stared at the pulse in her neck for a beat before regaining his composure. "Oh, right. The cupcake, of course. No, thank you." He held up a suitcase. "I brought your things."

She eyed him carefully. He was heavyset with dark hair and kind eyes. He was also very meticulously dressed in a dark suit and blue shirt opened at the neck.

"I love your outfit," he told her. "You have great fashion sense. So do I." He spread out his arms. "Who am I wearing, you ask. Tom Ford, of course. It's Tuesday. I try to wear Tom Ford on Tuesdays."

Keira's mouth hung open. This day was getting weirder and weirder. "Who are you?"

"I'm Bruce. Didn't Alex tell you I was coming?"

"He didn't tell me your name."

Bruce shook his head. "Isn't that just like him."

"Listen, you've got to get me out of here," she said desperately. "I'm being held against my will."

"That's terrible." Bruce's expression reflected his surprise. "I wish I could help you."

"You can help me. You're a vampire, right?"

"How did you know? Was it the open collar on my shirt? Too much?" He quickly fastened a button. "Wait, it was the cupcake comment, right?"

"You're not like the others."

Bruce frowned. "You mean because I'm gay?"

"No. I mean because you're nice."

"Thank you," he said, smiling at her, his chest puffing out just a little. "I pride myself on that. It's not always easy, you know." He set her suitcase down next to the couch. "Actually, I have a confession to make." He sighed before pausing dramatically. "When I went to your apartment to get your things I was forced to kill two other vampires. I tried to be nice about it, though."

Keira was speechless.

"They were stealing your things and trashing the place," Bruce said. "That really pissed me off. Still, I would have remained nice if they hadn't tried to kill me first. Don't worry. It wasn't messy. They disintegrated when they died." When she tried to speak, he held up his hand. "No, you don't have to thank me. I like to think anyone would have done what I did. Well, anyone who is a vampire." He paused. "Anyone who is a vampire in my clan, that is. Along with being nice, I do try to be accurate. Ask anyone, they'll tell you."

"No, they won't. No one around here is telling me anything."

"They aren't?" he said.

They don't trust me, she almost said before thinking better of it and just shrugging as if she didn't have a clue.

"That's such a shame. You seem like a nice person to me."

"Thank you." She couldn't believe she was standing here talking to a vampire who killed other vampires.

Her reporter sense must be on vacation. He looked harmless. He seemed empathetic. Maybe she could appeal to that side of him. "Will you help me?"

"Sure. Frankly, I think your fashion presence is pretty good on your own, but I'd be glad to give you a few tips—"

She interrupted him. "I need to get out of here."

He smiled at her fondly before shaking his head. "No can do."

"Why not?"

"Because you're The Executioner's granddaughter and as such you could possibly be a risk to our security." Her face must have shown her surprise at his words because he added, "Did you think I didn't know? I'm gay, not stupid, and I certainly wasn't born yesterday."

"No, you were probably born centuries ago," she muttered.

"I was not!" He was clearly affronted by her words. "You take that back."

"I'm sorry," she said automatically before stopping herself. "Hold on, no I'm not. You're the one who should be sorry. Holding me captive against my will this way."

"I'm not holding you captive. Alex is. I merely brought you some of your clothes, which as I already told you are very impressive given your limited budget as a reporter. May I say that I also liked a number of the songs on your playlist. I am a huge Andrew Lloyd Weber fan; I'm also a huge Imagine Dragons fan. And that Bastille song 'Pompeii.' Awesome. Or Lorde's 'Royals.' I also like 'Put the Blame on Mame' sung by Rita Hayworth in the classic film noir movie *Gilda*. What can I say? I'm a man of broad tastes."

"Whoa, how do you know what's on my playlist?" Keira said.

He pointed to her laptop. "Vamp Wi-Fi."

"So all you vampires know everything that's on my laptop?"

"No. I called dibbies on checking out your playlist. Tanya called dibbies on checking out your social media except for Pinterest. I got that one as well. You and I share the same fondness for furnishings and dream homes."

"This loft sure doesn't qualify," she muttered.

"I know. And so much could be done with it, right?"

Yeah, like escape from it, she thought. She finished the cupcake before wiping her hands on the paper napkin Sierra had left nearby.

"Does the loft belong to you?" she asked, already knowing it couldn't. As he said, he would have decorated it better. But her intention was to win Bruce over, and making polite conversation with him was part of that plan.

"No way. I would have taken this place in an entirely different direction. Less brick and industrial metal and more casual chic."

"Who lives here?"

"Alex."

"How well do you know him?" she asked as she looked around the kitchen for any sign of a knife or other means of self-defense. She didn't see anything on the countertops. That shouldn't surprise her. Vampires had no need for toasters or Cuisinart food processors.

"How well does anyone know anyone, really? I mean, we all project an image that we want others to believe. There's nothing there," he added.

"What?"

"No knives. No weapons. No garlic, not that garlic would hurt me."

"I wasn't—"

"Sure you were. That's okay. I understand it must be tough for you to take all this in. It's not like you knew your grandfather was a vampire hunter, or so I understand. That must have come as a big surprise."

"More like a huge shock."

Bruce looked around a bit nervously before confessing, "I've heard rumors that The Executioner once killed seven vampires in seven minutes. Wait. Maybe it was seven vampires in seven seconds. I'm not sure. I never heard all the details. No one wants to talk about his deadly deeds."

Keira had a hard time reconciling what she was hearing and what she'd read in her grandfather's journal with the man she'd known who'd read her Dr. Seuss stories at night. She'd ended up having to skim the parts of her grandfather's journal where he'd described his killing sprees. She'd skipped over sections because of the bloody violence.

"So vampires were never on your radar before?" Bruce was asking.

"No." She tried to turn the conversation away from her. "Are you a cop like Alex?"

Bruce laughed. "No way. I'm with Pat. I believe you met him earlier."

Keira nodded. "He didn't seem to like me."

"It's not personal," Bruce assured her. "He's naturally suspicious given your background."

"A background I didn't know I had until twenty-four hours ago."

"That's what Pat told me. He also said that you confronted Alex at work knowing he was a vampire. That was brave."

"Or stupid," she muttered.

"Or both brave and stupid." Although Keira was actually enjoying talking to Bruce, she knew she had to come up with a plan of attack; she was done playing the helpless victim. She might not be a hunter, but damn these vampires were going to regret messing with her.

"Where have you been all afternoon?" Alex's partner demanded when Alex returned to his desk in the police district. Craig Anderson was a fellow vampire and part of the Vamptown clan, as was Craig's vampire wife, Bunny. Craig and Bunny had been married fifteen years before they were both turned.

Craig was short and stocky with light-brown hair and a ready smile. Bunny had short curly black hair and had held on to a lot of her humanity despite the fact that she was a vampire. One example was the fact that Bunny never consumed human blood, only synthetic.

"Clan business," Alex said. "Did I miss anything here?"

Craig shook his head. "Just the usual murder and mayhem."

"I can deal with murder and mayhem."

"You can deal with anything," Craig said.

Alex didn't know about that. He was certainly having a hard time dealing with Keira. Why was that? Was it because of her connection to The Executioner? Or was this a sign of the premonition that his sire Mitch had warned him about? Was she really The One?

"Everything okay?" Craig asked. "I heard a woman came to see you earlier and that then the two of you took off."

"Her name is Keira Turner. She knew what I am. And she's The Executioner's granddaughter."

Craig's mouth dropped open.

"She claims I was next on his hit list," Alex added.

"So she came to do the job herself? I mean, The Executioner died a year ago. At least that's what we've been led to believe. There haven't been any killings attributable to him since that time."

"She didn't come to kill me. She came about the blood thefts. She said we weren't doing enough about it."

"Where is she now?"

"At the loft in Vamptown." Seeing Craig's surprised expression, Alex felt he had to explain. "She can't be compelled to forget. Besides, her apartment was trashed and vamps were on the fire escape clamoring to get in."

"Clamoring, huh?"

"Yeah. Anything new on the blood thefts?"

"Surveillance cameras are blank."

"Ditto for the one at the Evergreen Funeral Home," Alex said. "Neville is working on it but so far there's nothing. Which is not a good sign, as that camera was designed by Neville and his crew for the special needs of the neighborhood."

"Understood," Craig said. "What's our next move?"

"What about that biotech medical lab Bunny works in? Any word there? Anything from their management about concerns regarding the thefts?"

"Not that she's aware of. She said they did send out a mass email this morning warning everyone to change their passwords daily, but they didn't say it was because of the thefts."

"They're not going to admit they have trouble. It would affect their corporate stock price. No, they'd keep any breaches quiet. But I think it's more than a coincidence that they'd send out an email like that. We should talk to their head of security. See what you can find out about him."

Craig nodded before heading to his own desk. He returned a few moments later.

"That was fast, even for you," Alex said.

"Thought you'd want to know, I just heard over the scanner that there's a fire."

"At Bunny's biotech company?"

"No," Craig said. "At Keira's apartment. The fire department and EMTs are on the scene now."

"Shit." Alex zoomed out at vamp hyper speed. A second later he stood in front of Keira's apartment building, speaking to the firefighter in charge. Alex flashed his badge at him. "What's going on?" Alex said.

"A fire."

"I got that. Any injuries?"

"No. The occupants all seem to have been at work. The lower two apartments have water damage but the fire started in the top apartment. It's pretty much destroyed. Too soon to officially nail down a cause but I would definitely label it as suspicious. The place reeked of gasoline."

Vampires hated flames. Fire was one of the few ways they could be destroyed. Staking them merely paralyzed them. Only burning and beheading caused death and obliteration.

So why would vampires start a fire in Keira's apartment? They wouldn't. But maybe they'd hired someone to do it. They could easily compel a human to do their dirty work.

Why destroy her apartment? Had they found what they were looking for when they'd trashed the place earlier? If so, why come back?

Whatever the details, this definitely upped the ante in the troubles going on between vampire clans.

"How stable is the building?" Alex asked.

"Stable enough. We caught and contained it fairly early. No structural damage to the walls. The roof will need some work but it won't collapse. It's not habitable, though."

Looking the firefighter in the eye, Alex said, "Forget I asked you anything. Forget you met me."

He could tell from the semi-glazed look that his compulsion had worked.

Moving away from the crowd, Alex called Bruce on his cell. "Are you still with Keira?"

"Yes. She's not a very happy camper," Bruce said.

"When did you leave her apartment?"

"About an hour and a half ago. Why? The place was trashed before I got there and those two vamps disintegrated so there shouldn't be any trace of them."

"What two vamps?"

"The ones I had to kill. It was self-defense."

"Were they from the Gold Coast clan?"

"I didn't recognize them. I'm not sure where they came from. They weren't our clan, I know that for sure. Why? What's going on?"

"Keira's place went up in flames."

"Oh my! Well, I certainly didn't do that," Bruce stated emphatically.

"Do what?" Alex heard Keira demanding in the background.

"Keep her calm. I'm on my way," Alex said.

Before leaving, Alex checked out the surroundings for any trace of vampire presences. He picked up the scent of those vampires from the fire escape earlier but he thought it was weak enough to indicate they hadn't returned. What he was smelling was probably from their earlier appearance. He didn't sense Lynch's unique scent, but that didn't mean the Gold Coast clan leader wasn't responsible for this mess.

"I didn't tell her," Bruce assured Alex the instant he entered the loft moments later.

"Tell me what?" she said.

"There was an incident at your apartment," Alex said.

"I know. Vampires ransacked the place."

"There's more."

"Bruce told me he had to . . . uhm, kill some hostile vampires. Although frankly you all seem hostile to me," Keira added defiantly.

"I'm hurt you would think that way," Bruce said, putting a hand to his heart.

"There's more," Alex said.

"You killed more vampires?" she said.

"No."

Her eyes widened with horror. "You killed humans?"

"No. Of course not."

"Why of course not? For all I know you could be killing people all over the place," she shouted.

"Stop the dramatics."

"Then tell me what happened," she growled.

"There was a fire."

"A fire?" she repeated blankly.

"In your apartment."

Her expression reflected her shock and disbelief. She turned to Bruce. "Did you leave the stove on or something?" Not waiting for his reply, she returned her attention to Alex. "Was there a lot of damage?"

"The contents of your apartment are nothing but ashes now," he said bluntly.

Her face turned even paler than usual, if that was

possible. Alex stepped forward, ready to catch her if she fainted again. He felt guilty for breaking the news to her so roughly.

Putting her hand out, she gave him a look that could have singed him with its fiery anger. "Did you burn it to keep me from going back?"

Her accusation angered him. "I am not an arsonist."

"Which doesn't answer my question."

"No, I didn't set your apartment on fire."

"I need to see it. I need to see what happened."

He held up his phone and showed her some video he'd taken at the scene.

She was not appeased. "You could have faked that. I need to see my apartment in person."

"That's not going to happen."

"Why not?"

"Hostile vampires are after you," he said.

"Hostile vampires are holding me captive."

"I'm not the enemy here," he said.

"You look like the enemy to me," she retorted.

"I'm not the one who trashed your apartment."

"No, you're the one who burned it down."

"I didn't burn it down. The building is still standing."

"Why are you doing this? Is it because of my grandfather?"

"Yes."

"He thought you'd protect me," she whispered. "That's why I came to you. He sent me to you."

"His mistake," Alex said coldly. He couldn't afford to let her get to him. It didn't matter if she was The One for him. There was more at stake here. Like the prevention of an all-out war between his clan and the Gold Coast vampires. Like keeping Keira alive when dangerous enemies were after her. He couldn't give in to these feelings washing over him. If being tough protected her, then that's what he had to do.

Bruce defended him. "Alex is protecting you."

"I don't believe you. And I don't believe that my apartment and everything I own is gone." Her voice was raw.

"Including your grandfather's journal?"

"I refuse to answer that question." She lifted her chin with stubborn determination, but Alex saw the sheen of imminent tears in her eyes.

One tear started to fall down he cheek, and it took all of Alex's willpower not to reach out to her. He was a vampire, and normally he was immune to human tears. But nothing about this situation was normal. Why was that? It had to be the damn connection between them.

Maybe if she saw the damage to her apartment she'd realize the seriousness of her situation and stop being so difficult. He liked that justification more than the idea that he was giving in to her because she was about to cry.

"I'll take you, but there are some ground rules," he said. "First, you stay close to me. No yelling for help. You do and you put others at risk. Understood?"

She nodded.

"Second, we leave when I say we leave. We won't be staying long."

"Are you going to do that freaky fast vamp transportation thing again?"

"It's not a transpor . . . yes, I'm doing that again." This wasn't the time to go into semantics.

He wrapped a large navy-blue scarf around her head. "I don't want anyone recognizing you." He removed his shirt and handed it to her. "Put this on."

She was about to argue when she caught the look he gave her and took the shirt. It covered most of her.

"Now she looks like a homeless person," Bruce said. "I suggest she put on something from the clothes I brought her. Or better yet, just cloak her."

Cloaking was a talent that Alex possessed. Not all vampires were able to hide from humans. Usually their fast speed meant they were barely a blur and undetectable. But that only applied when they were moving. The ability to hide from humans while standing still required cloaking, but that took energy that he needed to reserve at the moment. "Vamps would still be able to see her," Alex pointed out.

"They're able to see her in that dreadful outfit you have her in now for sure," Bruce said.

"I'm a cop, not the fashion police," Alex said impatiently.

Keira removed the scarf and then his shirt, returning it to him. Great, now it smelled like her. Fresh and lemony.

"Which is why he's the best for the job of protecting you from other vampires," Bruce pointed out. "I'll just wait here for you two and get you settled in."

Alex tossed his shirt on the leather couch and went to the chest in the corner to remove a black T-shirt to pull over his head. He couldn't afford to be distracted by her scent on his shirt.

"Let's go." He pulled her close and wrapped his arms around her.

"Last time you picked me up," she said.

"Last time I was in a hurry to escape attacking vampires."

"This time I'm in a hurry to see my apartment," she said.

"Great. You want to be picked up, then I'll pick you up." He lifted her in his arms.

"If I'm too heavy . . . ," she said.

"Shh," he growled. "And hang on."

The trip took a second, but it was enough for him to be aware of her breast brushing his chest and her hip pressed against his waist. Her head rested on his shoulder. His reaction was twice as intense as it had been the last time he'd traveled with her.

They arrived in the deserted alley a few doors down from her apartment building, near the Dumpster behind the Korean twenty-four-hour market. He focused his hearing on her apartment. There was lots of noise from the front of the building, but her place seemed quiet.

He took her as close as the fire escape outside her gutted apartment. The acrid smell of smoke stung his throat. His heightened senses also picked up on the smell of gasoline, charred wood, and melted plastic. "We aren't going inside. There may still be hot spots," he warned her.

She looked around and trembled. "It's all gone."

"But you're still here. They're just things," he said.

"My things," she said with despairing fury. "They were my things. My memories! My photographs!" She hit him with her clenched fist. He ducked so she whacked his shoulder instead of his face. "My mother is gone and now her things are gone, too." She started sobbing.

"I told you this wasn't a good idea," he muttered even as he took her in his arms. "Seeing all this is just upsetting you. I shouldn't have brought you here."

She pulled away and scrubbed the tears from her face. "I'll tell you what you shouldn't have done. You shouldn't have kidnapped me in the first place."

"You wish I'd left you here for the vamps on this fire escape to take you?"

He didn't wait for an answer. Instead he lifted her in his arms and once again took off.

Chapter Seven

When Keira opened her eyes, they were once again in the loft. And so were her things.

"My couch." Keira ran her shaking hands over the microfiber upholstery. "My lamp." She touched the stained glass with her fingertips. "How did you get it all here? Never mind. Why didn't you tell me you saved some of my things? You must have arranged to get them out before the fire, right? The way you sent Bruce to get some of my clothes." She choked back a sob. "The Swedish horse." Her voice turned unsteady. "You saved the little wooden horse my mom got me. And the framed photo of my mom." Tears ran down her cheeks.

Alex wiped them away with his thumb.

"Thank you," she whispered.

"You're welcome," he whispered back.

His hands cupped her face.

Maybe it was the emotional roller coaster she'd been on since meeting him. Maybe it was the way he made her feel safe and secure when he touched her. Or maybe it was the way her body responded to him, yearning for his caress.

Placing her hands on his chest, she felt the warmth of his body. She wanted to grab hold of him and kiss him. She wanted to forget the danger swirling around them. She wanted to forget the sight of her home in ruins. She wanted to thank him for getting some of her belongings out in time.

He kissed her. Or maybe she kissed him. She only knew they were kissing and she was loving it. This moment had been a long time coming. The heat had been building beneath the surface from the moment she'd seen him. She'd tried to block her reaction but there was no hiding it now.

He curved his hand over her nape before sliding his fingertips into her hair and tugging her closer. She went willingly. When he licked the seam of her lips with his talented tongue she parted them to allow him entry.

Everything became hotter and faster. The shift of his hands to the small of her back and the curve of her derriere. She was pressed tightly against his hard body and felt his arousal. Her tattoo seemed to reflect the heat flickering through her.

This didn't feel like a first kiss. This felt like a reunion of long-lost lovers who had once shared the most seductive intimacies. It wasn't tender and exploratory. Maybe it had been for a split second before veering off into new rawly erotic territory.

Instead of being shocked, Keira responded with a wild abandon that she'd never felt before. Her tongue skirmished with his, all sexy swirls and tempting tangles. She slid her fingers though his dark hair, loving the feel of the silky strands.

Her knees were like Jell-O as she sank onto the couch. Her couch. He followed her, covering her, sliding his leg between hers. Now she could feel how much

he wanted her even more than before. They were hori-
zontal and she was on fire. He slid his hands beneath
her floral top and brushed his thumbs over her satin-
covered breasts. Her bra intensified his touch.

A tiny part of her brain realized things were going
too fast. But the rest of her didn't care. This felt too good.
He felt too good. He tasted too good. He was too damn
good, period.

Then it was over as fast as it had all begun. Swearing under his breath, Alex pushed off of her and left her
spread out on the couch yearning for more.

Lynch sat at his ornate desk with his hands calmly
folded before him as he faced Konrad Weissmutter, the
new acting director of operations. "Explain to me again
why you thought burning the target's apartment was a
brilliant idea."

"I never said it was brilliant—" Konrad denied.

"You also never asked for or received my approval
for such an idiotic plan." Lynch waved his left hand in
the air. "But forget that for the moment. Tell me why you
burned the apartment."

"Doing so forced the target to leave her home."

"That is true. Now instead of grabbing her from her
home we are faced with having to deal with getting her
out of Vamptown, where Sanchez has no doubt taken
her into protective custody. And this is an improvement
because . . . ?" His mocking question held both aggravation and anger.

"I may not have thought the plan through suffi-
ciently," Konrad said.

"You think?"

Konrad didn't answer.

"Clearly you didn't think," Lynch said. "There was no need to burn her apartment."

"It was a sign of intimidation," Konrad said.

"It was a sign of ignorance. Your ignorance."

"I didn't actually burn the apartment myself," Konrad hurriedly said.

"Of course you didn't. Vampires and fire are not a healthy combination. Neither is having fledgling mercenary vampires trying to set a fire. And where are these heroes now?"

"The fledglings did not set the fire. I personally compelled a gang member to do that after our mercenaries were killed by one of Vamptown's residents. Bruce is his name, I believe."

"Bruce did me a favor then."

Konrad looked confused. "He did?"

"Yes. He saved me from having to eradicate the fledglings for screwing up their job of grabbing Keira. Which just leaves you." Lynch reached for the tungsten knife on his desk. "You know how fire and beheading are normally the only means of eradicating vampires?"

Konrad nodded nervously.

"You might be interested to learn that I've recently developed another means. It requires perfect aim and precision. Luckily that isn't a problem for me. But it is for you." Without another word, he sent the knife flying through the air and into Konrad's throat.

Keira still couldn't believe how fast Alex left after kissing her. Which was silly since she knew he could move at what seemed like the speed of light. He'd growled something about Sierra staying with her while he was out.

Keira didn't have the luxury of taking off the way he did. Not only did she not move fast, she also no longer had a home. At least she had some of her belongings. She sat on the couch along with Sierra.

"I'm sorry to keep interrupting your work. I'm sure you'd rather be writing," Keira said.

"That's true. No offense."

"None taken. I'd rather be writing as well. But I can't do that when Alex has my laptop. How can I write under those conditions?"

What are you working on now?"

"I have to do a piece about the Taste of Chicago. I have a fast-approaching deadline on that, as in it's due tomorrow. I've had to write my first draft out by hand. But it's not just work stuff I should be dealing with. There's the matter of contacting my insurance agent about the fire. My cell phone is useless and I don't see any landline here. I'm not sure how I'm supposed to explain how my living room furnishings managed to escape the inferno."

Sierra remained silent as if unsure what to say.

"Can you talk to Alex about allowing me a phone call?" Keira asked. "Even a prisoner is allowed one call."

"You're not in prison," Sierra said.

"It sure feels like it."

"Think of it more as protective custody."

"Yeah, somehow that isn't helping."

"I'm sorry."

Sierra looked so remorseful that Keira felt a pang of guilt. "No, I'm sorry. I don't mean to make you feel bad. This isn't your fault. It's mine. I'm the one who opened this Pandora's box by going to see Alex in the first place."

"I think I told you before that that took guts. At least

when I moved here I had no idea vampires existed. But you went looking for Alex knowing he was a vampire."

"Yeah, that doesn't seem so bright to me in hindsight. I didn't plan on telling him I knew what he was. But his attitude got me and before I knew it the words were flying out of my mouth. Not that he compelled me. He can't. There was just something about him. There still is." Keira had only met Alex a few hours ago. She shouldn't be this emotionally invested in him, not to mention physically attracted.

"He gets to you."

"He does," Keira admitted. "Why is that?"

Sierra smiled. "I don't know. Maybe it has something to do with his sexy dark looks?"

"Even his voice is dark and deep and smooth." Keira couldn't talk about his kiss, which was all three of those things and more. So much more.

But it was damn hard not to when her lips still throbbed from his touch. What had she been thinking, kissing him that way? Kissing him any way was definitely not a good idea. Almost as bad an idea as going to confront a vampire in the first place.

But damn it had felt good. Okay, it had felt incredibly crazily awesome.

"I wish I could figure out what's going on," she muttered.

"I think you know what's going on," Sierra said.

"I do?"

Sierra nodded. "You're attracted to Alex."

"I just met him."

"Yeah, well, as I told you before time has a different meaning when applied to a sexy vampire."

"So Alex has done something to make me fall for him?"

"He's just been his normal self."

"I didn't feel the same way when I met Damon."

"Good thing," Sierra said. "Because Damon is definitely taken."

"By another vampire?"

"No."

"So humans have relationships with vampires here?" Keira asked.

"Most humans don't know vampires are here," Sierra pointed out.

"What about Alex? Is he taken, too?"

"He appears to be quite taken with you," Sierra said. "He also appears to be quite determined to protect you."

Keira silently wondered who would protect her from the overwhelming attraction she felt for Alex. It wasn't just his hot looks or lusting after his hot body. There was more to it than that. There was some sort of indescribable link between them. Despite what Sierra said about loving a vampire, Keira didn't know if she'd be able to make such a statement with equal enthusiasm. The big difference being that Sierra didn't have a legendary vampire hunter for a grandfather. Maybe it would be easier loving Alex if she didn't have a path of dead vampires in her family's background.

Whoa. Who was she kidding? There was no way loving Alex would be easy . . . or advisable. That was the bottom line here. Love was not an option. The thought was definitely a wild one and not anything she should consider. That would create an impossible situation for sure.

Alex walked into Zoe's rental house fuming. "Did you use magic?" he demanded.

Zoe looked at him and shrugged. "You're welcome," she said.

"She's going to wonder how her things got to the loft. Right now she thinks we brought her stuff like Bruce brought her clothes, but I'm not sure how long that will last." He squelched the guilt he felt at accepting Keira's thanks, not to mention that kiss they'd shared.

He'd had to leave the way he had because the truth had hit him like a grenade. Keira was The One. She was The One his sire Mitch had warned him would forever change Alex's life—for better or for worse. How twisted was that? The one woman in the world who had the power to get beyond his defenses was a vampire hunter's granddaughter. That was definitely freaking twisted. Still, another part of him felt this was meant to be. The kiss they'd just shared proved that. Her mouth had been so sweet and passionate.

He'd sworn his loyalty to his Vamptown clan. That should be his priority. But now Keira was his priority as well. It had taken her no time at all to get to him. She both fascinated and infuriated him.

"I'm not saying I approve of what Zoe did," Damon said as he joined them.

"But you understand my reasons, right?" she said.

Damon nodded. "You're a softie. You take care of your grandmother, your cat familiar, and . . . me," he admitted gruffly. "You're always thinking of others."

"Aww." Zoe's face lit up. She kissed Damon before turning to face Alex.

Seeing Damon with the love of his afterlife made Alex wonder what it would be like to have someone gaze at him so adoringly without being compelled to do so. Not that he'd compelled women to go all googly-eyed on him. He hadn't.

But he was surprised at the direction his thoughts had taken. This wasn't the first time he'd seen a public display of affection between Damon and Zoe—but it was definitely the first time he'd felt a pang of regret that he didn't have anyone who cared about him that way. Just because Keira had returned his kiss didn't mean she adored him or even liked him.

Yet he sensed she did care for him even if she didn't want to do so. He could understand her conflicted feelings. He was equally conflicted about being tough with her in order to protect his vampire clan and being protective of her in order to save her from harm. Not to mention how warm her lips felt. He shouldn't have kissed her. But she'd responded in ways he hadn't anticipated or expected but longed to experience again. When he'd left her, her lips were swollen from his kiss and her eyes hazy with passion. That image was imprinted in his mind and messing with his concentration. He was hot for her. There was no denying that.

But it was more than mere physical attraction. He didn't just want her, he wanted to know more about her. And not just because he was investigating this case.

Zoe's voice brought him back to the present. "Sierra told me that Keira lost her mom a few months ago. Her grief has got to be intense. I know when my mom passed, it was a very long time before the darkness of that loss lifted. The hole in your heart gets smaller over time but never disappears."

"We agreed that Keira shouldn't be told that there are witches in Vamptown," Alex said.

"She doesn't have to know that I'm the one who created her furniture."

"How did you get it here?"

"I didn't. I used the photos she posted on her Pinterest page of her living room to re-create the furnishings, including the framed photo of her mom on the end table."

"She was happy to have that," Alex said.

"I figured she would be. So again I say, you're welcome."

"My job isn't to make her happy. It's to keep her safe," Alex said curtly.

"Why?" Damon said. "Because you're a cop?"

"Because hostiles are after her."

"Bruce said he had to kill two vamps at her apartment."

"La-la-la," Zoe said, putting her hands over her ears. "I'd rather not hear those kinds of details. I'm going up to my studio and working on my new autumn line of seasonal soaps."

Damon waited until Zoe was upstairs before speaking again. "Tell me what's going on here, Alex."

"You know what's going on."

"Why did you use the term *hostiles* instead of *vampires*?"

"We can't rule out the possibility that demons are behind this."

"Behind what? The fire in the hunter's apartment?"

"She's not a hunter," Alex said.

"Fine, she's a reporter. And I'm a Demon Hunter. If demons were involved, I'd know."

"Would you?"

"Yes. What about The Executioner's journal? Was it destroyed in the fire?"

"I don't know," Alex admitted. "Whoever set the fire may have taken it."

"Legend has it that there are notes in that journal about vampire blood that could destroy us all. The Executioner's journal supposedly included a Manifesto with information dating back hundreds or perhaps even thousands of years. There is no proof, though, since no one has ever seen his journal aside from Keira."

"I am aware of that."

"Did she read the entire journal?"

"She hasn't said."

"Make her say. If she read it, then she can tell us about the blood notes."

"The blood thefts happened before she discovered the journal," Alex reminded him.

"I still think there has to be a connection between the two," Damon replied.

"You know my partner Craig's wife, Bunny, works at a medical research facility."

"That's where she gets her blood, right?"

Alex nodded. "She's a strong advocate of the use of synthetic blood instead of the real thing for vamps. But maybe someone at the facility has other ideas."

"It's not a vamp facility."

"Not entirely, no. I plan on talking to her. Meanwhile Neville is trying to unscramble the video feed that Bruce set up when he visited Keira's apartment this afternoon."

"Did you get an ID on the vamps Bruce got rid of?"

"Not yet. They may have been mercenaries from out of town. So far there were no hits on facial recognition software of the two Chicago clans." Alex paused before adding, "Lynch knows more than he's saying."

"That's always the case with him. But what about you?"

"What about me?"

"There's something about this girl reporter that gets to you. Why? Does she have some kind of hold over you?"

"Hell, no," Alex automatically denied, although if she was The One then the link between them would be powerful indeed. He was still having a hard time accepting that what Mitch had told him about The Longing and The One was really true. At least, his brain had a hard time processing it.

"Then what's the deal?"

"There is no deal."

"Yes, there is. You're not telling me something and I want to know what it is."

"It's just lore."

"You're too young to have lore," Damon retorted. "The vampires I know who have lore regarding them were turned hundreds of years ago. You were only turned what . . . sixty-some years ago?"

"On the battlefield in the Pacific in World War Two. Iwo Jima to be specific."

"And?"

"I was a medic. I was there to help people. To save them."

"And that's why you feel you have to save the reporter?"

"No. You don't get it. I didn't have a choice."

Damon frowned. "You were turned against your will? That's against the rules. Unless . . ."

"Unless you're in that part of the Pacific," Alex said. "There are certain rules for Europe and North America, but they aren't the same for the rest of the world."

"Ronan was turned against his will in the trenches in World War One in northern France."

Alex waved his words away. "He was indentured. That's different."

"So your sire Mitch turned you against your will? He died under mysterious circumstances. Maybe he was killed by The Executioner. I would think that would be reason enough to eradicate the vampire hunter's only remaining kin. Unless you wanted your sire killed because of the way he tuned you?"

"Mitch did what he thought was right. He did his best to help me deal. I wasn't a great student. In the beginning I was incredibly angry, I thought I was a monster, so I acted like one. There were things I did . . ."

Alex paused, his throat tight at the memories he thought he'd buried. The years after he turned were so dark and bloody, if he didn't forget them it would drive him mad.

"We've all done things we aren't proud of," Damon said quietly. His eyes darkened at his own terrible memories.

Alex knew Damon had been turned on day three of the battle at Gettysburg. He rarely talked about it. None of the vamps turned on the battlefield did—not Nick, Damon, or Ronan. War changed them.

He shoved those memories away, locking them up as he normally did and focusing on the matter at hand. "I'm a cop, you know how I am about solving a crime. Someone or something is stealing blood. We need to figure out who or what is behind the thefts and stop them before this blows into a full-out vamp war."

"Which could be what The Executioner wants."

"You used the present tense."

"Because I'm not convinced yet that he's dead," Damon said. "Horace Turner's remains were cremated and spread over Lake Michigan. So there's no way to verify his death or that he even really was The Executioner."

"How would Keira know about The Executioner otherwise? And there haven't been any killings attributed to The Executioner since Horace's death."

"True," Damon readily acknowledged. "I'm just saying I'm not completely convinced he's gone. Not yet. But enough about that. Tell me what ties you to Keira."

Alex took a deep breath. Instead of answering directly, he said, "Mitch selected me for a reason. Have you ever wondered why there are so few Latino vampires?"

Damon frowned. "So you're saying Mitch turned you in order to diversify the vampire community?"

"Something like that."

Damon's frown intensified. "You're not telling me everything. Why did he turn you?"

"Mitch said that there was something in my ancestral past that linked me to the vampire world."

"And that is?"

"I don't know. Mitch was killed before he could go into more details."

"You've had decades since then to figure it out."

"Those first twenty were spent trying to deal with becoming a vampire," Alex retorted. "Like I said, my transition was not an easy one. After Mitch was killed, the next twenty were trying to find a way to blend my new world with my old one as a medic. The temptation of human blood was too strong. I didn't have the self-control required. I still don't, which is why I'm a better cop than a doc."

"You're still exposed to human blood," Damon pointed out.

"Not that often. I can handle it because I can make a difference."

"So you're the caped crusader bent on saving humankind? You've seen too many superhero movies."

"That's not it. I know I can't find every killer in this city. I can't save everyone who is attacked. But I save those I can," Alex said.

"You do realize that vampires traditionally aren't into saving humans unless it's for their next meal."

"Yeah, I'm aware."

"And is this Keira the latest human you intend to save?"

"Yes, she is."

"What if saving her hurts Vamptown?"

"That won't happen."

"If it does?" Damon persisted. "Your loyalties better lie with us, Alex."

"They do."

"You took an oath. Yes, you took an oath as a cop as well. But a human oath is nothing compared with a vampire oath and that's what you swore to us. Do not forget that."

"I won't."

"Good. Because you know the punishment for breaking a vampire oath, correct?"

Alex nodded. "The punishment is death."

"So don't go losing your head over this Keira or you could end up literally losing your head by decapitation."

Alex's jaw clenched. He was sick of Damon treating him like some kind of disobedient schoolboy. "Have I ever let this clan down in the ten years I've lived here?"

"No."

"I'm not about to start now, so back off."

Damon held out his hands in a gesture of appeasement. "I'm just trying to do what's best for Vamptown."

"So am I," Alex said. "So stop breaking my balls and let me get back to work."

Chapter Eight

Half an hour after arriving, Sierra jumped up from the couch and headed for her tote bag. "I almost forgot. I brought more cupcakes. A dozen this time." She flipped open the container's lid and displayed the contents. "And a bigger selection. We've got cookies and cream. Pink lemonade. Blueberry with red, white, and blue frosting and sprinkles in honor of the Fourth of July tomorrow."

Sierra's words took Keira back to the luncheon she'd attended a few hours ago for the city's Taste of Chicago, scheduled to take place after the Fourth of July. Her life had still been relatively normal then. Yes, she'd read her grandfather's journal and was aware of the probability that vampires were real. But she still had her freedom and her apartment.

A thousand cupcakes couldn't make this situation better.

But they couldn't hurt, so she took the pink lemonade cupcake. She dipped her finger in the icing for a preview taste before contemplating what Sierra had told her so far. "I still don't get how you can be okay living with vampires."

"I'm actually only living with one. The others are neighbors."

"You know what I mean."

"You think vampires are evil."

"I don't think they are choirboys," she retorted.

"No, definitely not choirboys," Sierra agreed.

"Alex claims there are good and bad vampires like there are good and bad people."

"He's right."

"I don't understand. How can a vampire be good?"

"By fighting evil. They are better equipped than humans to fight the darkness that is out there."

"You write mysteries. You're good at figuring out clues. Who do you think is behind these blood thefts? Is that the kind of darkness you're talking about?"

"It's not anyone from here. I'm sure of that."

"How can you be sure? You said yourself that you haven't been here very long. What about the blood? Where does it come from for the vampires here?"

"That information is on a need-to-know basis. And I don't need to know."

"So you have no idea where the vampire you love gets his blood?"

"Let's get back to the blood thefts," Sierra said firmly. "The most likely suspect is the rival vampire clan."

"Do you know someone named Lawrence Lynch?" Keira asked.

"Why do you ask?"

"Because he came to the police department when I was there. He came to speak to Alex. I'm assuming he was a vampire since he made a comment about me being lunch."

"You need to ask Alex about that. I'm not sure how much I'm supposed to tell you," Sierra admitted.

"Alex doesn't tell me much."

"That makes sense. He doesn't know if you can be trusted."

Keira took a bite of her cupcake. "These are good." She looked at the box. "Heavenly Cupcakes. I did a story about them a few months back. Are they nearby?"

"Yes, they're . . . No you don't." Sierra caught herself. "Nice try but I'm not going to get into trouble for revealing something I shouldn't."

"It's just a cupcake shop," Keira said. "Or is it?"

"It's definitely just a cupcake shop with outstandingly delicious cupcakes and a wonderful owner."

"She's a friend of yours?"

Sierra eyed her cautiously.

"What?" Keira said. "What harm could come from you saying you're friends with . . . her name is Daniella, right? Daniella Delaney."

"That is her name."

Keira abruptly changed the subject. "What about you? What are you working on now? Would you be interested in my doing a story about you?"

"About me living with a vampire? No thanks. Not that you could write that anyway."

"Why couldn't I?"

"When I first found out about the vampires surrounding me, Ronan dared me to include that fact in an email to my publicist, Katie. She's an awesome publicist, by the way. The best in the business. Anyway, nothing I typed about it came through. Nothing I texted. It didn't work. Now, of course, I'd never try something like that."

"But I might. And I might be more successful." Keira reached for her laptop, which she'd been charging and had plugged in now.

"Go ahead," Sierra said, looking unconcerned. "Give it your best shot."

"I will. No Internet connection?" She looked at her screen with a frown. "What happened to vamp Wi-Fi?"

"It's reserved for vampires," Alex said as he strolled into the room. "Are you ladies having fun?"

"Buckets of fun," Keira retorted sarcastically. "Too bad you missed it."

Alex dramatically placed both hands over his heart. "I am so incredibly saddened to hear I missed out."

"I'll leave you two alone," Sierra said. "I've got another five pages to write yet today. Oh, Keira wants to know who Lawrence Lynch is. You should tell her. Bye for now."

"So you want to know about Lynch, huh?" Alex said. "Wasn't he in that journal of your grandfather's?"

"Not as far as I know, no."

"What do you mean not as far as you know? I thought you read the whole thing."

"Most of it."

"And Lynch was never mentioned?"

"I already told you."

"You haven't told me much."

"Right back atcha," she said. She licked pink lemonade frosting off her fingertips before saying, "So you're holding me near Heavenly Cupcakes, huh?"

"What gave you that idea?"

"Sierra."

"She told you that Heavenly Cupcakes was nearby?" Keira nodded.

"Liar." He rubbed his thumb across her bottom lip. "Shame on you."

Her entire body lit up with desire. Even so, she refused to let her wild attraction to him get in the way of information. Taking a step back, she irritably said. "Stop trying to seduce me into behaving."

"You're angry because you want me."

"I'm angry because I've been abducted by vampires and had my apartment trashed and then torched. It's been a hell of a day and not in a good way."

"Same here."

"And Sierra did tell me that the cupcake shop was nearby. Granted, she did so accidentally, but I wasn't lying. I've been honest with you, which is more than I can say about you."

"You haven't been honest about your grandfather's journal. You said you'd show me where it is right before you kneed me." He pointed to his crotch with both index fingers, which of course directed her attention to that area of his body.

She noted the bulge beneath the zipper of his black pants. She'd felt how hard his erection was. She'd felt him against her body. She still wanted him even though she shouldn't. But then she'd been doing plenty of things all day that she shouldn't. But not this. She was not having sex with a vampire, no matter how much her body wanted to. She returned her attention to his police badge attached to his belt.

"I did that because you were manhandling me and threatening me. It was self-defense," she said.

"Maybe," he allowed.

"Definitely."

"At least you didn't get a black eye from hitting the invisible defensive wall when you tried to escape." He tenderly brushed his fingers over her face.

"No thanks to you."

"Hey." He gently tapped his finger against her chin. "I didn't want you hurt. I gave you an ice bag for it."

Damn. He was hot enough when he was being bossy; when he showed a slight tenderness, he was nearly irresistible. A mere tap to her chin, over in an instant yet still registering in her sensual memory bank.

She had to stay focused here. Not focused on seeing Alex naked. Not focused on peeling his shirt from his chest and kissing her way to his navel. No, none of that was allowed. No thinking about it. No fantasizing about it.

She needed to be practical. "If you're forcing me to stay here overnight then we need to discuss the sleeping arrangements," she said.

"Go right ahead."

"I'm sleeping on my couch."

"Fine by me."

She eyed the huge bed in the far corner of the loft. "Where do you sleep?"

"Hanging upside down like a bat," he drawled.

Her eyes widened. "Really?"

"No, not really. Didn't your grandfather's journal detail the sleeping habits of vampires?"

"Not *your* sleeping habits, no."

"Yet I was next on his hit list. Didn't he do his research?"

"There wasn't much info on you at all."

"I find that hard to believe."

"There may have been some information about umm, you being a marine in World War Two."

"I was a medic fatally injured on Iwo Jima in the Pacific."

"He didn't go into details."

"Neither do I," Alex said curtly.

"You don't like talking about how you became a vampire. I get that."

"That doesn't stop you from being curious about it, though," he said.

"True," she admitted.

"How about this, I tell you something about that time and you tell me something about your grandfather?"

She thought a moment before agreeing. "Okay. You go first."

"They told us that we could take Iwo in three days. Instead it took thirty days and thousands of marines were killed."

"Including you."

"Including me for a brief moment."

"What happened?"

He shook his head. "I told you something. Now it's your turn to tell me."

"My grandfather had a streak of white across his hair."

"That's not information," he said.

"It's more personal than your factual statement was."

"You want facts? I'll give you facts." His voice was harsh. "Like the fact that nothing could prepare you for the horror on that godforsaken island. Constant shelling and sniper fire. Limbs being blown off. Skulls exploding. The enemy was booby-trapping their injured and dead with explosives so that we'd be blown to smithereens if we tried to move them."

"It must have been horrible," she whispered.

"It was beyond horrible."

"I'm so sorry."

"Yeah, so am I."

"Sorry that you became a vampire?"

A tick in his jaw indicated that he was holding his emotions in check. "Enough about me," he said curtly. "What about your grandfather?"

"He was there for the Chicago Fire, in 1871. He was alive then. And not a kid, either. Is that usual for vampire hunters? To have that kind of longevity?"

"If they're good at their jobs, yes."

"The hospital told me that he died of a sudden brain aneurysm. Is that true?"

"I don't know."

"Would you tell me if you did know?" she demanded.

"Maybe. We didn't know The Executioner's identity until today when you told us."

"You said hunters lived as long as they were good at their job. Did a vampire kill my grandfather? Did they compel the ER doctor to tell my mom and me that it was an aneurysm?"

"I'd need to know more details about the time right before his death. Were you with him?"

"No." Just hours ago she would have stopped there and revealed nothing more out of fear. But that fear was changing and morphing into a shared sense of . . . she wasn't sure what to call it. Trust? She'd sensed the depth of Alex's anguish when he'd talked about the battle. The more time she spent with him, the more she felt she knew him in ways that defied logic but were too true and too strong to ignore.

She nervously fingered her evil eye ring. Her grandfather used to tell her to trust her gut. She was doing that with Alex . . . up to a point. "The hospital called and said he'd collapsed on Michigan Avenue and had been brought into their emergency room. They said we should come as quickly as possible because his condition was critical and he wouldn't last long. He was already dead when we got there." She had to pause a moment to collect herself. Although her grandfather had died a year ago, the memory was still difficult to manage. It also reminded her of her mother's much more recent passing.

Taking a deep breath, she continued. "What about his age? Wouldn't the doctors have noticed something? As far as I knew he was seventy years old. But now I know he was much older than that. He looked to be thirty or forty in the photo with the smoldering debris from the Chicago Fire behind him, and like I said that was almost a hundred and fifty years ago."

"He didn't write about his early life?"

"He was rather mysterious about it. All he said was that he had no choice. That he *had* to become a hunter. That he had to make things right. After that point he merely wrote that he was fighting evil."

"He killed vampires, period. He didn't care if they were good or evil."

"He considered them all to be evil."

"Do you share that belief?"

She wasn't sure what to say. She didn't believe Alex was evil, but she couldn't find the words to express her emotions.

"Never mind," he growled. "Your silence says it all."

"No, it doesn't. I don't know about all vampires but I don't think you're evil," she said softly.

"I'm glad you realize that," he replied.

Keira also realized that she wasn't going anywhere anytime soon so she might as well try to make the best of the situation. Once leaving the loft was removed from the visual equation, she noticed more about the details of her surroundings. A series of framed landscape paintings on the front brick wall were the first thing to grab her attention. She moved closer to get a better look. They were colorful watercolors.

"These are lovely," she said. "Did you paint them?" After all, Alex did have artistic hands with long fingers. She'd admired that about him from the first moment she'd met him.

"No. They belong to a friend."

His answer surprised her. Not that he wasn't the artist but that the paintings weren't his. That's when she realized she didn't know much about his romantic history. "A girlfriend?"

"No."

Keira moved from one painting to the next before casually asking over her shoulder, "Do you have a girlfriend?"

His smile was sexy and potent. "No. How about you? Is there a boyfriend waiting in the wings?"

A few hours ago she might have lied and said yes, that the man in her life was a Special Forces dark-ops specialist who fiercely protected her. But she figured Alex had his ways of investigating her past so there was no point in fabricating anything. "I suspect you already know the answer to that question, but no. I'm not currently seeing anyone."

Or kissing anyone. The thought flew through her mind as the memory of his lips on hers sent the blood rushing through her body. To distract herself from those romantic images, she continued her exploration of the loft, skipping past the large bed with the black satin sheets. But that was difficult to do considering how easily she could imagine Alex on that bed, on those sheets, with her in his arms.

One kiss shouldn't get her thinking along those lines so quickly. But there was something about Alex that besieged her defenses and got to her.

Tearing her eyes away from the bed, she noted that

the depressed leather couches and chairs had disappeared, replaced by her furniture. She hadn't realized that her things had made his disappear. She wondered how he felt about that.

"Do you think I'm girling up your man cave?" she asked.

One dark eyebrow rose. "Girling up?"

"Replacing your leather couches and chairs."

"They belonged to my friend."

"Does anything here belong to you?"

You. You belong to me. It was almost as if she could hear his words in her mind. Her breath stopped. The feminist part of her didn't want to belong to anyone, but there was a tiny part of her that responded to his silent claim, providing he'd belong to her in return.

She moved closer to the worktable where he'd dumped out the contents of her messenger bag earlier. She'd carefully returned her belongings to their rightful place while he was gone. For the first time she noticed the pile of books on one side.

"Yours?"

He nodded.

"Favorite author?" she asked him.

"Lee Child," he instantly replied. "What about you?"

"Jayne Ann Krentz."

"I like her books, too," he said before smiling and adding, "You seem surprised."

"I am. She writes romances."

"I know she does. I like romance."

"You do?"

He nodded again. This time a lock of his dark hair tumbled over his forehead, giving him a bad-boy roguish look. "You couldn't tell by the way I kissed you?"

"I could tell you're good at it," she said. "Kissing, I mean."

Her gaze was held by his. His brown eyes were dark with passion. It was difficult to look away but she forced herself to do so before she ended up in his arms.

"What about cards?" she said a tad desperately, picking up the box on the worktable. "Are you good at playing cards?"

"I am."

"Care to play a game?" she said.

"You're on." Alex opened the box and expertly shuffled the deck with all the dexterity of a dealer at a Vegas casino. "Poker? Texas Hold 'Em?"

"Go Fish," she replied. At his blank look, she added, "Let's play Go Fish."

He appeared disappointed. She wondered if he'd hoped she'd want to play Strip Poker or something. While the prospect of having him remove his shirt did have its appeal, she was trying to be strong and not give in to temptation.

"If you really want to play Go Fish—"

"I do," she said.

"Then that's what we'll do." He dealt her the required number of cards. "Ladies first."

And so they began. "Got any sevens?" she asked.

"Go fish. Got any twos?"

She handed over her two of spades. "What about music?" she asked. "What music do you like?"

"Benny Goodman. Big-band music," he replied. "Got any threes?"

"Go fish. I like Coldplay," she said.

"They're good," he agreed.

As Alex looked down at his cards, she noticed the thickness of his dark eyelashes. He had such a strong face that the sweep of those lashes caught her by surprise. So did the curve of his lower lip. She studied the hint of stubble appearing on his jawline.

"Do you want some?" he asked.

She blinked.

"Music," he elaborated. "Did you want to hear some music?"

Did she? She didn't know for sure. She was only certain that his kiss had branded her in a magical way that left her wanting more.

Alex was well aware of the looks Keira had been giving him. Aware and aroused by them.

"Music?" he repeated.

"Sure."

He reached for the small remote that activated the sound system. "Counting Stars" by OneRepublic blared out. He could tell she was surprised by the way her eyes widened slightly. This was clearly a song she knew and enjoyed. He watched her lips moving as she started lip-synching along.

The memory of their kiss refused to leave his mind. So did the flash of her smile when she eventually beat him at cards or the sound of her laughter when he cracked a classic cop joke.

There was so much more to her than he'd initially realized.

Alex felt like a heel for being so mean to her but he'd had to protect his clan. Now his focus was shifting to protecting her, and that was dangerous. Not just for him but for her, too. Vamptown was counting on him to figure out who was stealing blood to prevent tension with the Gold Coast clan from spiraling out of control.

And what was he doing? Playing Go Fish with Keira. Getting to know her better and feeling closer to her each minute. He should regret doing that. Part of him did. The other part was the problem.

He'd never considered a romantic relationship with a human woman before, let alone one with her bloodline. But there was this thing between them. She must be feeling it, too. She'd certainly responded to his kiss with passion and enthusiasm.

She was so damn smart. He wished the circumstances were different so they could work together to solve these thefts. But he wasn't naive enough to think that would be an easy option.

As if reading his mind, she said, "I've been wondering . . . what do the thefts have in common? I mean, aside from the fact that they're stealing blood. What else is a common denominator here? The location, for sure, as most of them took place in the same general area."

"I can't talk about the case."

She sighed irritably. "Can't or won't? You've already talked about it with me."

She had him there. He was set on automatic default to reject her curiosity.

"Come on," she coaxed him. "Talk to me."

Too many others were depending on Alex for him to risk confiding in her further until he was certain she could be trusted. He couldn't just base his decision on his gut or his libido. There were still too many unknowns regarding her relationship to her hunter grandfather and his journal for Alex to reveal more of what he knew about the case—like the fact that they suspected vampires had wiped the video feeds clear.

Yes, Keira knew there was surveillance video from the theft sites, and yes she'd attributed that to vampires, incorrectly suggesting that it was because vampires couldn't be filmed. That wasn't the case here. But he couldn't give her additional information at this point.

"I can't tell you any more," he said.

"I guess that means our temporary truce is over."

"I guess it does," he said.

"It's your loss," she replied.

He tried to squelch the pang of regret he felt but it stayed with him as she gave him the silent treatment after that.

Later that night, Alex texted Neville to dig deeper in Horace Turner's past, going all the way back to the Great Chicago Fire. It was possible he was using another name in those days. Alex wanted details and he wanted them fast.

Looking at Keira now, curled up like a kitten on the couch, you'd never guess that she was related to one of the most vicious vampire hunters of all time.

He was amazed at the ease with which she fell asleep. But then much of what she did and said amazed him. He'd never met another woman like her. He'd known from the first moment he'd seen her that she was trouble, and that instinct had only intensified when she'd leaned across his desk at the police station and murmured, "Your vampire heritage."

But he'd never anticipated that she'd be The One. He wished his sire had told him more about what that entailed. But Mitch had always avoided that conversation. And frankly Alex had had a hard enough time trying to adapt to being a vampire.

He'd been dedicated to saving lives as a human. But when he became a vampire that changed. He'd seen so many of his buddies die that he'd thought he'd become immune to the finality of death. But the pain of their loss had hit him with the force of a tidal wave. He'd gone on a killing rampage across Asia. Even after the war he'd kept killing with a rage that went clear to his soul, had he still had one.

He'd done bad things. Things he regretted. The vampire life wasn't a natural fit for him. Mitch had chosen him for a reason but that reason was never completely clear to Alex, and that was incredibly frustrating. All Mitch had said was that something in Alex's ancestral past linked him to the vampire world. He had never gone into specifics.

Yes, Alex had abilities that some other vampires didn't, from being able to drink beverages besides blood to his ability to cloak. But he didn't know why. He only knew that he was meant to be where he was right now with this woman sleeping nearby.

He moved closer to her, leaning down to slide her hair away from her cheek.

She sighed and grabbed hold of his wrist. "More," she whispered.

He suspected she was in that twilight place between sleep and alertness. But he allowed her to tug him down so she could kiss his lips. She tasted delicious.

She'd started to trust him when they'd talked earlier. He'd sensed that. He couldn't betray that trust now by taking advantage of her. She didn't know what she was doing, but he did. She was driving him wild with the sweet seduction of her tongue. This had to stop.

It took every ounce of self-control he had to pull away. She sighed and turned her head, nuzzling into the blanket he'd lent her. She'd changed clothes in the bathroom, exchanging her skirt and top for a pair of pajamas printed with typewriter keys. Her movement had dislodged the part of the blanket by her feet and it was only then that he realized she was still wearing her shoes, as if planning on making a swift getaway in the night.

She was tough, he'd give her that. But he was tougher, and he'd have to be to keep this situation from becoming even more dangerous than it already was.

Chapter Nine

Keira woke slowly the next morning. Why was she on her couch instead of her bed? Had she fallen asleep watching *Perry Mason* on classic TV last night? It wouldn't be the first time. There was something about those vintage black-and-white shows that she found soothing.

Then it all came back to her—her grandfather's journal, the vampires on her fire escape, her apartment in ashes. And Alex. Hot, sexy, brooding Alex.

Had their temporary truce last night been a dream? Had they played cards and laughed and joked? Was that real? Had he kissed her again or had that only taken place in her imagination?

Her eyes flew open to find Alex standing over her, grinning. "How is our intrepid girl reporter today?" he asked. A quick glance at her watch told her it was just after six AM. He was entirely too cheerful for a vampire this early in the morning. Now that she was sitting up, she realized she had a crick in her neck from sleeping on the couch. She hadn't felt awkward last night wearing pajamas in front of him since they covered more of her skin than her skirt and top had. But for some reason she felt vulnerable at the moment and that irritated her.

Was she the only one who'd been affected by their kiss yesterday? Last night they'd bridged their distrust long enough to . . . what? How would she describe what they'd done? Play cards and talk. How groundbreaking was that? Not groundbreaking enough for him to really confide in her . . . or for her to really confide in him. Her irritation grew.

"I am *not* intrepid. I'm no Lois Lane!"

"No?" he drawled. "She did tend to get into some pretty dangerous situations."

"Meaning I've done the same thing?"

He just gave her a look.

"Okay, I admit coming to see you without a real plan may not have been my brightest moment."

"Ya think?"

"Yes, I do think, contrary to what you are insinuating. I usually do think things through before acting on them, although there are times when I just take a leap of faith. This was one of those times."

"If you hadn't come see me, you might have been home when those vamps came to get you."

"Maybe that wouldn't have happened at all if I hadn't opened up this vampire thing by coming to see you. That vampire, Lawrence Lynch, who came to talk to you while I was there may have been behind the break-in at my place."

"I never gave him your name."

"Maybe he already knew."

"Had you seen him before?" Alex asked.

"No. But now that I think about it I did feel like I was being followed. I didn't see anyone specifically. It was just a weird feeling. Nothing concrete, and it didn't last long."

"When was this?"

"After I left the Taste of Chicago press lunch, right before I confronted you at the police station."

"You should have told me earlier."

"I didn't think it was real," she admitted.

"Why are you rubbing your neck?" he asked her.

"I must have slept on it funny."

The next thing she knew, he was sitting next to her and gently massaging her neck. "Where does it hurt? Here?"

She nodded.

"You're all tense," he murmured.

Whose fault is that? she would have said had his touch not made her feel so good. He was so close that she could hear him breathing. Then he abruptly stopped and moved away.

Clearing his throat, he said, "You still haven't explained why your grandfather sent you to see me. Was it only because I was next on his hit list? I would have thought that would be enough to keep you away. Or did you come to warn me?"

"Warn you about what?"

"That I was next?"

"He wrote that I'd need your help."

"Help doing what?"

"He wasn't real specific," she said.

"And that didn't raise a red flag for you?"

"Forgive me if I act on it when I read that all hell is going to break loose if I don't contact you."

"Contact me, a vampire whom your grandfather

planned on killing. A vampire when your grandfather believed we were all evil."

"Hey, I didn't say it was logical," she shot back.

"None of this is logical."

"You can't keep holding me prisoner here. People are going to know I'm missing. I have work deadlines. I have co-workers and friends. They're going to look for me."

"Maybe."

"No maybe about it. They've probably already reported me missing."

His expression remained impassive.

She pointed an accusing finger at him. "They did report me, right? And you covered it up."

"Who knew you came to see me?"

"Lots of people." In retrospect, that would have been a smart thing to do. Not to reveal the vampire stuff, but at least to tell someone she was checking out a story at the police station.

"Liar," he said.

Telling someone probably wouldn't have made a difference anyway. Alex would just have compelled his cop buddies to forget it.

"Why is a vampire masquerading as a Chicago cop?" she demanded.

"I'm not masquerading."

She'd done some minimal research on Alex before confronting him. She knew he was in charge of some special case division but couldn't get any details on what that was. Thefts from blood banks seemed to be a special case to her, so it made sense for her to go see him as her grandfather had instructed. Not that her grandfather could have known about the thefts; they'd happened after his death.

She was getting a headache trying to figure this all out. Besides that, she was starving. The only food she'd had since the press luncheon yesterday was a cupcake. She'd checked the kitchen but found only containers of blood in the fridge. That had taken away her appetite pretty fast, so she hadn't bothered checking the cupboards.

Wait, she did have some of those cupcakes left. A huge cup of coffee would sure be nice.

As if on cue, Alex offered her one of the two mugs he held. "Do you take it black?"

"What is it?" she asked suspiciously.

"It's coffee. I can drink a variety of things, including wine and coffee." He took a swig from the mug he'd kept for himself.

"Is that normal? For a vampire, I mean." She'd asked him before but he hadn't really answered.

"Not necessarily."

"What makes you so special?"

His smile was seductively inviting. "Why don't you tell me?"

"The fact that you're bossy and arrogant."

"Nah, most vampires are bossy and arrogant. That doesn't make me special. Try again."

She belatedly took the mug he'd offered her earlier. "Yesterday Bruce said something about you being able to cloak. I'm assuming that means the ability to avoid detection. Is that a common vampire ability?"

"You read your grandfather's journal. What did he think were common vampire abilities?"

"He certainly didn't mention drinking wine and coffee. Or anything about cloaking."

"Your curiosity is a dangerous thing," he told her.

"It's why I became a journalist."

"Not exactly a booming job market at the moment."

"Like being a vampire is?"

"Point taken." Alex flashed her another one of those trademark smiles of his.

"So tell me why you have these special abilities."

His smile disappeared. "Because the vampire who sired me had them."

"Where is he now?"

"Dead."

"What happened?"

Alex looked away from her to check his phone, which had just indicated he had a text. "I've got to go to work. You can take a shower if you want."

Did that mean she smelled? Was he trying to tell her that she *needed* to take a shower? She could feel herself blushing so she lifted her coffee mug and focused on drinking from it. Not only was Alex a hot and sexy vampire but he also made a damn good cup of coffee.

"Sierra will be coming to stay with you while I'm gone," he said.

As he walked past her toward the door, she smelled his scent. It was spicy and fresh and triggered the memory of her dream last night that he'd kissed her and left her wanting more. Maybe that was left over from him leaving her that way earlier yesterday.

"Any news on the blood thefts?" she asked him. She was losing it here. She had to keep the focus on the case and not on Alex. But damn, it was difficult to do that when he radiated sexuality.

"That's why I'm heading to the station."

"Maybe I should come with you," she said, eager to get out of the loft.

"You'd just be a distraction," he told her bluntly before walking out the door.

Alex wasn't in a good mood when he walked into his office. Craig's wife, Bunny, was sitting next to his desk waiting for him. "I did it," she stated dramatically. "I'm responsible for the blood thefts."

Alex stared at her in amazement. "What the hell are you talking about?"

"It's my fault."

Alex guided her into the empty interrogation room, the one he used for vampire-related business. He'd disabled the cameras so they wouldn't record and then compelled the human cops to avoid that room.

"What is this all about?" he demanded.

"I told you."

"Why would you steal blood? You don't even drink it. You go for the artificial stuff, right?"

"We're doing experiments to improve the artificial blood currently available. I've indicated that I think a better blend could be attained."

"So you broke into the blood bank and stole blood?"

"I didn't actually steal it but I might as well have."

"Did you hire someone else to do it?" Alex asked.

"No."

"Compel someone else to do it?"

"Of course not."

"Then I fail to see how you are to blame for the thefts," he said.

"Because I put it out there."

"Put what out there? Doesn't your facility have access to blood?"

"Yes, but the research grant for the project I'm

working on was recently cut because of a lack of funding."

He sighed. "It always comes back to money, doesn't it?"

"We couldn't procure the blood we needed."

"So someone stole it."

"They must have."

"Any idea who? It would have to be someone who knows about the work you're doing." He pushed a yellow pad toward her. "I'm going to need names."

"I can't blame anyone else for my mistakes," Bunny said, wringing her hands.

"What mistakes?"

She shook her head.

"Maybe I should bring Craig in here."

Now she really shook her head. "Don't do that!"

"Why not? He's your husband. Are you suggesting he has something to do with the thefts?"

"No. He'd never do something like that."

"Bunny, I've got a lot going on right now. We've got a potential vampire war breaking out between us and the Gold Coast vamps. Someone torched Keira's apartment yesterday, and we have multiple hostiles looking for her grandfather's journal. I've got to get to it before someone else does. So I really don't have time to sit around trying to figure out what you're talking about."

She picked up a pen from the table and started to write. "Warren Driscoll is a research assistant."

"A human?"

"For the most part. He has some vampire blood but not much. Not enough to interfere with his work."

"Does he know you're a vampire?"

"We've never discussed it."

"That doesn't really answer my question. What makes you think he might have something to do with the thefts?"

"He was very upset when he got the news about the grant funding being cut," Bunny said.

"How upset?"

"Quite upset."

"Did he suddenly show up with batches of blood?"

"No, nothing that obvious. He did seem to indicate that he might have access to a supply of blood that was outside the normal suppliers."

"I'll bring him in and talk to him."

"Don't hurt him."

"What is it with everyone thinking I hurt humans and burn down apartments?" Alex said impatiently.

"I never said you burned down an apartment."

"Keira thought I did."

"You seem to have formed a strong connection with her in a short period of time," Bunny said. "That's the way it was with me and Craig. We met when I was sixteen. He moved in across the street from me and the first time I met him, I knew we'd be married. We didn't know we'd be vampires."

"How did that happen, again?"

"Craig was run over by a horse and carriage."

"Horse and carriage? I thought you were turned in the 1950s."

"We renewed our vampire vows in the 1950s. We couldn't keep the same identities forever. Humans would get suspicious. Craig has kept his name since the 1950s and just added *Junior* or *the Third* after his surname of Anderson."

"So when were you turned?"

"During the Chicago Fire. Craig's cousin from Romania was visiting. The situation was chaotic. I'll never forget that night." She shuddered.

Alex was only now realizing that Craig had never gone into details about when he was turned. He'd been vague, letting Alex assume that the date was the 1950s and not the late 1800s. He wondered if there was a reason for the secrecy. "Go on," he told Bunny.

"They said the fire was under control but it wasn't. By the time we realized that, it was too late. It was very windy. Embers were flying through the air, setting everything they touched aflame. We were heading toward Lake Michigan, as were throngs of others. Some had carriages filled with their belongings, or those they could grab in a hurry. Somehow Craig was shoved into the street in front of one of them . . ." She paused. "His legs were crushed." She cleared her throat. "Even after all this time it's still difficult talking about what happened. I stayed behind with Craig. His cousin said he could take away the pain but it would change Craig forever. I refused to let go of Craig's hand so his cousin was stuck with us both. He commandeered the carriage and loaded Craig into it. I'm not sure where he took us. He was new to the city yet he seemed to know where he was going. We escaped the path of the fire and ended up in a deserted house away from everything. That's where he drained Craig and then me before having us drink his blood."

"You weren't nervous about becoming a vampire?"

"I just wanted to be with Craig," Bunny said. "I confess I never did get used to drinking blood. I never bit anyone. Craig brought me containers of blood. I went to college in the 1960s and got my degree in chemistry and microbiology. I've been working on the creation of a workable synthetic blood ever since, using various names and working in various places."

"What about your sire?"

"He returned to Romania."

"Before the fire or after, did you know anyone by the name of Horace Turner?"

"I don't believe so."

Alex made a mental note to check with Craig as well as getting more info on the mysterious vampire cousin from Romania. "Let's get back to your assistant Warren. Where is he now?"

"He didn't show up for work this morning and he hasn't returned any of my calls or texts. That's not a good thing, right?"

"Definitely not a good thing," Alex agreed.

A shower and a change of clothes didn't give Keira a fresh perspective on her situation. But at least she smelled better thanks to the selection of artisan soaps in a basket in the bathroom. She pulled on a pair of comfy yoga pants and a black tunic.

When Keira opened the bathroom door she found Sierra in the kitchen putting away a bag of groceries. "Alex asked me to pick you up some food," she said. "I wasn't sure what you'd like so I got the basics for you—eggs, bread, frozen dinners."

"I'd like my freedom," Keira said. "Alex says I have to prove I'm trustworthy. I think it should be the other way around."

"Did he suggest a way to prove yourself?"

"Sure. He said I'd have to voluntarily let them take my blood."

Sierra looked stunned. "You mean to drink from you?"

"No, my blood is toxic to vampires because of my grandfather being what he was. Instead they want to take a blood sample the regular way with needles and a phlebotomist so they can learn more about me."

"Wow."

"I know."

"All I can say is that everyone is very stressed at the moment because of these blood thefts," Sierra said. "We could be on the verge of a turf war between vampire clans here."

"As I already told you, I met Lawrence Lynch briefly. He's in charge of the Gold Coast vamps, right?"

Sierra neither denied nor confirmed Keira's statement. Instead she said, "What was he like?"

"He gave me the creeps."

"I've heard he's pretty ruthless."

"Ruthless enough to torch my apartment?" Keira asked.

"I doubt he'd do it himself given the fact that vampires avoid flames. But he could certainly have compelled someone to do it. He could also have sent his minions to try to grab you."

"Minions?"

"Minions are mercenaries of a sort. I've heard he hires them to do some of his dirty work. I've only been in Chicago six months, so I'm not totally up on the details of the issues between him and Vamptown."

"You still must know more than I do."

"I don't know about that. You're the one who met Lynch, not me. I do know that Alex has really gone out of his way to protect you," Sierra said. "I know you don't think so, but it's true. The others aren't pleased that he brought you here. Alex has put himself at risk by helping you."

Keira's heart froze. "Will the others hurt him?"

"The hostile vampires would kill him. It's my understanding they were mercenaries. We don't know who hired them, but their mission was to grab you and to kill Alex if he tried to stop them."

"How do you know that?"

"Let's just call it the word on the street."

"So Alex is in danger?"

"I know he's a cop, but saving you from hostile vampires is above and beyond the call of duty or abilities of the average Chicago police detective."

"By average you mean human."

"Alex is above average even in the vampire world," Sierra said.

"How so?"

"He'll have to tell you himself."

"Is that why he was next on my grandfather's hit list? Because Alex is 'above average,' as you put it? Does he have powers that other vampires don't, and if so what are they? Other than drinking wine or coffee and being able to cloak, I mean. I know about those. Does he have additional abilities?"

"Ever the reporter, huh?"

"I'm not asking because I'm a reporter. I'm asking because . . ."

"Because you care about Alex. You might as well admit it. I saw the look on your face when you realized he is in danger."

Keira wrapped her arms around her middle, trying to stay warm when her body felt like ice. Yeah, it was cold in the loft with the air-conditioning cranked way up but she was wearing yoga pants and a black tunic top with long sleeves. It's not like she had on a tank top and shorts. She shouldn't be on the verge of trembling. Concern for Alex was making her react this way. He was so strong and powerful that she hadn't considered the possibility he could be hurt. "I never should have gone to see him," she murmured.

"If you hadn't, you'd be dead by now," Sierra said bluntly.

Before Keira could respond, the door to the loft flew open. Daniella Delaney rushed in and yelled, "War is coming!"

Chapter Ten

Keira looked around in dismay. "Where?"

"Here. Right here," Daniella exclaimed before adding, "I think."

"Okay, let's just all take a deep breath before we panic," Sierra said. "No sirens have gone off so we should be okay for now."

Daniella nodded and inhaled.

"In and out," Sierra said, putting an arm around the woman. "That's it."

"You're Daniella Delaney, right?" Keira said, just wanting to confirm her facts. "You own Heavenly Cupcakes. You were written up in the *Chicago Tribune*. I did a story about you for *ReadIt* a few months ago."

Daniella perked up. "That's right."

Keira had heard of *Cupcake Wars*. Surely that must be what Daniella was talking about. No way could she be referring to a vampire war. No way the cupcake maker could be a vampire, right?

"I have premonitions—" Daniella began.

Sierra held up her hand to stop Daniella midsentence.

"I don't know how much we're supposed to share with Keira."

"My premonition involves her," Daniella said.

"Maybe we should wait for Alex to return," Sierra suggested.

"He was in it, too," Daniella said.

"Then we should definitely wait," Sierra said.

"But this is urgent," Daniella said. In a lower voice, she added, "It's not like the sex premonition I had about Damon and Zoe."

"That's a relief." Keira didn't need any sex premonitions added to the chaotic mess that her life had become in the past day. "You do know I'm being held here against my will, right?"

"Of course I know that," Daniella said.

"Being held against my will by vampires," Keira elaborated.

"Yeah, that sucks," Alex said, appearing out of nowhere.

"War is coming," Daniella told him before frowning. "Or maybe Warren is coming." She rubbed her forehead with a flour-dusted index finger. "You know my premonitions aren't always completely clear. They can be a bit fuzzy sometimes."

"Did you tell Nick about your premonition?" Alex said.

"Not yet. I rushed right over here to tell you and Keira because the two of you were in it."

Clearly Daniella knew about vampires—Keira's comment about them hadn't startled her in the least.

"It wasn't a sexual premonition," Daniella told Alex.

"How reassuring," Keira said sarcastically.

"Isn't it, though," Alex agreed.

"Anyway, something dangerous is coming," Daniella said.

"More dangerous than vampires?" Keira said.

"It could be vampires," Daniella acknowledged. "That's one of the fuzzy bits. And just for the record I don't approve of holding you against your will, Keira, but I understand that these are troubling times."

"To put it mildly," Alex said.

"And troubling times can require extraordinary measures." Daniella glanced at her watch. "Yikes, speaking of measures, I've got to get back to work. I've got six dozen cupcakes to finish measuring and baking for a graduation party we're catering."

"I'm going to take off, too," Sierra said. "I've still got five more pages to write today."

"I'd like to take off myself," Keira said. "Unfortunately I'm being held hostage here."

"I'll tell you what's unfortunate," Alex said once they were alone. "The fact that it's been hours since your mouth has been on mine."

Keira blinked in surprise. "I thought we decided that kiss was a mistake."

"Did we? I don't recall saying that." He looped his arms around her waist.

Her hand on his chest prevented him from pulling her closer. Well, it probably didn't truly prevent him. He was certainly stronger than she was and he could have taken her in his arms no matter what she said. But she sensed that he wouldn't do so.

Was she stupid for trusting him? There had to be a reason for her grandfather to have sent her to Alex. "What are you doing here? I thought you said you were going to work."

"I *was* at work. And I'm going back later. But right

now I'm more interested in you." He brushed a strand of hair from her cheek.

"Why?" she asked suspiciously.

"I'm trying to make sense of all this."

"Me too."

"Then talk to me."

"You're just trying to seduce your way to my grand-father's journal."

"Am I?"

"Yes."

"And how am I doing?"

"Too damn well," she muttered before reaching out with both hands to slide her fingers through his dark hair and tug him closer. A second later his mouth covered hers.

There was no resisting him. She'd initiated the kiss but he intensified it tenfold as she parted her lips to invite him in. He combined the thrust of his tongue with seductive swirls that woke something deep within her. She wanted him so intensely that it was almost painful. Yet it was also powerfully magnetic.

His dark hair was like silk and his lips were made to drive her mad. He was a vampire—dark and dangerous and sexy as hell. Oh yeah, and immortal.

"We can't keep doing this," she whispered against his mouth.

"Why not?"

"Because it could lead to trouble."

"Trust me, we're already in trouble," he said huskily.

"I know, but if this gets more intense . . . more intimate . . . having sex with you would complicate things. Or maybe it would just complicate things for me and make things easier for you," she said.

"How do you figure that?"

"This is a serious situation."

"Definitely." He nibbled on her earlobe.

"I mean it. Your vampire friends aren't happy that I'm here, and your vampire enemies are out to get me."

He leaned back to gaze into her eyes. "I won't let them."

She believed him. She shouldn't, but she did. That didn't change the other problems facing them. "You're out to get my grandfather's journal, no matter the cost."

"What makes you think there will be a cost? What aren't you telling me?" he said.

"There's a lot I'm not telling you."

"What about the Chicago Fire? Did he write about that time? About any vampires from that time? Did he name names?"

"I'm not sure. He didn't write a lot about that. The journal begins right before the fire."

"What about later? Did your grandfather plan on having a vampire war to save him the trouble of killing us all himself?"

"I don't know," Keira said. "He can't be behind the blood thefts. He died a year ago."

"Did he really?"

"I don't know," she whispered, rubbing her forehead. "I don't know what to believe anymore."

"Believe this." Leaning closer, Alex kissed her again. Every time his lips touched her, the sizzling desire she was experiencing got wilder in her most intimate places. Nothing could have prepared her for this. The taste of him was an addictive aphrodisiac.

"What's going on?" she asked unsteadily. "Why do I feel this way?"

"What way?" he whispered against her lips.

"Like this was meant to be."

"Maybe it is." He backed her up against the brick wall and held her wrists over her head with one hand while he caressed her breasts with the other. When the black tunic she wore got in his way, he simply slid his hand beneath it to unsnap her bra. He cupped her bare skin in his palm before brushing his thumb over her nipple.

She shivered with the fierce pleasure created by his caress. His body was pressed against hers, allowing her to feel his arousal and igniting her passion even more. He kept kissing her as he lowered his hand over her stomach to the waistband of her pants and lower.

Her knees almost gave way as he threaded his fingers through the crisp curls on her mound before fingering her clitoris with the tip of his thumb. Every pulse in her body was beating with wild anticipation of the shards of rapture to come. The friction he created was driving her mad.

She gasped with excitement and held her breath waiting for his next move. Her entire body was vibrating on the verge of something spectacular when Alex's phone pinged, indicating a text.

"No." She would have grabbed his hand to prevent him from answering but he held her wrists captive.

She mourned the loss of his darkly intimate touch.

He swore as he read the message. He released her. "I have to go."

He was gone in an instant, leaving her breathless, frustrated, and yearning for more yet again.

Alex couldn't believe how powerful his feelings for Keira were becoming. He'd gone home to see if there was a tie between Craig and Bunny and The Executioner's journal. Instead he'd been distracted and compelled to kiss Keira. He'd been ready to take her against that brick wall and she'd seemed happy to let him do so. She was passionate and fierce despite the fact that she knew he was a vampire. This was a first for him. Something as highly inflammable as his desire for Keira was a dangerous thing. Why did she have to be The One? The why-her, why-now questions kept flaring through his brain as he raced at vamp speed back to the police station.

The text he'd received was an urgent summons in regard to the blood thefts. It had come from Thomas Wentworth, the Chicago police detective in charge of the special cases unit in the Gold Coast district.

Thomas was waiting for Alex at Alex's police district station. The two of them entered the specialized interrogation room where Alex had spoken to Bunny earlier.

"We're on neutral ground here," Thomas said. "Not on Vamptown or Gold Coast turf."

Alex got right to the point. "Have you used your cleanup crews to hide evidence in these blood thefts?" The vampires in each clan had the means to correct any situation that might reveal their existence. They also had the ability to create new identities as needed.

"I came to ask you the same thing," Thomas said.

"Why would we try to rob a location on our own turf?" Alex said.

"Why would we?" Thomas countered. "The blood banks are on our turf. The funeral home was on yours. The South Shore vamps have been noticeably quiet on this."

"You've got a point."

Even though Thomas was part of the Gold Coast clan, Alex had always had a relatively good working relationship with him.

"I've got some of my team watching the South Shore clan," Thomas said.

"You've probably got some watching our clan as well."

"Affirmative," Thomas said. "Just as you're watching us."

"Are you aware that Lynch came to see me yesterday?"

Thomas nodded. "I am aware, yes."

"Were there any reports in your area about more thefts?"

Thomas's expression remained impassive but Alex picked up on something. "There was, wasn't there."

"We took care of it."

"How?"

"That's our business."

"Not if it involves humans. You know that our treaty requires us to remain under the human radar," Alex reminded him.

"As I said, we took care of it."

"Do you have someone in custody?"

"Not in police custody, no," Thomas said.

"Dammit, you know that wasn't what I meant."

"And you know I'm not at liberty to reveal Gold Coast intel."

"Does the person you have in custody have ties to the South Shore vamps?" Alex asked.

"None that I could discover, no."

"Do they have ties to Vamptown?"

"Yes."

"You're holding Warren," Alex said. No wonder the research tech hadn't shown up for work today. "Is he still alive?"

"Affirmative."

"And you think he is behind all the thefts?"

"He was behind the one last night. We caught him red-handed," Thomas said.

"He's not a member of our clan," Alex pointed out.

"He works for a member of your clan."

"Wrong. He works for the same medical biochemical company as a member of our clan. There's a difference."

Thomas shrugged. "If you say so."

"Have you tied him to the other thefts?"

"He appears to have an airtight alibi for the one in Vamptown."

"Which serves to prove that there is still someone out there trying to steal blood," Alex said.

"Or you could have staged the robbery at the funeral home as a red herring. After all, no blood was removed from that site. In fact, it is the only attempted theft out of the five so far."

"We could have, but we didn't." Alex abruptly changed the subject. "What about the fire?"

Thomas didn't pretend not to know what Alex was talking about. "The fire at the vampire hunter's apartment? I have no knowledge of that."

"No knowledge" was the vampire's way of saying *maybe I did it, maybe I didn't.*

"She's not a vampire hunter," Alex corrected him.

"She's dangerous to all who would protect her," Thomas said.

"Why?"

"I've already said too much."

Alex could tell that he wouldn't get any more information out of Thomas on that issue so he returned to the thefts. "What about Warren? What are you going to do with him?"

"Turn him over to you. Maybe you can get more out

of him than we did. But before I do that, there is still the matter of The Executioner's journal. We want it."

"I'm aware." Alex deliberately used the same words his Gold Coast counterpart had.

"If you have it, I recommend turning it over to me."

"I can't do that."

"Can't or won't?" Thomas said.

"Won't."

"So you *do* have it?"

Alex just smiled.

"I don't envy you, my friend," Thomas told him. "I have a feeling things are going to get very rough around here very soon." With that warning, Thomas was gone, leaving Alex wondering what the hell was coming next.

Lynch stood looking at the spectacular view of the Chicago skyline from his penthouse apartment. The windows were specially treated to block out the worst of the sunlight. Turning to face his temporary acting head of operations, Pierre Dubois, he said, "Vamptown won't know what hit them." He paused a moment before happily admitting, "I'm looking forward to messing with them."

He was still peeved that he hadn't discovered the means by which the vampires in Vamptown were able to tolerate sunlight with such ease. While it was true Gold Coast vamps didn't sizzle when in the sun, that ability was a drain on their system. But his current medical project was much more important. The blood thefts were a necessary component of his experiment, which was cloaked with the utmost security. He was the only one who knew the details. The time was quickly coming when the world would know of his brilliance, but for now the information remained highly classified by him.

Eyeing Pierre, he said, "There's nothing you're keeping from me, is there? And remember the new protocol of calling me master."

"No, master. I'm not keeping anything from you."

"I'm asking because your predecessor's predecessor Douglas should have come to me with his suspicions about Keira. Instead he had her followed from the press luncheon to the police station without telling me anything about it. Had he informed me of his actions, I could have grabbed her at that time."

"He wasn't certain of her tie to The Executioner."

Lynch glared at him. "You're not defending him, are you?"

"No, master." Pierre hung his head.

"Good." Lynch was running out of qualified applicants for the position of director of operations. He'd hate to have to terminate another so quickly. But he would do so if necessary.

"Can you fill me in on your master plan, master?"

"I could but I don't think I will at this point," Lynch replied. "It is rather brilliant if I do say so myself . . . and I do."

"I'm sure it is, master."

"I'm aware that there were those in the Gold Coast clan who doubted my ability to run things when I took over. But since that time I've tripled our wealth in a relatively short period of time. And that's nothing compared with what is going to happen soon. My medical project is projected to increase our wealth a thousand-fold. I'm the only one who is capable of these accomplishments. No one else. No other chemist. No other innovator. No other leader. Just me."

"There is no one like you, master," Pierre quickly acknowledged.

"Exactly. I'm glad we see eye-to-eye on that fact."

"If there is anything I can do to be of assistance, master?"

"Just do your job," Lynch said. "That's all I ask of anyone. Do your job perfectly and there won't be any problems." He paused for a moment before smiling. "Unless you live in Vamptown, that is. In which case you'll be dealing with plenty of problems. As I said earlier, they won't know what hit them."

"I'm getting stiff from just sitting around doing nothing," Keira told Bruce, who had joined her within moments of Alex leaving. Actually most of her restless body aches were Alex's fault for leaving her on the verge of orgasm. Not that she was sharing that with Bruce. "I need to get some fresh air and take a walk."

"I've got the next best thing," Bruce said. "A Pilates workout DVD. I'm qualified as an instructor. I took an online course."

"I'm not interested in a workout," she said impatiently. "What about the news? Have there been any other incidents?"

"Incidents?"

"Trouble. Alex lit out of here . . ."

"As if on fire." Bruce completed the sentence for her. She grimaced.

"Sorry," he said. "Bad choice of words given your apartment fire."

"I'm glad you got some of my things out. The photo albums in the bookcase mean the world to me."

She opened one up but the pages were blank. "What?" She could hardly frame the word. "Who took the photos out of here? I want them back." She jabbed her finger against Bruce's chest, wrinkling his impeccably pressed lavender shirt. "Hand them over!"

"I don't have them."

"Then who does?"

"I don't know," he said. "But we've got bigger problems at the moment."

"Like what?"

"Like that siren going off."

Keira frowned. "I don't hear anything."

"Only vampires can hear it."

"Why is it going off?"

"Because we're being invaded," Bruce said.

Chapter Eleven

"Invaded?" Keira repeated in alarm. "What are we supposed to do?"

"Stay calm," Bruce said. "I'm pretty sure we are supposed to stay calm."

"Who is invading us?"

"Hostiles of some sort. We have to head for the shelter."

"What shelter?"

He rushed over to the bed and pushed a brick above the intricately carved headboard. A panel in the wall slid open, revealing a dark entryway.

"Come on." Bruce held out his hand. "We've got to move fast."

She vehemently shook her head. "No way. I'm claustrophobic. I am not going in there."

"Yes, you are," Alex said, appearing out of no place as he so often did. "Keep her safe," he told Bruce before shoving her into the dark confines and closing the panel.

Alex was ready for battle. "What have we got?" he demanded even as he activated the loft's flat-screen TV monitors, which were tied into Vamptown's security command center. Thomas had just warned him that things were going to get rough. Moments later Alex heard the Vamptown siren go off. Vampire hearing was such that even though Alex was outside of the limits of Vamptown, he wasn't outside the range of the siren system installed to protect them all.

"Unknown hostiles," Nick replied through the system.

Alex watched the screen as shadowy figures walked with rapid precision down the street. There were multitudes of them. A small army with daggers and swords.

Alex was downstairs in a flash with his own weapons in hand. Damon met him at the door leading outside. "Where are they?"

"I'm not seeing or sensing anything," Damon said.

"You're a Demon Hunter. If they were demons, you'd sense them, right?" Alex said.

"Right."

"So they must be something else. Maybe they have cloaking abilities to make them invisible," Alex suggested, keeping his back to the wall as he quickly surveyed their surroundings. "What about the humans in the vicinity?"

"Neville sent out a text alert that this area is under a tornado warning and to seek immediate cover. Hopefully that keeps them indoors."

"We know what you did." The message—at a frequency only vamps could discern—floated in the air all around them.

"What the hell is that supposed to mean?" Alex said. The message sounded personal. Was it directed at him or all of Vamptown? Was it referring to the blood thefts or something else? "Who is protecting the funeral home?"

"Nick and Ronan are in charge of that," Damon said.

"Everyone else is in the shelter, right?"

"Right." Damon said.

Alex blocked out the raw panic he'd seen in Keira's eyes as he'd shoved her into the tunnel. He couldn't think about that now. He needed to focus on the imminent attack.

"Something is off about this," Damon said.

"Did you get that message about knowing what we did?"

Damon nodded.

An eerie howl filled the air.

"What the hell?" Alex had never heard anything like it. "Demons?"

"I don't think so."

"I'm not standing here waiting for something to happen," Alex growled before stepping onto the deserted sidewalk. "Bring it on!" he yelled. "Show yourselves, you bastards!"

"I need to get out!" Keira's words came out as a gasp instead of the shout she'd intended. "Get me out!"

"So you really are claustrophobic?" Bruce asked a tad nervously.

"Yes!" She was in full-blown panic mode now. "Out! Get . . . me . . . out!" She frantically scratched at the wall.

"This way out." Bruce pulled her close and did that vamp-super-speed thing down some stairs and then through a maze of dark tunnels.

"Who goes there?" someone shouted out.

"Doc, that's the wrong security question," Bruce said before coming to a stop. "You're supposed to say 'Identify yourself and your first pet's name.' "

"Identify yourself and name your first pet and who's that slung over your shoulder?" Doc demanded.

"It's Bruce, pet was Brutus, and this is Keira." He set her down. "Not sure about the name of her first pet."

"It's not in the system," Doc said.

"She has claustrophobia," Bruce said.

"Too bad she can't be compelled," Doc said. "That would have cured her symptoms. Uh, what's she doing now?"

Keira knelt down in pain. Her head felt as if it was about to explode, and she couldn't breathe.

"Don't panic," Bruce told her. "Doc is a doctor."

"I'm a dentist actually. Currently, anyway. Doc Boomer at your service," he said.

The pounding in her head was so bad that Keira could barely hear him.

"Do something, Doc," Bruce said, sounding very far away.

She was aware of someone putting a hand on her back and then her arm before sliding it down to her wrist. She tried to pull away.

"I'm just checking your pulse," Doc said in a deep loud voice. "No big deal."

She was in a confined space surrounded by two vampires. The confined part was enough to set her off even without the cheerful bloodsuckers. Hell yes, this was a big deal.

"Talk to me," Doc said, much the way that Alex had earlier.

This was all his fault. Alex was to blame for her being in pain. He was to blame for her home being torched. He was to blame for everything.

Her fingertips burned. She closed her eyes and saw flames leaping from the floor of her apartment up the drapes and over the furniture. Her emotions flared, consuming her in their vividness.

"I thought you said she wasn't a witch," Doc said.

"She's not supposed to be a witch."

"Then how is she able to do that?" Doc pointed to the lights that were flashing and flickering.

"Are we sure she's doing it and not someone else?" Bruce said.

"Let me out!" she screamed, standing up and stretching out her hands. A second later she'd blasted a huge hole in the wall in front of them.

"What the hell?" Alex said. There was no sign of anyone or anything appearing on the sidewalk or streets where the screens of the security system indicated they should be. "Where are they?"

"There's trouble beneath the funeral home," Neville told Alex and Damon via their secure system.

An instant later they joined Nick and Ronan. "A wall from the tunnel beneath has been compromised," Nick said.

"Compromised? It was blown to hell," Ronan said.

"Did you catch the hostile that did it?" Alex asked.

"Yeah." Nick pointed to Keira, who was shivering in a corner of the corridor in the funeral home basement.

Alex rushed to her side. "What did they do to you?"

"You!" she growled, slapping his hands away. "You did this to me. I told you not to lock me in there."

"She's claustrophobic," Doc said.

"What happened?" Alex demanded.

"I'm not sure," Doc said. "I suspect her panic triggered some sort of paranormal response in her. An extremely pissed-off paranormal response. She wanted out so she made that happen."

"I have a headache," she moaned.

Daniella joined them, giving them all a reprimanding look. "You're lucky we didn't have a funeral in progress. I don't know what we would have done in that case. I'm assuming someone compelled my father, stepmother, and brother to stay in the funeral director's office until further notice. How is that supposed to be a safe place during an invasion? And what the hell happened to Keira?" She moved closer to offer a sympathetic word but Alex held his hand out to keep her back.

"She was in the tunnel," he said.

"We all have bad memories of those tunnels," Daniella said. "Miles held me captive down there when he was in charge of the Gold Coast clan."

Nick put an arm around Daniella. "I know it's difficult for you, but Miles is gone. Eradicated."

"By me. Maybe this is his clan's way of getting back at us all," Daniella said. "Have you considered that?"

"Considered and rejected," Nick said curtly.

"What about the invasion?" Daniella asked.

"It was a false alarm, according to Neville," Nick said, checking his smartphone. "Someone hacked into our system and created the image of an invasion. Neville and his crew are working on fixing the problem. The most damage was what the hunter's granddaughter did to the tunnel."

"She has a name, dammit," Alex growled in frustration. "Her name is Keira and she's no hunter."

"Careful," Doc warned him. "I wouldn't get any closer to her if I were you."

"You're not me," Alex said before returning his attention to Keira. "*Mija*, it's me. It's okay. You're safe now."

"No I'm not!" She slapped his hands away.

"I warned you," Doc told Alex.

"Where am I?" Keira looked around.

"The basement of the funeral home," Bruce said helpfully.

Her eyes widened. "Did Bruce bring me here to kill me?" She got to her feet and looked ready to make a run for it.

Alex quickly got to his feet and curled his fingers around hers for reassurance. "No, nothing like that. I've got you. You're safe."

"This is where you get your blood," Keira said out of the blue.

"Uh-oh," Bruce said.

Alex took her in his arms and rushed her back to the loft. "Shh, I'm not using the tunnels," he assured her.

She felt the rush of thick, humid air before the chill of the air-conditioning hit her. Opening her eyes, she looked around, searching out reassuring items like the photo of her mom. What would she think of this situation?

One thing was certain. Keira's mom would tell her to stay strong. So Keira took a deep breath and shoved the remaining fear down. Even though it wasn't easy, she had to regain control. Her tongue was so dry it felt like it was stuck to the roof of her mouth.

"I'm sorry," Alex said, handing her a cold unopened bottle of water from the fridge. "I didn't know—"

"Yes, you did." She took the bottle. "You heard me tell Bruce I had claustrophobia. You didn't care."

He cupped her cheek with his hand. "I do care."

She moved away. "Sure you do. You care about my grandfather's journal and that's it."

"Not true. I do care about the journal but I care about you as well."

His warm words washed over her. She wished she could believe him. A part of her sensed that she could. But that wasn't logical. The bond she felt with him had to be the result of some sort of vampire thing.

Yes, he was a damn fine kisser. Yes, he was powerful and sexy. Yes, looking at him made her weak in the knees, which was why she was now sitting down on her couch. "If you think you can romance the journal from me, you're wrong."

"You're too smart for a con like that."

"That's not what you thought this morning when you called me Lois Lane."

"My bad."

"And not your only bad," she said bitterly. "You shoved me into that dark hole."

"We were under attack. The tunnels were the safest place for you."

"No place feels safe," she retorted. "Not my apartment with rabid vampires at the door. I thought vampires had to be invited in. Maybe they would have stayed on the fire escape if you hadn't grabbed me."

"They were fledgling mercenaries."

"What does that mean?"

"It means they don't wait for invitations."

"What's the point of having rules if everyone doesn't obey them?" she growled in frustration. "So fledgling mercenaries can do whatever they want?"

"No. They can do whatever they are paid to do. That's what they were created for."

"Someone paid them money to come after me?"

"No. Someone promised to pay them with blood. That's why they seemed so rabid. They hadn't fed in a long time, and that kind of starvation is particularly difficult during the fledgling period." He paused a moment before asking, "What made you say what you did about the funeral home and blood?"

"It's the truth, isn't it?"

"That's not what I asked."

"It was the only location that had an attempted robbery. I checked the police records."

"The specifics weren't in the police records."

"They weren't?"

"No. But you knew that already."

"I did?"

"Don't get cute with me."

"Trust me, I'm not feeling very cute at the moment," she muttered, holding the cold bottle to her sweaty and pounding forehead.

"I'm finding it hard to trust you when you refuse to tell me the truth," Alex said.

"I'm a reporter. I keep asking questions until I get a reasonable answer."

"Reasonable? Really?" he mocked her. "None of this is reasonable unless Damon is right and your grandfather is still alive."

Keira blinked in surprise. She couldn't believe what she was hearing. "That's ridiculous!"

"Is it?"

"So you're saying my grandfather sent those rabid fledgling vampires after me and then torched my apartment?"

"Maybe he did."

"Why?"

"To make me feel sorry for you," Alex said.

"You . . . you . . . ," she sputtered, so angry she couldn't speak properly. The lights started flickering.

"Did I hit a nerve?" he said. "Too close to the truth?"

"Too ludicrous to even contemplate," she shot back. "My grandfather would never do that to me."

"Do what? Put you in danger? He sent you to me, didn't he? You don't think that was a risky move?"

"Unless he knew you wouldn't hurt me," she said. "Maybe he knew you and I had some kind of connection."

"Or maybe he knew that starting a war between vampire clans would kill more vampires than he ever could on his own."

"Maybe he did. But I'm not part of that plan if there ever was one."

"Or *is* one," he said.

Keira refused to accept the possibility that her grandfather was still alive. While a part of her would welcome his return to her life, another part of her couldn't believe that he'd put her through the pain and grief of losing him. Or that he wouldn't have come forward when her mother died two months ago. No, he had to be gone.

As for the Evergreen Funeral Home, she'd guessed that was the location of the attempted blood theft, hoping Alex's reaction would tell her if it was true or not. She narrowed her eyes at him. He'd shoved her into that dark space with no regard to her feelings, and that infuriated her.

The lights flickered again. Had she done that? What the hell was going on?

"When are you going to discuss the elephant in the room?" she demanded. "Don't give me that look. You know what I'm talking about. The fact that I blasted my way out of that tunnel. I went all Princess Leah minus the blaster in my hand."

"Tell me exactly what happened."

"I had to get out. My panic kept growing until I couldn't breathe. I couldn't control it."

"Has anything like that happened before?"

"No."

"Are you sure?"

"I think I'd know if I knocked a hole in a wall just by putting my hands out and having bolts of energy shooting from my fingertips," she noted sarcastically.

"What else did you feel besides the panic?"

"Anger. Then my head started pounding and my fingertips felt hot. The lights started flickering like they did here a minute ago. I couldn't breathe. I think I screamed something. I put my hands out . . ." She demonstrated and the plastic water bottle in her hand burst open, spraying water over them both.

"Okay, I am officially freaking out now," she said. "What did you do to me to make this happen?"

"I didn't do anything," Alex said.

"The other vampires, then. What did they do?"

"Nothing. It's your heritage. Your hunter heritage."

"That's ridiculous," she said. "Nothing weird ever happened to me until I met you."

"A blood test could confirm it."

"Confirm what?"

"That fact that you have a powerful strain of hunter blood in you. I don't know if it's the percentage or something else. If you read your grandfather's journal then you should know that the blasting ability you experienced is one of his tools of the trade."

"You mean he used it to blast vampires?" She must have skipped over that part.

"Yes, and before you try it on me, he was only able to do so after decades of training and learning to focus his abilities."

"I wouldn't try it on you."

"Wouldn't you?"

"Why did he send me to you?" she said. "And don't give me that feeling-sorry-for-me shit."

"I don't know. I suspect it was because he knew I would protect you."

"From what?"

"From whatever danger faced you."

"That's not logical. My vampire hunting grandfather sends me to a vampire to protect me? And not just any vampire, but the one at the top of his hit list."

"Like you said before, there is a connection between us." Alex smoothed her damp hair off her cheek. "You feel it, too. I know you do."

Her nipples tightened at his touch. His gaze lowered from her eyes, to her mouth, to her breasts. Her wet tunic top was plastered against her and provided no protection.

Droplets of water sparkled on his lashes. She followed the path of one that dropped onto his cheek and ran down to his mouth, where his tongue darted out to lick it away.

She burned deep inside. Cupping her cheek with his warm hand, he brushed his thumb over her lips. She did the same to him. He licked the ultra-sensitive skin between her fingers before drawing her thumb into his mouth and gently nipping the ball of her thumb before soothing it with the tip of his tongue.

"We can't do this," she said even as she reached for him. Freeing her hand, she slid it through his thick dark hair.

"I know." He placed a string of ravishingly delicious kisses along the curve of her lips. "And we won't. We'll stop."

"Not yet," she murmured, deepening the kiss.

"No, not yet." His voice was muffled against her mouth.

"Soon?"

"Mmm. Not too soon." He lowered his hands to the small of her back in order to tug her closer to his aroused body.

She felt a flare of wild desire that surged and pooled at the juncture of her thighs. She was awed by the power of her response. Awed and stunned. What was she doing?

She wanted him so badly. Why shouldn't she have him?

The protection tattoo on the small of her back burned beneath his hand, not in a sexy way but in a warning way.

"I'll do it," she gasped as she broke free of his intimate embrace. Putting a hand on his chest, she clarified her statement. "The blood test. I'll do it."

Chapter Twelve

Alex released Keira. He'd felt her protection tattoo burning beneath the palm of his hand. His body was wound so tight, his arousal still intense. Walking to the kitchen, he turned the faucet on cold full blast and splashed his face with the icy water. He'd prefer to douse his entire body but there was no time for a cold shower now. Yes, the water bottle had sprayed him, but that was nothing.

Cupping his hands, he splashed more frigid water over his head.

"Are you okay?" Keira asked from the other side of the room. Wisely, she hadn't followed him to the sink.

"Just peachy." His voice was curt. Grabbing a towel from the top drawer, he rubbed it over his wet hair and face. "What made you change your mind?"

"I thought we agreed that we were going to stop—"

"I meant about the blood test," he interrupted her. He was in no shape to talk about the kiss they'd just shared.

"Right. The blood test." She straightened her shoulders and stood to face him. Her top was still wet and displayed her nipples for his visual appreciation. "The quest for knowledge. I want to know what's going on with me. And it all seems to come back to blood, doesn't it?"

"Yes, it does." Blood and sex. He wanted to grab the satin cover off the bed and wrap it around her from head to foot. He also wanted to tear her clothes right off her and enter her in one slick thrust. He was holding back but it took more energy than he was accustomed to requiring.

"Like the fact that you get your blood from the funeral home," she was saying. "How does that work? Is that why the funeral home was broken into?"

That got his attention. "It was an attempted break-in. You still haven't said how you heard about it."

"You mentioned an attempted robbery although you didn't go into details when I came to the police station yesterday. Someone told me more when you first brought me here. Pat or Damon, I'm not sure which."

That was possible. Or she could just have been guessing. She was so damn clever; he had to admire the way she figured things out.

"So is Lynch after your blood supply?" she asked, going all reporter on him.

"He's got plenty of his own."

"He has his own funeral homes?"

"No." Alex tossed the towel onto the countertop. "You ask too many questions."

"I wouldn't be a good reporter if I didn't."

He should just walk away but he couldn't. She was a fire in his blood. He was throbbing with his desperate desire for her. He wanted her so badly he could hardly think straight. This went beyond the physical, though. He admired her guts, her vulnerability, her courage.

His time as a medic had taught him to shut down his emotions because feelings got in the way of doing what had to be done. This power she had over him was dangerous. Maybe the answer was in her blood. Maybe getting a sample tested would give him options so this link between them would never control him.

Reaching for his smartphone, Alex texted Neville about getting a human phlebotomist to come get a sample of Keira's blood. Neville responded with an ETA of fifteen minutes.

"Are you going to answer my questions?" Keira said.

"Probably not," Alex replied.

"Then why should I answer yours? Because I'm the victim in this play and you're the vampire?"

"You're not a victim."

"Damn right I'm not. Just because I have claustrophobia doesn't mean I'm a wimp."

"I never thought you were a wimp," he denied.

"So what's the deal with this blasting stuff?"

"You tell me."

She sighed, obviously peeved with his answer. But instead of challenging him, she changed the subject. "How long will it take to get results from the blood test?"

"Not long," Alex said. "Doc Boomer will evaluate it immediately."

"You sure he won't drink it first?"

"Hunter blood is toxic, remember?"

"Right." She rubbed her forehead. "So what happens if I cut myself and a drop of blood touches you?"

"Nothing happens. It's only when the blood is ingested that trouble occurs."

"Can you tell when someone is a hunter?"

"The fact that they're trying to kill me is usually a pretty good sign," he noted drily.

"That's your only sign?"

"I can usually sense trouble. Most vampires can."

"Yet you didn't sense it with me."

"Oh, I sensed trouble with you right away."

"You knew I was related to a vampire hunter?"

"Not specifically."

"Then what kind of trouble did you sense with me?"

"All kinds of trouble."

"What's that supposed to mean?" she demanded.

A knock on the door saved him from answering. Neville was there with a woman at his side and Doc Boomer behind him. "This is Molly," Neville said. "She's here to take blood."

Alex could tell by the slightly glazed look in Molly's eyes that she'd been compelled. But her movements were efficient as she set to work, tapping the vein in Keira's arm. "This looks good." She tied a tourniquet around the top of Keira's arm. "Make a fist, please."

"You okay?" Alex asked Keira. He didn't want her panicking and sending the small tubes of blood splattering all over the place. He also didn't want her hurt.

"I'm fine," she said.

"Done," Molly said a few moments later. She handed the tubes of blood to Neville, who took them gingerly before gladly handing them over to Doc Boomer. He put them in a steel suitcase and departed as quietly as he'd appeared.

Once they'd left, Keira looked down at the Band-Aid on her arm. "She did a good job. That didn't hurt at all."

"I'm glad."

"She was compelled, wasn't she? That's why she had that funny look in her eyes."

"Yes."

"You can compel humans to do whatever you want?"

"Most humans, yes."

"With great power comes great responsibility. For Spider-Man and vampires alike."

"Spider-Man and vamps don't share many similarities," Alex said wryly.

"You're both outsiders who hide your true identities, right?"

"I suppose. I never thought of it that way." Probably because Alex didn't see himself as any kind of hero, let alone a superhero. Yes, he did have some super abilities. And yes, he tried to use them at times for the greater good.

But there had been times in his afterlife when that had not been the case. Times when his rage and thirst for revenge had consumed him like a fever. The fact that he was dependent on human blood to survive had been hard to swallow at first. Then he'd welcomed that hunger and fed it with utter excess. Those dark years lived on in his nightmares, leaving him shivering in a cold sweat like those times in a shallow foxhole on Iwo Jima with explosives banging, flashing, and crashing all around him. Dig your foxhole too deep in the sandy areas and you'd be buried alive when it collapsed. Dig it too shallow in the areas with lava and you'd have your limbs blown off by enemy fire. He'd thought that island was hell on earth . . . until he'd been turned into a vampire and made his own hell on earth.

Keira interrupted his dark thoughts.

"Will Doc Boomer be able to tell me what is happening to me?" she asked.

"That's the plan."

"Plans don't always work out. I had a plan when I came to see you at the police station, you know."

"What was your plan?"

"That we'd work together to find whoever is stealing the blood and then stop it."

"That's still the plan."

"Yeah, but I didn't anticipate being threatened by vampires on my fire escape. I didn't expect you'd kidnap me or that my apartment would be torched."

"Life is full of the unexpected."

"Was your life like that?"

"Hell yes." He'd never dreamed he'd end up as a vampire. Yet here he was, still unsure what the purpose was in his being turned.

His mother died when he was five. He'd been raised in a series of foster homes before finding the Kendalls. He'd been a bitter thirteen-year-old when he'd arrived on their doorstep. Bill Kendall was a pharmacist while his wife, Jill, was a homemaker. They were the reason Alex felt shame for the evil things he'd done in his early years as a vampire. They'd given him a sense of moral values that remained with him even now.

Doc returned a short time later. "I have some preliminary results." He had an iPad in his hand. "She definitely has hunter blood in her. A very intense and virulent strain of hunter blood. The rest of her blood is human for the most part. The interesting thing is the slight percentage of hybrid blood that I found."

"Hybrid? What's that supposed to mean?" she demanded.

"I'm not done testing yet, but I think the hybrid element is what has made your hunter blood as intense as it is. The components in the hybrid mix include one percent druid, not enough to show up on our scanner but enough to affect the totality of your traits."

"Am I suddenly going to try to blast vampires?" she asked nervously.

"No. Becoming a vampire hunter is a conscious decision and requires years of training," Doc Boomer said.

"Why can't I blast my way out of here?" she said.

'Because at some deep level you feel safe here," Doc Boomer said.

"Do you have any hypotheses about the blood thefts?" she asked him.

He blinked at the change of subject and paused before answering her. "I don't think it's for vampire consumption."

"Why not?"

"There is sufficient supply in the pipeline."

"Maybe there's been a stoppage at some point that you don't know about," she suggested.

"We'd know."

"Would someone or something else be trying to consume the blood?"

"I don't believe so," Doc said. "Demons don't consume blood. They consume souls. Black magic . . ."

"Black magic?" she interrupted him. "You mean like witches?"

"Thanks for your help," Alex said, hurrying Doc to the door. "Text me when you get more info."

"Wait a minute," Keira said. "Doc, in the tunnels you said something about me not being a witch. Does that mean there are witches here?"

"Of course," Doc said. "How else do you think your furniture was re-created if not by a spell?"

"What do you mean re-created? This is my furniture, isn't it?" Keira turned to Alex. "Isn't it?"

"Sure looks like it to me," Alex said before rushing Doc out the door.

"These are my things." She picked up the small red horse. "And these are my photo albums." She opened one, but the pages were blank. "Where are the photos?" She remembered asking that question right before the sirens went off for the invasion warning. No one had answered her then. Instead she'd been shoved into that damn dark hole.

"Why did you get rid of Doc so quickly?" she asked suspiciously. "What were you afraid he'd say? That he'd tell me about the witches in the area?"

"He's a busy man."

"You mean he's a busy vampire."

"Same thing."

"Not really. Yet again, you still haven't answered my question about my photographs. Where are they? Did you take them as part of your investigation of me?"

His phone rang. Checking it, he said, "I've got to go."

"Of course you do," she said sarcastically.

Alex opened the door to find Zoe standing there. She waved at Keira. "Hi, there. My name is Zoe. I just ran into Doc outside the building and he told me you know about the furniture spell."

Alex swore under his breath. His foster mother Jill frowned upon cursing out loud in front of a lady. He'd picked up plenty of colorful language while in the marines. None of which was relevant at the moment. He needed to focus here.

The problem was, Zoe talking about the furniture spell. Alex didn't want Keira knowing details about her surroundings or the people in Vamptown like Zoe, who was indeed a witch. But that ship had obviously sailed. He'd have to minimize the damage.

"There's been another blood theft. I've got to return to the police station," Alex said. "Have Sierra come stay with Keira."

"No can do," Zoe said cheerfully. "Sierra is having tea and cupcakes with her publicist Katie at Heavenly Cupcakes. Katie is in town for a family wedding and

took a few extra days off. It's her first time in Chicago
and Sierra is showing her around."

"Does Katie know about the vampires?" Keira asked.

"No way."

"What about the witches?"

"What about them?" Zoe said.

"Does Katie know about those? Does Sierra?"

"Sierra does. Katie doesn't," Zoe said.

"And that's the way we want to keep it," Alex said as
he headed out. "Behave," he warned Keira and Zoe both
before leaving.

"So I heard you have special zapping powers," Zoe
said as she took a seat on the couch.

"Did you do this?" Keira pointed to the couch. "Doc
said a witch's spell re-created my living room furniture.
Was that your doing?"

Zoe nodded.

"So you're a witch?"

Again Zoe nodded.

"Are there many of you?"

"Here in Vamptown? No."

"Wait a second. Vamptown? Is that where I am? I
thought I was still in Chicago."

"You are. Vamptown is a neighborhood, like Greek-
town."

"Only it's full of vampires instead of Greeks?"

"This is all off the record. Sierra said she already told
you that you can't reveal what you know, that you can't
share it or write about it."

"No one would believe me," Keira muttered. "I barely
believe it myself. How did you know how to re-create
my living room?"

"Bruce showed me your Pinterest page. You had a
photo of it posted there."

"And the photo album?" Keira opened it and showed Zoe the blank pages.

"I'm sorry about that, but I couldn't re-create what I couldn't see."

"So all my family photos are gone." Keira wasn't even aware that she was crying until she tasted salty tears on her lips.

"I'm so sorry." Zoe patted Keira's arm. "I'd hug you but I wouldn't want to freak you out, being hugged by a witch you just met and all."

"Distract me," Keira said, impatiently wiping away her tears. "Tell me how you ended up surrounded by vampires."

"I moved here from Boston with my grandmother."

"Is she a witch, too?"

"Yes."

"Why come here?" Keira asked.

"She knew Nick, and he invited us to come. We were looking to relocate so things worked out."

"Do witches and vampires get along?"

"Most don't," Zoe replied.

Keira changed the subject slightly. "Sierra told me she's in love with a vampire."

"That's right. His name is Ronan and he's a sweetie."

Keira had a hard time imagining a vampire as a sweetie. "What about you?" she asked Zoe. "Are you in love with a vampire?"

"With a vampire Demon Hunter," Zoe said proudly.

"How is that different from a vampire?"

"Didn't your grandfather go into that in his journal?" Zoe asked.

Keira immediately got suspicious that Zoe was after the journal and would somehow use her witchcraft to get it.

"Relax." Zoe patted Keira's arm again. "I can't locate your journal."

"How did you know . . . ?"

"Your expression. Going back to my question, you don't know about vampire Demon Hunters?"

"I may have skipped over some stuff," she admitted. "And some pages were written in what looked like an ancient language."

"Interesting. Do you know why your grandfather became a vampire hunter? Was it something he decided to do, or was he born to do it?"

"He wasn't real clear about that."

"Men never are."

"Do witches live a long time? Are you immortal like vampires?"

"Normally no. But my life hasn't been normal since I met Damon."

"He scares me," Keira admitted.

"He scared me, too, when I first met him. But I fell for him anyway."

"You mean Damon is . . . ?"

"The vampire Demon Hunter that I love. Yes, he is."

"You're a braver woman than me," Keira said with a shake of her head.

"I don't know about that," Zoe said. "Sierra told me you walked into Alex's police district building and confronted him knowing he's a vampire. That was very brave of you."

"Or stupid, as Alex takes great pleasure in telling me over and over again."

"He wasn't happy with me re-creating your furniture," Zoe admitted. "He didn't want you knowing I'm a witch."

"He doesn't trust me."

"Can you blame him? Your grandfather killed vampires."

"I thought he was an accountant. I only had him and my mom, and she passed away two months ago. They were my only family." Keira bit her lip as emotion threatened to overtake her again. Zoe seemed nice enough but Keira didn't want to continue showing weakness. She needed to keep her wits about her.

"Did your mom know about your grandfather's secret?"

"He left me a note saying she didn't know anything about it. He sent me to Alex if there was trouble. The blood thefts seemed like trouble to me so I went."

"I heard about your godson and his blood disorder."

"Benji is the greatest little kid you could ever imagine. I don't suppose you have a spell to cure him?"

Zoe shook her head regretfully. "I wish I did," she said softly. "There are so many children dealing with life-threatening or fatal diseases."

"His mom and I are hoping that he can be part of a new drug trial to treat him."

"I'll certainly send white light and positive karma Benji's way."

"Thanks."

"You're welcome." Zoe paused a moment before adding, "I don't mean to be a Debbie Downer here but we need to discuss what the procedure is should we get another invasion warning while I'm here with you."

"I'm not going back in those caves," Keira said.

"They are tunnels, and trust me I'm no fan. I had a demon strap me to a table and threaten to cut me into little pieces in those tunnels."

Keira's eyes widened. "There are demons down there?"

"Not anymore. That was a onetime deal. Damon eradicated the demon."

"How do you know there aren't more?"

"Because Damon is an awesome Demon Hunter and no demon would dare come around here."

"But apparently one did and tried to hurt you."

"True but that was a onetime deal, like I said."

"How do we know that demons aren't behind these blood thefts?" Keira was rather proud of the calm way she was absorbing the information that Zoe was sharing. If vampires existed, why not witches and demons? Yes, both had been mentioned before, but not in any detail.

"Demons are more into stealing souls than blood."

"What other creatures are there?"

Zoe looked insulted.

"I'm sorry," Keira quickly said. "That came out wrong. I wasn't insinuating that you are a creature or that witches in general are creatures."

"What about vampires?"

"What about them?"

"Do you consider them to be creatures?"

"I consider one of them to be too damn sexy," Keira muttered.

"I know. Damon is incredibly sexy but as I said, he's mine."

"I was referring to Alex."

"Oh. Okay then. Alex is sexy, too, and not mine, so you go, girl." Zoe grinned and offered a high-five that Keira accepted because not doing so seemed rude.

"What is it like, loving a vampire?" Keira asked.

"The sex is off-the-charts incredible," Zoe said.

"That's not what I meant exactly."

"I know. But you were wondering, right?"

Keira didn't know how to answer that so she remained silent.

"It's natural for you to think about it," Zoe said.

"Is it? So all women who come in contact with Alex wonder what it would be like to have sex with him?"

Zoe grinned and nodded. "Probably."

"Because it's a vampire thing."

"Actually women have been falling for Alex most of his human life, since before he became a vampire. Or so I've heard."

Keira was desperate to change the subject. "Are the vampires here related in some way?"

"They are part of the same clan but they aren't brothers per se."

"How many are there?"

"Why do you want to know?" Zoe countered.

"I'm a reporter. I'm naturally curious."

"So is Sierra. Curious, I mean. Must be a writer thing."

"It is."

"I'm a former librarian myself. Now I own an artisan soap company. Bella Luna."

"There is a basket of your soaps and body lotions in the bathroom here. I really liked the citrusy one."

"Thanks. It's called Revive and it's one of my best sellers. But let's get back to our game plan for the next invasion warning. The only safe place is in the tunnel."

"What if the invasion comes from the tunnel? That demon who terrorized you got into the tunnel," Keira reminded her.

"He was coming from hell. He escaped through a portal my grandmother and I inadvertently opened. But that's been closed now."

"I don't want to talk about this anymore." Keira turned the conversation to Zoe. "What made you want to become a soap maker?"

Zoe countered with, "I'd rather answer your earlier question about what it's like loving a vampire."

"That's okay, that was too personal—"

"Yeah, it was, but I'm going to answer anyway."

"You already did."

"That was about the sex. Which is incredible but there's more to love than that. I can't say what it's like to love a vampire. I can only say what it's like to love Damon. We share a special kind of connection that I can't even begin to explain, you know?"

"Yeah, I do know." Keira knew because she was feeling the same way about Alex. But she was no witch with special powers. Or was she? Not the witch part, but the special powers part. She'd blasted a huge hole in that tunnel. "But I need to know how to control my powers. Can you teach me?"

Chapter Thirteen

"What's the emergency?" Alex demanded as he joined Craig in the interrogation room reserved for their use.

"There's been another blood theft."

"Where?"

"At the biotech medical lab where Bunny works. They just discovered the theft an hour ago."

"It happened in broad daylight?"

"We don't know that. It may only have been discovered now but taken place last night."

"Any suspects?"

"None in custody," Craig said.

"What about the research assistant Warren?"

"He's disappeared."

"The Gold Coast vamps questioned him but released him. You work on trying to track him down. I'll head over to the lab."

"Bunny is pretty upset about Warren's disappearance," Craig said.

"She came to see me yesterday and said the thefts were her fault."

"That's shit."

"I know."

"Why would she say something like that?"

"She felt guilty. Not because she'd stolen blood but because she suspected that her lab tech Warren had. Apparently there were budget cuts that stopped their research project funding."

Craig nodded. "I know about that but I didn't realize Bunny's feelings were that intense. I've been married to her for decades so you'd think I'd know her by now."

"That's another thing. I didn't realize you guys were around during the Chicago Fire."

"We don't talk about those days much."

"Why not?"

"You don't talk about the days before your transformation."

"Keira said her grandfather's journal started right before the fire."

"What's that got to do with us?"

"That's what I'm trying to figure out here."

"I'm not aware of any connection."

"It's the stuff we're not aware of that worries me," Alex said.

That was still the case when he pulled into the parking lot of the biotech company. He flashed his badge at the security guard, who gestured for him to him pass through a metal detector. Since Alex had vamp weaponry like daggers on board, he wasn't about to do that.

Looking into the guard's eyes, he said, "You will not make me go through the detector." Then Alex pointed his hand at the security camera, pausing it in a way that would not alert the security person watching it. "What do you know about the blood theft?"

"It wasn't my fault. I wasn't on duty."

"What have you heard?"

"That everyone suspects the lab tech in that department."

"Warren?"

"Yeah, that's him. He's usually here first thing in the morning but he didn't show up for work today."

On the way over, Alex had asked Neville for background checks on the security crew. Neville could do it faster and with more detail than going through official police lines. No doubt doing so broke all kinds of privacy laws, but it had to be done. The situation was too risky with the threat of a turf war with Gold Coast vamps.

"What else can you tell me about Warren?"

"He was on the nerdy side. Most who work here are. But he was weird. Had a strange look in his eyes."

A strange look as in someone who had been compelled? Alex had seen the ID photo of Warren, who'd looked like someone who'd be right at home in one of Alex's fave sitcoms, *The Big Bang Theory*. He hadn't noticed anything strange about his gaze.

"Did he always look that way?" Alex asked.

"No."

"When did you notice him appearing different than before?"

"Yesterday."

Alex tried asking a few other quick questions but decided he'd gotten all he could from this particular guard. "You won't remember me asking you any questions."

His next step was to return the security cameras to their normal operation before going to the lab area where the blood was taken. Bunny met him at the door to Lab 7 with its huge RESTRICTED sign.

He did his thing on the security camera in the corner aimed at them before speaking.

"Any sign of Warren?"

"No. I'm worried."

"Right."

She put her hand out to stop Alex from going through the doors into the lab. "When was the last time you fed?"

He frowned. "Why?"

"If you haven't fed lately the scent of blood can be overwhelming given our heightened sense of smell."

"It's not like I carry a six-pack of blood with me," he said.

"And it's not like you can drink from one of the human employees."

"Of course not."

"Then you'd better have this." She handed him a beaker filled with a red liquid.

He eyed it suspiciously. "What is it?"

"Something I've been working on."

"That doesn't tell me much."

"You need to drink it."

"Hold on," Craig said from behind them.

"What are you doing here?" Alex said.

"I thought you might need this." He handed Alex a certified bottle of Vamptown blood.

"I wanted him to try my special blend," Bunny said.

"I love you, hon, but that stuff tastes awful," Craig said.

Alex downed the blood and handed the empty bottle back to Craig.

"Let's get this done," he said, nodding toward the door.

Bunny swiped her employee ID card on the security panel as well as putting her finger on the scanner. Inside, the place was full of scientific and chemical equipment all beyond Alex's understanding, but it did remind him of Doc Boomer's lab. Bunny was right. The place was permeated with a strong scent of blood. Even though he'd just fed, the smell was distracting, almost making him forget to address the security cameras in this area.

"Where do you store the blood?" Alex asked Bunny.

She showed him the refrigerated unit.

"How much is missing?"

"All of it. A total of several hundred units."

"Have the crime scene investigators come and looked for fingerprints?"

Bunny nodded. "They were here earlier."

"I checked with them when I left," Craig said. "There were too many prints on the doorway to lift anything definitive. Warren's prints were included, though. So were Bunny's and a several other employees."

"When did you discover the theft?" Alex asked Bunny.

"Around ten this morning when I went to access some for our project," she replied.

"We will consider this an official police investigation as well as a Vamptown investigation," Alex said before checking his smartphone for a text. "Neville didn't find anything suspicious among the security staff or the rest of the lab employees, either. Just Warren. He apparently had some bad habits."

"Bad habits?"

"Very bad. The kind that can get you killed."

Keira focused on the bottle of water on the kitchen counter. Stretching out her hands, she focused on it.

"You need to focus," Zoe said. "All powers require intense focus."

"I am focusing," Keira said. She squinted but nothing happened to the bottle of water. It stood there mocking her.

"Uh-oh," Zoe said. "The sirens have gone off."

"I thought only vampires could hear them," Keira said.

"Vampires and witches," Zoe said.

"So you're not the only witch? There are others?"

"There's my grandmother Irma. I told you we both moved here from Boston."

"And there's me," a disembodied voice said.

Keira looked around and saw no one.

"Down here," the voice said.

There at her feet sat a gray cat.

"Is this your cat?" Keira asked Zoe.

Zoe nodded and reached in the pocket of her maxi skirt for a small bottle. "Sniff this," she told Keira.

Keira shook her head and took a step back. "No way."

"She's a feisty one."

Keira looked at the cat.

"Yes, I talk," the cat said. "Get over it. We've got more urgent issues to manage. Like the fact we're under attack."

"I am not going back into that damn tunnel," Keira said vehemently.

"This is just lavender. A calming scent," Zoe said, waving the uncorked bottle under Keira's nose.

Keira felt the effect instantly. Her rising panic was stilled.

"It's just lavender . . . and magic," the cat said.

Zoe reached for the brick over the bed that opened the hidden entrance to the tunnel before returning to Keira and putting an arm around her. "It will be all right," Zoe said. "We just need to get to our safe place."

Keira blinked as the cat leapt or floated onto the crook of Zoe's other arm.

"Maybe you should have sniffed some of that soothing spell yourself, Zoe," the cat said. "My name is Bella, by the way, Keira. Can she hear me?"

"Yes, I can hear you," Keira said. She felt as if she were floating on a cloud—like something out of a hazy dream.

"We're going the wrong way," Bella said as the door into the tunnel closed behind them and they started moving forward. "We're supposed to go left, not right."

With a jerk of her head, Zoe jacked up the lights, intensifying them to almost sunlight brightness. "Are you sure?"

"Yes," Bella said.

"You're trusting our safety to a cat?" Keira said.

"Don't knock it until you've tried it," Bella said. "Now we go right at the next intersection and down these stairs. Careful now."

"Where are we?" Keira asked, suddenly confused.

"Where do you think we are?" Zoe said as she guided Keira along.

"It looks like we're in a park near Lake Michigan. The gardens at Millennium Park."

"Your happy place?"

"Is it real?" Keira whispered.

"Does it matter?

"You drugged me and now I'm hallucinating."

"But you're not panicking and that's a good thing," Zoe pointed out.

"What about you, Zoe?" Bella sounded worried. "Are you panicking?"

"Nope," Zoe said in a nervous rush. "I refuse to panic. No panicking allowed. No one is allowed to panic. Are we clear on that?"

"You're hyperventilating," Bella said.

"You're okay." Keira felt the need to reassure the witch who'd put a spell on her. How bizarre was that? She should be fighting to escape, not trying to be empathetic and patting Zoe's hand.

"If you two are done with that touching besties display, the all-clear just sounded," Bella said.

"That was fast," Zoe said.

They quickly retraced their steps. Once they reentered the loft, Keira saw a woman with white hair waiting for them. She reminded Keira of Betty White. At first she wondered if she was channeling some sort of *Golden Girls* hallucination.

"Gram, what are you doing here?" Zoe said.

Then the woman spoke. "Is everyone okay?"

"Yes."

"I had to make sure."

"Was there another attack?" Zoe asked. "The all-clear came fast."

"No attack. It was another false alarm. If the truth be told, I really wanted to meet the girl who has Alex and Damon so riled up."

"That would be me," Keira said with a big grin as Zoe guided her to the couch.

"I had to give her a soothing lavender spell," Zoe explained. "She doesn't like small places and didn't want to go into the tunnel."

"I heard she blasted a hole in the tunnel," Zoe's grandmother said. "It's been fixed of course."

"So vampires do freaky-fast construction repairs, too?" Keira said.

"Why yes, they do," Gram said.

"I'm hungry," Bella said as she leapt from Zoe's hold to the back of the couch and sat next to Keira. "I don't suppose you have any caviar in the fridge, do you?" She blinked up at Keira with adorable anticipation.

"I haven't looked in the fridge lately," Keira said.

Bella's ears perked up. "So there could be caviar in there?"

"Doubtful," Zoe said.

"Come with me, Bella." Zoe's grandmother gathered the cat in her arms. "We'll go home and have some eye of newt. Just kidding."

Shortly after they'd made their departure, Alex appeared.

"Another hard day at the office, dear?" Keira greeted him.

He eyed Zoe suspiciously. "What are you doing here?"

"She's babysitting me," Keira piped up.

"Zoe, I told you to get Sierra," Alex said.

"And I told you that she is busy," Zoe said. "You've got to stop ordering us around, Alex."

"I tell him that all the time," Keira said.

"There's been another theft," he said.

"Here in Vamptown? What?" Zoe said in answer to his angry glare. "She knows about Vamptown."

"You told her?"

"Yes."

Alex swore under his breath.

"Why were you trying to keep that secret?" Keira asked.

"That intel was on a need-to-know basis," Alex said. "And you didn't need to know in the beginning. Keeping it secret was a way to keep Vamptown safe. As we used to say in the marine corps, 'Loose lips sink ships.'"

"Vampires tend to be pretty suspicious," Zoe said. "They don't trust easily."

"We especially don't trust witches or vampire hunters easily," Alex said.

"Yet we are able to work well together in the end," Zoe said cheerfully.

"How much did you tell her?" he demanded.

"Everything," Keira said.

"Not everything," Zoe corrected her. "Just some of the highlights. I'm not sensing any danger from her," she added.

"Thank you," Keira said. "Right back atcha."

"High five." Zoe fist-bumped Keira.

Alex couldn't believe what he was seeing. "I only left you alone for a few hours."

"Not alone," Keira said. "You left me with Zoe."

"It's not like I let her escape," Zoe said. "I could have done that but I didn't."

"I've decided escaping might not be in my best interests after all," Keira said.

"Ya think?" Alex drawled.

"Zoe said I had to learn how to manage and control my powers before trying to go solo."

"Actually I said that going solo was not a good idea given the fact that you couldn't control your powers," Zoe corrected her.

"So now you think you're Wonder Woman?" Alex said.

"Of course not. Besides, if we are talking about superheroes then Spider-Man has a special place in my heart. He's . . . he's Benji's favorite." The thought of her godson was enough to put a lump in her throat.

"You're not going to cry, are you?" Alex eyed her with equal parts alarm and concern.

"I've got to get going," Zoe said. "And I'm sure you two can get along just fine without me."

Keira was so distracted by the intensity of Alex's gaze that she didn't even say good-bye to Zoe. She distantly recognized that the witch had departed the loft, but most of Keira's senses were focused on Alex. Had he looked this good when he'd left this morning? Or was her attraction to him growing each time she saw him?

She remembered the silky feel of his dark hair between her fingers and longed to touch him again.

"Tell me about the latest theft," Keira said somewhat desperately. It was either that or plaster herself against his hot body.

"I've got to do this first." Tugging her into his arms, he kissed her with sensual skill and total confidence. She didn't know if those were natural attributes of his or a result of his vampire heritage.

"This is something special," she whispered against his mouth. "You feel it, too, right?"

"Oh yeah." He ran his hand down her spine to caress her bottom.

"Is this some normal vampire thing?"

"No, this is something unique."

"This is going to get complicated, isn't it?"

"It already is," he said.

"I know. But I can't seem to fight it," she muttered as she nibbled her way around his lower lip. "I don't want to fight it. I just want you."

"I want you, too."

"I know you do." She could feel his arousal pressed against her. Whatever this was between them, it was wild and raw.

Alex deepened the kiss, stroking her tongue with his. She moaned with pleasure. He was a master at the art of seducing her with his mouth, knowing just when to thrust and when to slide.

Cupping her derriere with both hands, he lifted her. She wrapped her legs around his hips so that her moist core was pressed against the throbbing power beneath his zipper. The shot of desire was like a high-voltage shock that coursed through her entire body. She was achingly aware of every move he made. She wanted him inside of her right now.

She was hot and throbbing from the erotic friction he was creating. His heart beat with raging power against her. So did the rest of his body. There was so much raging power going on her that all she could do was eagerly respond to the pounding, pounding, pounding . . . Wait, was that pounding on the front door?

The noise seeped through her sex-hazed senses. So did the voice. "Open up, Alex! It's Pat. I have urgent news!"

Chapter Fourteen

Swearing under his breath, Alex released Keira and went to the door. "This had better be good," he growled as he let Pat into the loft.

"It's not good," Pat said. "It's bad. Very bad."

"Go on."

"We have reason to believe that The Executioner is still alive," Pat said.

"My grandfather is alive?" Keira repeated. "But how is that possible? Where is he? Is he okay?"

Pat said, "He's okay enough to have obliterated two vampires a few hours ago, including Thomas Wentworth from the Gold Coast clan."

Keira took a step back at the look of hatred that Pat shot her way. "I don't understand. How could he come back from the dead?"

"Easy if he never died in the first place," Pat retorted.

"He had an aneurysm," she said. "He was dead by the time we got to the hospital."

"Did you see the body?" Pat demanded.

"Yes," she said unsteadily. "I didn't get to say good-bye

to him while he was still alive so I told him after he passed."

Pat remained unmoved. "Everything you say could be a lie."

"Why would I do that?" she said.

"To catch us off guard," Pat said. "Like the Trojan Horse, you come into Vamptown and then attack."

"I haven't attacked anyone except for the tunnel, and that was as much a surprise to me as it was to all of you," she said.

"So you claim."

"I'm telling you the truth. Give me a polygraph test. That will prove I'm telling the truth."

"Hunters can lie so well that they can't be caught."

"I'm not a hunter," she said. "I'm a reporter."

"Nick and Damon want to see you," Pat told Alex. "Immediately."

"Wait," Keira said. "There must be a way to prove that I'm not lying."

"There is one way," Pat said.

"No," Alex said. "I'm not putting her through that."

"Through what?" she said.

"You don't want to know," Alex said.

"Of course I do. I wouldn't have asked if I didn't."

"This isn't the time," Alex told her curtly. "Go on," he said to Pat. "I'll follow in a moment."

Pat looked like he might argue before turning and leaving.

Alex immediately grabbed Keira. "Hang on! We're leaving."

"What? Why?"

"Because it's too dangerous here."

She couldn't voice another word because he took her in his arms and they were off. She rested her cheek against his shoulder and closed her eyes as buildings rushed by. She wondered how he made it out of the loft without being stopped by Pat but couldn't ask him. She couldn't ask him anything, like where they were going.

He held her securely, and she felt strangely safe—which was ridiculous, considering the fact that she was being transported at freaky-fast speed to who-knew-where by a vampire.

When he finally lowered her, she looked around in dazed amazement. "Where are we?"

"The Lovers Hideaway honeymoon suite."

She looked at the mirrored ceiling. "Are we in Vegas?"

"No."

"What are we doing here?" she asked nervously.

"Not what you think," he retorted.

"Aren't you going to get into trouble for taking off this way?"

"Hell yes."

"Then why did you do it?"

"To save you."

His words left her speechless.

"No one would think to look for us here," he said.

"What are you saving me from?"

"My clan."

"What were they going to do to me?"

"You don't want to know."

Probably not, but she had to ask anyway. "Were they going to kill me?"

"Yes."

A shiver went down her spine. Not a happy shiver. This was a holy-shit-that-was-a-close-brush-with-death kind of shiver. Coldly scary. "But why?"

"Because you're a threat."

"I didn't do anything. I gave them blood for them to test. Didn't that prove anything?"

"It proved that you have the ability to be a good liar because of your powerful hunter blood."

"Then why do you believe me?"

"Because we have a link," Alex said.

"The sexual attraction between us."

"No, it's more than that."

"Did you bring me here to have sex with me?"

He cupped her face with his hands and directed her attention away from the huge heart-shaped bed. "I told you, this isn't about sex."

"I heard you."

Yeah, she heard him but now that his hands were on her it was very difficult to concentrate. Vampires weren't just after her; now they wanted to kill her. And those were the friendly ones. God only knew what the enemy vamps wanted to do to her.

She started shaking and couldn't seem to stop. Rubbing her hands up and down her arms helped, but when Alex did it she got warm very fast. She got downright hot, in fact.

Her surroundings weren't helping. They weren't in some clinical setting. They were in the middle of a love hotel. Not the kind of place that charged by the hour. It wasn't that in-your-face obvious, although it was rather over-the-top with the heart-shaped bed and the mirrored ceiling. "Why did you pick this place? Did someone commit a murder here?"

"No. Damon and Neville might track former crime scenes. An acquaintance of mine in vice investigated an alleged high-end prostitution ring operating here."

"High-end prostitution?" Keira pointed to the leopard-print wallpaper. "I find that highly unlikely."

"She told me the place was interesting."

"She? Was she a vampire acquaintance?"

"No, a human one."

"Did you ever bring her here?"

"No. We have a working relationship, that's all."

"And what kind of relationship do we have?" Keira had to ask. She didn't really want to . . . well, sort of she did. She wanted to know the answer even though she doubted she'd get one that she'd like.

"A complicated one."

True enough. Yep, not the kind of answer she was hoping for. Nothing new to report there. It's not like he went down on one knee and vowed his undying love for her. *Undying* being the key word. How did things work between a vampire and a human? And not just any human, but a human with vampire hunter blood and some mysterious kind of hybrid mix. She felt like one of those new gasoline mixes.

"This is all such a mess." she said, shaking her head. "Is my grandfather really still alive?"

"My gut tells me it's unlikely."

"How accurate is your gut?"

"Fairly accurate."

"Then why can't you just tell your vampire friends that?"

"Because you're being framed. Someone wants us to kill you. I think that's why this entire issue about your grandfather has come up."

"What does this have to do with the blood thefts?"

"It could be a distraction to keep our attention away from tracking down whoever is really stealing blood."

"Nice to hear my death would be nothing more than a distraction."

"It would be a hell of a lot more than that to me."

"Why?"

Tilting up her chin with his index finger, he gazed down at her with those sexy dark eyes of his. "We have a connection. You feel it. So do I." He gave her a brief but incredibly hot kiss with plenty of tongue action before setting her aside. "I don't have time to go into the details now. I have to go compel the manager to register us for this room using fake names."

"I'll bet most people using this room use fake names," she muttered before putting space between them so she wouldn't throw herself into his arms and do something crazy involving handcuffs and nudity.

"Sorry it's not the Four Seasons but that and the rest of the luxury hotels are too close to the Gold Coast clan for now."

"Is this place in Vamptown?"

"No. We'd never allow a place like this in our neighborhood."

"I rest my case."

"We won't be here long. We will need to keep moving until we get this thing figured out." He turned her to face him. "I need your word that you won't try to leave while I go compel the manager. This isn't a game. Your life depends on this. It depends on you trusting me."

"There's no good reason why I should trust you given the fact that I've only known you for a day or two." She put her fingers on his lips when he would have protested. "But I do. I'm trusting my gut, like you said. You have my word. We're in this together now."

"Good. And you do have plenty of reasons to trust me, like the fact that I've saved your life on more than one occasion," he said before kissing her wrist.

She almost asked him if he was tempted to suck her

blood when he was that close to her artery but remembered that her blood was toxic. She hoped the rest of their relationship wouldn't be equally dangerous before silently admitting that it already was. She had feelings for him. Feelings that ran deeper and were more powerful than they should be.

"Thanks," she whispered.

He looked up with a smile. "Are you thanking me for the kiss or for saving your life?"

"Both."

He kissed the palm of her hand and closed her fingers around it. "Stay here. I'll be right back."

He was true to his word. She'd barely had time to check out the bathroom when he returned.

"What do we do now?" she asked.

He reached into the back pocket of his black pants and pulled out a burner phone. "I keep this for emergencies."

"I'm sorry," she said.

He frowned. "Sorry that I have a burner phone?"

"No, sorry that you have to use it. That I've put you in this position." While he was gone, even though it was for a very short time, she'd been hit with a bout of guilt. "I shouldn't have come to see you. I should have let the police do their thing."

"Their thing is to ignore the blood thefts."

"Are they being compelled to do so?"

"It's a possibility," he said.

"Which would mean that vampires are behind the thefts." She paused as another thought occurred to her. "Why would the Vamptown vamps kill me when they want my grandfather's journal? If they kill me, then they can't get it."

"You're a more immediate risk. They figure they

could eventually track down where you hid the journal by retracing your steps from the time you got it from the bank until you came to see me."

"They can do that?"

"There are security cameras all over belonging to the city of Chicago or to private businesses. We hack into those and get the info we need."

"But I thought you said the cameras were not functioning."

"That was only for the thefts. We need to get that journal before someone else does."

Red flags went up for her. What if he was only pretending to save her in order to gain her trust so she would reveal where the journal was. What if this was all an elaborate setup?

But Pat had come to the loft all furious and sending threatening vibes. Wait, what if Pat was part of the con? What if this was all an elaborate setup to get her to trust Alex and confide in him?

She was getting a headache. To trust Alex or not to trust him? To have sex with him or not to have sex with him? To love him or not to love him?

That last question frightened her the most. Which was stupid, because the trust thing involved her safety and this was all a matter of life and death so you'd think she'd be more focused on security issues than sensual ones.

But she was in a cheesy love hotel, after all. And just in case she forgot that fact, there were little placards on the table and the dresser to remind her.

"I'm hungry. I wonder what they have for room service." She picked up the menu and opened it. "The daily special today is . . . ," she read aloud before abruptly stopping.

"Go on," Alex said. "You talking about food won't upset me."

"What about oral sex?"

"I'm all for it," he said. "Why do you ask?"

"Because it's the daily special."

"Really?" He flashed her a wicked grin. "Tell me more."

"Read it for yourself."

"I'd rather you read it to me."

"Let's just say it involves edible chocolate body lotion along with whipped cream."

"Sounds interesting."

"Can you do whipped cream?"

"Why are you asking? Are you interested in ordering the daily special?"

She used the closed menu as a fan to wave in front of her red face. "I was just curious, that's all."

"Right. Because you're a reporter and reporters are naturally curious. So are vampires, by the way. Naturally curious, I mean."

"There could be a story in this," she said.

"I'm sure there is."

She picked up a brochure from the table. "This says a love hotel is a place for secret assignations."

"Really? They used the word *assignations*?" He came closer to read over her shoulder.

"They have them in Japan and Brazil." She sounded breathless—but then who wouldn't with a sexy badass vampire leaning over her shoulder. Actually his ass was mighty fine. She'd noticed that on numerous occasions.

"What do they have in Japan and Brazil?" His breath was warm against her ear, which tickled slightly and aroused mightily.

"Sex."

He laughed. Had his laugh always sounded so sexy and sardonic? She'd read that casinos in Vegas piped oxygen into their gaming rooms to keep people alert. Was this place doing the same thing only with pheromones or some other sexual inducement? Or was Alex inducement enough?

"I figured they had sex in Japan and Brazil," he said.

"I meant love hotels. You know . . . where people have . . ."

"Sex?"

She tossed the brochure back onto the table. "Never mind. What were we talking about before?"

"Before we got distracted by sex?"

"Yes, before that."

"I have no idea," he readily admitted.

"The case. We were talking about the case. So we both agree that we think vampires are behind the thefts?"

"That seems a likely scenario."

"But not Vamptown vampires."

"Correct."

"Because they would never do something like that?"

"Also correct."

"They'd only do nice things . . . like kill me." She smacked her hand against the table, knocking that damn brochure on the floor. "I don't see why you can eliminate them from the list of suspects when they are willing to resort to murder."

"Only because they've been led to believe you are a threat."

"So it's okay to murder someone who is a threat?"

"It is in vampire culture," Alex said.

"Well, it's not in human cultures," she said emphatically.

He gave her a look.

"Well, most human cultures," she said.

He raised an eyebrow.

"Well, some human cultures," she amended before waving her hands. "Never mind. I say we keep them on the suspect list. And what's the deal with that funeral home?"

"Not that again."

"Yes, that again."

"You ask too many questions."

"That's my job."

"No," he immediately corrected her. "Your job is to stay alive. Keeping you alive is also part of my job, so forget about the funeral home."

"You're hiding something."

"I'm hiding a lot of things," he readily admitted.

"Because you don't trust me?"

"Because it's better that you don't know some things."

"Why?" she repeated.

"It's for your own safety."

"Not trusting me is for my own safety? I find that hard to believe."

"Yet you found it easy to believe in vampires."

"It wasn't a matter of believing. It was a matter of being convinced by my grandfather."

"By his journal, you mean?"

She nodded.

"Everything seems to bring us back to that journal."

"Not everything. This thing between you and me . . . that isn't connected to the journal, is it?" Her direct stare dared him to confirm it.

"Not that I'm aware of."

"What kind of answer is that?" she demanded.

"The only kind you are going to get for now."

"Which implies that this thing between us is involved with my grandfather's journal," she said.

"Since I don't know what's in your grandfather's journal, I can neither deny or confirm that."

"Oh." She guessed that made sense in a vampire kind of way.

"You said you trusted me. You said we were in this together now," he reminded her.

"I know." She rubbed her forehead. "I need some fresh air. I've been locked up in your loft for ages." She pointed to the window, where a slash of sunshine came in. "Do these rooms open to the outside?"

"Yes."

"Then can we just open the door for a minute? I promise not to run."

"I'd catch you if you did."

"I know. I'd let you. Because I'm safer with you than without you. I know that. I'm not sure I like it, but I do know it."

"As long as you know that, I guess it wouldn't hurt to open the door." He turned the knob. "Don't make me regret this," he warned her.

She reached up to kiss him. "I won't."

Alex opened the door. The first thing she noticed was the cool breeze, which felt so good against her face. She drew in a deep breath then frowned. "I smell something strange. Do you smell it, too?"

His face darkened.

"What's wrong?" she asked.

A millisecond later she saw what was wrong. A vampire stood a few feet away with an ice bucket in his hands and blood dripping from his fangs. "I came here for the daily special. This place is a fave of mine. I never expected to find you here, Sanchez. There's a bounty on your head," the vamp said, licking his lips and showing his fangs even more with a hiss. "On both your heads. This must be my lucky day."

"Or not," Alex growled, launching himself at his adversary.

Chapter Fifteen

Keira watched with stunned horror as Alex changed before her very eyes. Any trace of the Chicago cop was gone, replaced with a feral warrior whose fangs were fully emerged. His growl was duplicated by the vampire with the ice bucket, who threw it at Alex before grabbing a dagger from his boot.

The other vampire wielded his weapon with fury. Alex reached for his own dagger from his boot. He slashed with precision and power, using martial arts techniques that Keira had only seen in the movies. Then, with one raw slice of the other vampire's throat, it was all over. An instant later the vampire disintegrated.

Alex kept his face turned away from her as he returned to the doorway. "Get inside," he growled.

"Are you okay?" she whispered even as she obeyed.

"I didn't want you to see that."

She sensed a certain disgust in his voice. Was he upset that she'd seen him go full vamp, so to speak? While the violence had shaken her, the fact that Alex was safe was all that mattered to her.

"My grandfather described vampire fights in his journal."

"Words are different than images," Alex said, washing his dagger under the bathroom hot-water faucet.

"Who was that?"

"It doesn't matter."

"Was he from Vamptown?"

"Of course not. There's no way they'd—"

"They'd what?" she interrupted him. "Try to kill you? You said they wanted to kill me."

"They don't *want* to. They just think that you are a threat to them."

"Oh, that's okay then. As long as they don't *want* to kill me, everything is just peachy," she shot back. Maybe she wasn't as calm as she thought.

"They're not the only ones who want to kill you."

"What happened to that vampire you just fought? He disintegrated. Does that mean he's dead?"

"He's not coming back, that's for sure."

"Maybe you should have let me question him before you killed him."

"Right. Like that would have worked."

"It might have. We'll never know now. He said we had a bounty on our heads. Who do you think set that up? I feel like we are wanted by everyone."

"Several names come to mind."

"Maybe to your mind. Not mine. And since I can't read your mind, I have no idea who is on your list."

"I'll tell you later." He returned his deadly dagger to his boot. "Let's get out of here."

"Where are we going?" she said.

"Neutral territory."

"Switzerland?"

"Lake Michigan," he said.

"I can't swim."

"Then it's a good thing we're heading for a yacht. No swimming required."

"Wait!"

"For what?"

"For an explanation. Like how we're going to get to this yacht."

"The same way we got here," he said.

"You can walk on water?"

"No, but I can levitate above it for short periods of time."

"How short?"

"Short enough to get us on board."

"How can you be sure? Have you done this before?" she demanded.

"Not exactly."

"What does that mean?"

"It means not exactly. Come on. We don't have all day."

"It's the evening, actually."

"Fine, we don't have all night then."

Keira paused to take a deep breath. The day was starting to take a toll on her.

Alex turned and looked at her with a question in his eyes.

"I've never seen a vampire fight before," she said quietly. "You're right. The image is different from the words."

"Is that what has you spooked?"

"*All* of this has me spooked."

"Good. Maybe that will inspire you to stay close to me."

She was already inspired, as he put it, to stay close

to him. Too close. Seeing him battle that other vampire had scared the hell out of her on numerous levels. She'd been afraid of the vicious hatred in that other vampire's glowing eyes. She'd been afraid Alex would be hurt or killed. She'd been afraid that the vampire she loved . . . whoa.

"You're thinking too much," Alex told her as he took her in his arms. "Let's go."

"What do you mean they got away?" Lynch viewed the four vampires in his office with deadly anger. They were members of his clan. They had sworn allegiance and obedience to him. Their duty was to accomplish whatever order he gave them. "As temporary acting director of operations, this is on you, Pierre. I'm terminating you effective immediately." One precise throw and one throaty gurgle later resulted in Pierre disintegrating.

"Our guy only ran into them by accident," the tallest of the three remaining vampires said. Lynch knew his name was Robin but he liked to be called Yuri, which is why Lynch didn't call him anything at all. It was all about maintaining discipline and power. Lynch got to decide how to address his underlings.

"So you've said. 'Our guy,' as you so poetically refer to him, was at this questionable hotel indulging in questionable sexual activity when he stumbled upon Sanchez. A stroke of luck," Lynch said.

"That's right."

"Yet he wasted an excellent opportunity presented to him by fate."

"He paid for that mistake with his life."

"I am aware of that. I saw the video our guy took with his smartphone before he was obliterated. Thankfully all video feeds from Gold Coast vamps go through my office or I might never have known about this mishap."

"True."

"Forcing Sanchez to leave Vamptown is the best way to capture this hunter's granddaughter. But it's only a matter of time before they figure out what is going on. That would be a very bad thing for our operation. Do you understand?" Lynch said.

"Yes, master."

"Then you must understand that I can't allow these kinds of mistakes." Lynch's voice turned kind.

Robin aka Yuri had been around Lynch long enough to know that kindness was not a good thing. His face reflected his fear. "But master, I'm just the messenger."

Lynch nodded in commiseration. "I know that saying about not killing the messenger. Normally I might believe it. But not today."

"But—"

"Silence! It's nothing personal. It's just business." With one swift move, Lynch stood and killed the tall vampire, who disintegrated into tiny bits before disappearing. Reaching for the white napkin next to the shot glass of blood on his desk, Lynch wiped Yuri's blood from the knife he'd just used on him.

"Do the rest of you comprehend the seriousness of this situation?" Lynch asked the three vampires who remained in his office with him.

"Yes, master."

"I can't hear you."

"YES, MASTER!"

"Just so we are perfectly clear, I will not tolerate stupidity or mistakes. Understood?"

"YES, MASTER!"

"Good. I'm relieved to hear that. I really don't enjoy

having to slash throats, and it's petty of you to make me do so. Don't do it again."

Keira opened eyes that she had kept clamped shut since Alex had grabbed her at the hotel and headed for the lake. She didn't want to see him levitating over water. She didn't want to worry about the height of the waves on Lake Michigan or all the other vessels out there. She told herself she just needed to have blind faith in Alex and his abilities.

He'd certainly gone above and beyond to protect her.

They were a team. When she was in his arms, it was difficult if not downright impossible to keep a clear head anyway.

Her feet hit the deck with a gentle slap. Time to open her eyes and look around. She was no expert but this looked like a nice-sized yacht. Not billionaire-helicopter-pad big or sailboat tiny. "Nice ship," Keira said.

"It's a boat. You can fit a boat on a ship but you can't fit a ship on a boat. That's how you can tell the difference. A little something from my days as a United States Marine."

She wanted to ask him more about his days as a marine but realized he didn't like to talk about his past. Not that that had stopped her before. But she didn't feel like having Alex put up defensive walls right now. There was enough stress just trying to stay ahead of everyone after them. "Whose boat is this?"

"A guy who spends most of his time in Abu Dhabi."

"Is he a vampire, too?"

"Some would describe him that way. Come on, let's go belowdecks."

She made it down the steps leading to a salon with deep couches in a rich burgundy and what looked like original artwork on the walls when the first hint of claustrophobia hit her. There was a small galley kitchen with stainless appliances toward the back.

"Are you hungry?" he asked her.

She was too panicky to be hungry but knew she should eat.

"Won't the owner be upset with us trespassing on his boat?" she said.

"He'll never know."

"He will if we clean out his fridge. But if he's rarely on this boat, there probably isn't any food in there anyway."

"Good point. I've gotten out of the habit of thinking about food."

"You just think about blood."

"Not all the time," he said.

"Are you thinking about it right now?"

"Only as far as trying to figure out this latest blood theft and the killings. I knew Thomas. I just spoke with him earlier today. Why would someone want to obliterate him?"

"You're asking the wrong person."

"You're right. I am. I should be asking Lynch."

"I only met him for a brief moment but he didn't seem like the kind to confess his crimes."

"True. Listen, if you'd like to take a nap there is a bedroom below with a bath."

"No thanks. In fact, I'd rather get back on deck." She scrambled up the steps. The sky was getting darker now. "The fireworks should be starting soon."

"That's right. It's the Fourth of July. When I was a kid growing up in Chicago this holiday was a big deal at my last foster home."

"What happened to your parents?"

"My mom died when I was a toddler. I never knew my dad."

"I'm sorry."

"Don't be. There are worse things."

"Things like being a vampire?"

"So we're back to that, are we?"

"I'm just saying that it's a lot to process in a day or two."

"You're handling it well."

His compliment surprised her. "You think so?"

He nodded.

"It doesn't always feel like I'm handling it well. I kept my eyes closed the entire trip here."

"I know." He brushed his fingers over her cheek.

"I'm not a wimp."

"I know that, too."

"I got a little claustrophobic belowdecks."

"The first time I boarded a transport ship I hated it," he admitted.

"Did you get seasick?"

"That wasn't the problem. The sleeping bunks were on top of one another, three to a vertical row. Little did I know that would seem like luxury once we hit land and we had to dig foxholes."

"Are you saying you're claustrophobic, too?"

"I'm just saying I know what fear is."

"You didn't show any fear when you were fighting that vampire."

"Just because I don't show it, doesn't mean I don't feel it," Alex said gruffly before changing the subject. "If your grandfather is really still alive, do you think he'd come looking for you?"

She answered truthfully. "I would think so, but he's not who I thought he was so I can't be sure."

"We've got to get to his journal. There is information in it, or so legend has it, that pertains to how vampires process blood that would be extremely detrimental if it got out."

"It's in a safe place," she said.

"You still don't trust me enough to tell me."

She nervously fingered her evil eye ring. "I want to trust you completely."

"Then what's the problem?"

"This could be a con. Maybe you and Pat arranged to make it seem like we had to go on the run.

"You think too much."

"Before you told me that I didn't think enough. There's no making you happy." She held up her hand. "I know, I know. Handing over the journal would make you happy."

He took her hand in his and lifted it to his lips, where he kissed the center of her palm before caressing her skin with the tip of his tongue.

"That tickles," she warned him. It also made her seriously hot and filled with the urgent need to get naked with him immediately.

"Then I must be doing something wrong," he murmured.

"No, you're pretty much doing everything right," she told him. Wanting him to put his hands and his lips all over her wasn't practical given the logistics of the yacht. They'd have more privacy belowdecks, but that wasn't an option. Stripping up here wasn't an option, either. Yes, night was falling, but there were other boats on the water waiting for the fireworks.

Maybe there was a deck chair somewhere that would do the trick?

She saw his eyes darken even more, reflecting the sexual hunger she was feeling. She had to take a step back or she would have tossed caution to the wind. Had he attempted to hold on to her, she doubted she would have argued with him, but he let her go.

Alex's voice was calm as he returned their conversation to the case. "Is there someplace special your grandfather would go if he wanted to meet with you?"

"I assume he'd call my phone but I don't have that with me right now." She was rather pleased with how calm she sounded. "It's back at your loft. I still can't believe you think he's alive. We spread his ashes over Lake Michigan."

"You spread someone's ashes. I'm not sure they were his."

"You think he killed your friend Thomas?"

"Someone did and they made it look like The Executioner's style of beheading."

"Why would he fake his own death?" she asked.

"So no one would look for him."

"I thought you said there hadn't been any killings since his death."

"He could have just been biding his time."

"If he was alive, he would have come to my mom's memorial service," she said. Her throat felt like sandpaper as she said the words. "He would have been there somehow, someway."

"Are you sure he wasn't? Maybe he was in disguise."

"It was a very small ceremony and I knew everyone there."

"Maybe he watched from a distance."

"Or maybe he's being blamed for something he didn't do because he's no longer with us," she said.

"That is another possibility."

"If that's the case, then who would profit by such a con?"

"It could be a deliberate distraction to keep us off the blood theft case."

"There were more thefts, right?"

He nodded. "Last night and again this morning. The thief last night was caught and questioned."

"By the police?"

"By Thomas from the Gold Coast clan."

"And what did he discover?"

"Thomas told me Warren didn't talk."

"Is that the same Warren that Daniella was talking about in her premonition? You remember she said that war was coming and then added maybe Warren is coming."

"It's possible. He was a research assistant in a biotech lab. I'm still trying to track Warren down."

"How are you going to do that when you're on the run with me?"

"It will be a little more challenging," he admitted. "But not impossible."

Another thought occurred to her, stirring up new fear. "What about Benji and Liz? Will your clan go after them in an attempt to get to me?"

"No."

"How can you be sure?"

"That's not how we do things."

"Is it the way the Gold Coast clan does things?"

"Possibly, which is why I have someone watching out for your friends. I have since you first told me about them."

"Why didn't you tell me? Are they okay?"

"So far, yes."

"What do we do next?"

"I've put out a BOLO on Warren. Hopefully the Chicago police will pick him up, and when they do I'll take him off their hands."

"And do what with him? Disintegrate him like you did that vampire?"

"Warren isn't a vampire. At least not a full vampire." Alex ran an impatient hand through his dark hair. "It's complicated."

"Like anything about this is simple?" she said before looking over his shoulder. "Does your cloaking ability only work on humans?"

"Why?"

"Because something is crawling up the side of this boat."

Chapter Sixteen

"Not something. Someone," Alex said as he leaned over the railing to help the figure in scuba gear onto the boat. "What the hell, Craig. How did you know where to find us? Are you alone?"

Craig shoved his goggles away from his face. "Yes, I'm alone."

"Were you followed?"

"Only by a couple of carp," Craig said.

"Is that some kind of supernatural being?" Keira asked.

"No, it's an invasive species of fish in the lake."

"Right. That kind of carp. The Asian carp. I did a story about them."

"You must be Keira. I'm Craig." He held out his hand. "I'm Alex's partner at the police department."

She shook his hand. He had a firm grip and a direct gaze. "How did you find us?" she asked.

"It wasn't easy. I figured you might head for neutral ground. Or neutral water in this case. Neville has a face recognition drone going along the shoreline but it's not working now that it's dark. He doesn't have the model with night-vision capability. He is pissed because he ordered it that way but there was a problem. They had a tail on me but I lost him. I came because there's news."

"Which is?"

"Warren is dead. Bunny is devastated. She blames herself."

"Thomas told me that they caught Warren red-handed trying to steal blood from one of the blood banks in Gold Coast territory."

"And now both Thomas and Warren are dead."

"They knew too much," Alex said.

Craig nodded. "Bingo."

"Are they blaming Warren's death on The Executioner?"

"I don't know. But I did have a brief phone conversation with Warren before he was obliterated. He said to follow the money trail. That there was more to this story than he expected and he was very close to figuring it all out."

"Too close apparently," Alex said. "You still haven't said how you knew where to find me. There are a lot of boats out here. How did you know which one I was on?"

"The name."

"What's the name?" Keira asked.

"Latin Lover."

"He's lying," Alex said.

"I need to talk to you privately," Craig said.

Keira watched the two of them head for the front of the boat, out of earshot. As she did so she couldn't help wondering how ironic it was that she was spending Independence Day without any independence of her own.

Alex eyed his longtime work partner and close friend with concern. "You've put yourself at risk coming here."

"You underestimate my abilities."

"How unfair of me."

"Damn right!" Craig reached into the watertight bag he'd brought with him. "I figured you might not have fed recently so I brought you some blood from my own fridge."

"Thanks." Alex quickly downed the contents. "I appreciate it."

"No problem. But listen, something big is going on here and I'm not talking about the fireworks over Navy Pier."

"What have you heard?"

"The idea that The Executioner is still alive and out there has everyone worried."

"It's a red herring. Someone wants us focused on that instead of the thefts. How was Warren killed?"

"His throat was slashed."

"Any clues? He's not a vampire. Why would The Executioner go after him? And what about the money trail Warren talked about?"

"I haven't found anything yet, but then I'm no forensic accountant."

"And we can't call one in at this point."

"I'm afraid Neville may have hacked into the police department computers to get a fix on you."

"He probably has."

"So where do we go from here?"

"I've got a few tricks up my sleeve yet but it's best that I don't share them with you," Alex said. "Gives you plausible deniability. We should get back to Keira."

"Do you trust her?"

"We're working on that but yeah, basically I do."

"This is serious shit."

"I'm aware. I just killed a vampire who tried to attack us. It wasn't anyone from our clan," Alex said.

"Was it the Gold Coast clan?"

"No one I recognized, but I suspect it was one of Lynch's vamps."

"How did he know where you were?"

"He didn't. It was just bad luck that he was there."

"Where were you?"

"You remember when O'Reilly in vice had that high-end prostitution ring investigation?"

Craig nodded. "You went there? How was it?"

"We didn't really stay long enough to evaluate the place."

"What made you take Keira there?"

"It was the first place that came to mind," Alex said.

Craig grinned.

"What?" Alex glared at him. "It wasn't like that."

"Of course not."

"I wasn't trying to whisk her off to a bordello or something."

"Right."

"It's a love hotel. They have them in Japan and Brazil."

Craig's grin got bigger. "Nice to know."

"I had to leave Vamptown in a hurry."

"Sure you did."

"And I couldn't risk going someplace where Neville might track me down. Since that case wasn't one of ours, I thought we'd be safe."

"You thought you'd be safe in a love hotel with the sexy woman you have a thing for?"

"When you put it like that . . ."

"How would you put it?"

"Another way," Alex muttered. "Getting back to Warren, did he say anything else about the case?"

"Just to follow the money trail."

"Bunny said he was upset about funding being cut off for the work they were doing on developing artificial or synthetic blood."

"That's right."

"How is Bunny holding up?"

"As I said, she's blaming herself."

"Tell her she shouldn't."

"I can, but it won't make a difference."

"Understood." Alex glanced over his shoulder at Keira, who was standing by the railing, looking at the sky in anticipation of the upcoming fireworks. The runner lights were on, providing some illumination and preventing them from being ticketed by the authorities patrolling the lake for boating infractions.

"She's not your usual type," Craig noted. "You usually go for slinky hot female vampires in stilettos who follow the rules. No emotional involvement."

"There's nothing usual about Keira at all," Alex said. "She's special all the way."

Craig remained silent as they rejoined Keira. "Are they still upset with me in Vamptown?" she asked.

"The answer to that would be yes," Craig said.

"I thought they were supposed to be good vampires and not kill humans," she said.

"Usually they don't harm humans," Alex said.

"Well, I certainly don't want them breaking that rule for me," she said. "How much trouble are we in?"

"A lot," Craig said.

"A change of subject here," Alex said. "Bunny told me about how you were turned during the Chicago Fire, Craig. The Executioner was also alive during the Chicago Fire. I'm wondering if there was any connection between you?"

"I didn't know anyone by the name of Horace Turner."

"He may have used an alias," Alex said.

"Like what?" Craig asked.

"Like Russell Altman," Keira said.

Craig's eyes widened. "Russell Altman lived next door."

"He started becoming a vampire hunter around that time. Maybe if we could figure out why, that would help us," Alex said.

"Didn't he explain in his journal?" Craig asked.

"No," Keira said. "He was very vague. I don't even know if he was married or had a family before ours."

"If he was Russell Altman, he was married to Almina, who died tragically."

"What happened to her?"

"She was murdered," Craig said.

"By vampires?" Keira asked.

"I have no idea," Craig said.

"I asked Neville to research Horace's past. Do you know if he came up with anything?" Alex asked.

"Only that he had been using his Horace name since the early 1900s. Neville had no idea what happened before that time. Horace only married once and that was to Keira's grandmother Sally. They had one child, a girl."

Keira nodded. "My mother."

"Who had one child, a girl."

"Me," Keira said.

"The first time we are aware of that he made a kill was a year before the fire," Alex said.

"Could he have learned to be a vampire hunter in a year?" Keira asked.

"Unlikely. What about his parents? Did Russell ever mention his parents when he lived next door to you, Craig?"

"They were dead, that's all I know. It was a long time ago."

"Have Neville check into it," Alex said. "Say you recognized the photo from the Chicago newspaper that he has dating back to that time."

"What are you going to do?" Craig asked.

"It's better you don't know. Thanks for coming out here, bro."

"Are you going to swim back to shore?" Keira asked as Craig readied his scuba gear.

Craig shook his head. "I borrowed a friend's boat. There are plenty out here for the fireworks on Navy Pier later. The lake is a good vantage point for watching them. I don't have far to go. Bunny is waiting for me." Without further ado, Craig slid back into the water.

Keira stared down at the darkness of the lake. "I hope your friend doesn't get into trouble for helping us."

"He's good at what he does."

"So are you." She shifted her attention to Alex's face. "What's next? Or is it better that I don't know, either?"

"We can't get off this boat until after the fireworks are over and the crowd gets smaller," he said.

"I thought you could move fast enough that humans can't see you."

"I need the space to move."

"Where are we going from here?"

"I've got to pick up some supplies from a drop point," Alex said.

"Supplies? Do you mean blood?"

"I mean weapons."

"So you're not hungry?"

"I didn't say that." The blood Craig had brought was minimal. It was sufficient for now but wouldn't last all that long.

"Should I be nervous?"

"Yes, you should be very nervous," he said.

"Toxic blood, toxic blood," she said, laughing at his expression."

He grinned and looped his arms around her waist. "It's not your blood I'm after. It's you. Just you."

He shifted her so they were in the shadows as he pulled her closer. Cupping the back of her head with one hand, he used his other hand to cup her bottom and position her as she rubbed against him. The thin cotton of her yoga pants and underwear didn't get in the way of the friction created by the thickness of his arousal behind the placket of his dark jeans. Every thrust of his hips was matched by a thrust of his tongue entering her mouth the way she wished he'd enter her body. The heat was elemental, bypassing her brain and going right to the hidden juncture between her thighs.

"Fireworks," he murmured against her mouth.

"Mmm. I feel them."

"I meant in the sky."

Opening her eyes, she looked up. The display had started, with the percussions from the explosion reverberating through her chest.

Sensing something, she focused on Alex. "Are you okay?" She'd done a story on post-traumatic stress syndrome in veterans returning from Iraq and Afghanistan. They'd told her that certain noises could set them off—a car backfiring, thunder, or fireworks.

Yes, Alex had had more years to recover from his experiences on Iwo Jima, but did anyone ever truly recover from something like that? Or perhaps his memories were going back to his early days as a vampire. He'd basically told her nothing about that time in his life . . . or his afterlife.

There was so much she didn't know about him.

"I'll be okay when we figure this all out," Alex said, tilting her head back up to the fireworks in the sky. "Until then, just enjoy the moment."

She tried to but it was difficult when she knew that Alex was constantly on guard, his eyes checking their surroundings nonstop. Tension radiated from him. She wanted to kiss him and make it all better but knew that wasn't the answer. Not right now. Maybe it would be at some point. If so, she sure hoped it came soon, because her body ached with desire for him.

"Where the hell are they?" Lynch demanded of the three vampires who'd been in his office when he'd decapitated Pierre and what's-his-name. "Where are Sanchez and the hunter's granddaughter?"

"We don't know, master."

"It's your job to know," Lynch said in a pleasant voice. "You do remember what happens to those who are not capable of doing their job?"

"Yes, master."

Lynch adjusted the monogrammed eighteen-karat-gold cuff link on his impeccably starched and pressed French-cuffed pale-blue shirt. "It's really sad how you all keep disappointing me."

"Give us more time, please, master."

"More time? Why? So you can screw up even further? What is the point of that?"

"We can find them, I know we can."

"I'll tell you what I know. I know that I gave you a job and you didn't complete it."

"But, master—"

Lynch silenced him with a wave of his hand. "And even worse, you talk back when I am speaking to you.

That alone would be reason to discipline you. I'm the reason this clan is doing so well. I'm the reason it will do even better in the future. I will rule all the vampires in this city."

"Yes, master."

"And I will annihilate those vampires who refuse to go along with my terms. I will also annihilate those who are inept and just plain stupid. Like you."

Lynch stood and slit the vampire's throat. The other two who had remained silent didn't say a word.

"I'm growing weary of all this incompetence," Lynch said. "It's getting very messy." He pointed to a spot of vampire blood on his cuff before wiping the blood from his knife with the silk handkerchief in his jacket's top pocket. "Do better, gentleman, or there will be hell to pay."

"Are you ready?" Alex asked Keira. "Things have calmed down enough that it's safe for us to move now."

"Remember, I have claustrophobia. Do not take me someplace that is going to freak me out, like a tunnel or something," she warned him.

"Are you afraid of heights?" he asked.

"No."

"Good."

"Why?"

"You'll see."

She wrapped her arms around his waist and held on tight. A moment later Alex said, "You can open your eyes now."

She didn't realize she'd closed them. Looking around she realized they were on the sidewalk in downtown Chicago. "Where are we?"

"Look up."

She did. "We're outside the Willis Tower."

"I still think of it as the Sears Tower," he admitted. "But yes, that's correct."

"It's closed."

"Correct again."

"So how do we get in? Are you going to crawl up the outside of the building?"

"That's Spider-Man's thing, not mine."

"Guess I was getting my superheroes mixed up."

"I'm no hero, super or otherwise."

As far as Keira was concerned, Alex was increasingly displaying heroic attributes even if he didn't admit it.

"Spider-Man is Benji's favorite. I'm worried about my godson. What if the bad vamps go after him because of his connection to me?"

"I told you I've got that covered."

"When was the last time you checked to make sure they're okay?"

"On the way here."

"Wait a second." She belatedly released him. "You were texting and transporting at the same time? That sounds dangerous. Isn't there some law against that?"

"Not that I'm aware of."

"Not being aware of a law doesn't give you permission to break it."

"Vampires can multitask." Taking her hand, he pulled her around the corner to another entrance. When a security guard stepped out, Alex spoke to him. "You're going to let me inside."

The guard obeyed the compulsion order. Keira wasn't sure what special vampire abilities Alex used after that to disable security cameras as they rode the elevators up to the skydeck on the 103rd floor. "Are you sure it's safe?"

"I'm positive."

"It must be nice to be so certain about things."

"Have you been up here before?"

"I did a story when they first opened the skydeck. When I still had a job as a reporter. Since I never filed my story about the Taste of Chicago opening tomorrow they've probably fired me."

"They didn't do that."

"Because you compelled them not to?"

"Because I emailed your story to them after reading it first."

"When?"

"Your first night at the loft."

"Those were rough-draft notes."

"They sounded good to me. Your editor thought so, too. She said the story was good to go. And before you ask, no, I did not compel her to say that. I can't compel via email. It has to be in person."

"You could have gone to see her in person."

"No, I couldn't. I've been much too busy." He gave her one of his badass looks. "You could say, *Thank you, Alex.*"

"I suppose I could."

Crossing his arms across his chest, he waited for her to say the words.

"Okay, thank you, Alex."

"You're welcome." He tugged her into his arms. "Come look at the view."

The lights of the city were magnificent. Because the platform extended out beyond the building, you could see even more than from a traditional window.

"Not scared, are you?"

"Not of this," she said, stepping onto the clear glass floor that jutted out. "Pretty impressive, huh?"

"Very impressive." Alex was staring at her instead of the view.

The sexual tension that had been growing all night was there in spades. Everything, all the kisses and caresses, was leading up to this moment of simply gazing into each other's eyes. Her heart was streaking and her body hummed and ached with the need to have him buried deep within her.

"Are you in a hurry?" she whispered.

"No. We're here for several hours."

"Did you have something in mind regarding how we should pass the time?"

"Definitely." He lowered his head. "Here, let me show you."

Chapter Seventeen

Alex was a masterful kisser, there was no doubt about that. He did things with his tongue that were creative and masterful. Leisurely licks, sensual strokes, tantalizing twirls. He noted which she enjoyed the most and would elaborate further on that theme.

She responded with wild abandon considering she was standing on a ledge of glass. Her hands on his chest registered the pounding of his heart. She wasn't the only one losing control here. His growl told her that he was as on edge as she was.

His mouth covered hers with raw hunger before lifting for a second to allow him to peel off her T-shirt.

"What about security cameras?" she murmured against his lips as she resumed their series of kisses.

"I disabled them," he said while disabling her bra and tossing it aside.

His actions inspired her to remove his T-shirt and run her hands over the bare skin of his chest and abdomen. "You're so hot."

"So are you." He cupped her breasts in his palms, brushing his thumbs over her nipples.

She tilted back her head as pleasure coursed through her. "You like that, hmm?"

"Yes." More a gasp than an answer.

"Then you'll like this." He licked his way down the curve of her neck.

Clusters of erotic earthquakes shook her body. That was magical. That was vampire magic. She didn't want to know the details at the moment. She just wanted him to continue.

"More," she both begged and ordered.

He gave her more, licking his way across the curve of first one breast and then the other until he reached the aureole. He paused there, giving the sensitive skin his complete attention and giving her even more intense erotic quakes.

Her hands shook as she attempted to undo the zipper on his pants. She fumbled, muttering her frustration.

"Let me help," he whispered.

Using that super-fast vampire speed of his, he removed his pants and hers. Now only underwear—his black briefs and her lime-green cotton briefs—separated them.

Kneeling before her, he gripped her hips and tugged her closer. He stealthily introduced his fingers beneath the elastic of her underwear to cup her with the heel of his hand and rub against her. He licked the skin of her stomach above the waistband of her panties while thumbing her clit with a rhythm that gave her an orgasm that shattered her control.

His briefs were gone and so were hers. He pulled her down, shifting so his penis slid into her moist vagina. His thrusts were powerful and deep. The feel of him filling her was enough to send her over the edge as she came again. She never knew it was possible to feel such fierce bliss. Wave after wave of ecstasy consumed her.

She opened her eyes to see the feral hunger on Alex's face. A hunger for her. Not for her blood but for her body, heart, and soul. This was more than mere lust. This was something beyond her realm of human experience.

Alex stiffened in her arms as with one final upward thrust, he came. Lowering his head, he rested his forehead on her shoulder.

Neither of them spoke for some time. "Not feeling claustrophobic, are you?" he murmured.

"Nope."

"Good. I wouldn't want you busting out the glass a hundred stories up."

"A hundred and three stories up," she corrected him. "I did a story when they opened this attraction."

"Speaking of an attraction . . ."

She felt him hardening within her. "You don't have to speak. You can just show me."

He did. Then and again throughout the night.

"Can you keep your hands on the glass?" Alex asked her as she stood facing the window.

"Yes."

"Are you sure? Without blasting anything?"

"I'm sure."

"Despite me tempting you?"

"Tempt away." Her voice was heavy with anticipation.

"I will." He licked the nape of her neck and she was a goner.

Turning in his arms, she faced him and reached for him, holding him in her hand, rubbing the tip of her finger over the tip of his penis, before guiding him to the

part of her that ached and throbbed with the need to
have him fill her.

They came in unison, leaving Keira with the knowledge that her life was now forever changed.

"It will be daylight soon," Alex said a while later. "We
need to get dressed and moving."

"Does the sunlight outside of Vamptown bother
you?" she asked before answering her own question.
"You seemed okay with the sunshine at my apartment.
Wait, it was cloudy that day, wasn't it?"

"The Willis Tower will have people coming into it
soon. That's why we need to leave."

"Unless we merge with the crowd as they leave."

"That will take too long."

"Where do we go from here?"

"You'll see."

"Meaning you just had sex with me but you don't
trust me enough to even tell me where we're going next?"
she said.

"Meaning you just had sex with me but you don't
trust me enough to tell me where your grandfather's
journal is?" Alex countered.

"So we're back to that, are we?"

"Apparently. You're going to have to tell me the journal's location soon. Like I said, we're running out of
time."

"Why is that?"

"Because someone is not only stealing blood but
killing vampires."

"You're not still thinking it's my grandfather, are you?"

"I'm not ruling anything out," Alex said.

"Including me being a traitor of some sort out to destroy Vamptown?"

"No. I *am* ruling that out."

"Why?"

"Because of this." He lifted his T-shirt to show her the small of his back and the new tattoo there.

"When did you get that done?" She looked closer. "That almost seems to be like mine."

"It is exactly like yours. And I didn't get it done. It appeared on its own."

"Is mine still there?" She turned her head this way and that, trying to see.

"Yes, but it's changed a bit."

"Changed how?"

"There's more to it now."

"It's bigger?"

"It's more complex."

"I need a mirror."

"I don't have one."

"Because vampires can't see their reflections."

"I can see my reflection just fine. That mirror thing had to do with the fact that mirrors were backed with silver back in the day."

She pointed to the tattoo at the small of his back. "How did that happen?

"I suspect it's tied to the link we share."

"Sex?"

"More than that. I researched it. The tattoo isn't your standard Eye of Horus. This particular version of the protection symbol has an ancient Moorish design."

"My grandfather's journal did have some sort of ancient text that I didn't recognize," she admitted.

"All the more reason why we have to recover it."

She knew he was right. But she hated that their time together had shifted from erotic intimacy to practical matters.

"It's not over," he murmured, running his hand over her cheek.

"You mean it's not over until you get your hands on my grandfather's journal."

"No, I mean this is just beginning."

"What is?"

"You and me. This is just the beginning of you and me."

"How do you figure that?"

"I haven't figured it all out." He brushed the ball of his thumb over her bottom lip. "But I know we are meant to be together. You feel it, too. I know you do."

There was no point denying it. Not after the smoking-hot sex they'd just shared. He'd made her come more times than she could count. Well, actually it had been half a dozen times. She could count that far.

"Here, put this on." He handed her an oversized Chicago T-shirt from the duffel bag he'd retrieved from the ceiling air vent several feet away. "Stuff your top into the front of it."

"Is that your way of saying I'm not busty enough for you?"

"You're fine. We're trying to get a disguise together here. Work with me." He handed her a Cubs baseball cap.

"I prefer football and the Bears," she said. "Just letting you know for future reference."

"I'll be sure to make a note of that," he drawled. "I'll file it right under—" He stopped and put his hand over her mouth. Leaning close, he whispered in her ear, "Someone is coming. I'm going to cloak us."

He already had the bag slung over his shoulder as he pulled her tight against his body. Wrapping her arms around his waist, she hid her face against his chest.

A security guard walked past them. "Nothing to report up here," he said into his radio.

Alex waited until the guard entered the elevator and used his key to make it work. Keeping them cloaked, Alex took her in his arms and rushed to the elevator, hitching a ride down with the guard.

He waited until they were outside and a block away before undoing the cloak. "Glad that worked," he said. "I wasn't looking forward to climbing down a hundred-plus flights of stairs."

"Did I tire you out on the skydeck?"

"No way. Did I tire you out?"

"You were incredible."

His grin was downright wicked. "Glad to hear it. Unfortunately we don't have time to talk about it right now."

The street was deserted but it wouldn't stay that way for long. Soon hundreds of commuters would be filling the sidewalk and street in cars and on foot. The light seemed strange—and looking up, she saw why. Fog was rolling in from the lake, covering the tops of the taller buildings like the Willis Tower.

"Where to now?" she asked while tucking loose strands of her hair up under her baseball cap.

"A safe place."

"Safer than the love hotel and the boat?"

"A room at the Palmer House hotel," he said. "Safe enough for you?"

Keira nodded.

They walked into the historical hotel with a group of Japanese tourists and headed straight for an elevator. Alex cloaked the security cameras until he reached the room he'd selected.

"My grandfather wrote about this hotel in his journal. He used to bring me here every Christmas season to see how they decorated it," Keira said. "He told me stories about Potter Palmer, who built this hotel originally. It burned down two weeks later in the Chicago Fire. Potter rebuilt it as a fireproof hotel. Potter's wife, Bertha, was a huge supporter of the arts. She donated many of the impressionist paintings at the Art Institute here in Chicago. She also helped develop the brownie during the Chicago World's Fair. I'm talking too much, right?"

"You're fine."

"Am I? How do you know someone won't try to check into this room?"

He held up his phone. "I hacked into their reservation system. This room is taken for a week by us under an assumed name. Not that we have that long. We don't have seven days to figure this all out. At the most we have twenty-four to forty-eight hours."

She eyed the bed. "Then there's no time to rest."

"Vampires don't need much sleep."

"I haven't gotten much sleep since all this started."

"You certainly didn't get any sleep last night," he said in a husky voice that was like velvet over her skin.

"I didn't mind."

"I've got some logistical things to set up, so you can go ahead and rest for a few minutes," he told her.

"You're not going to leave me, are you?"

"No. I won't leave."

"Good," she whispered before crawling into the bed.

Alex wasn't sure how good things were. He was in deep shit here. He'd broken Vamptown rules, rules he'd been warned not to cross on pain of death.

He knew the policy and procedure despite the fact that the rule hadn't been enforced during his time with the clan. Nick, Damon and Ronan had all done things to protect the women they loved at all costs. Alex had merely done the same.

Just his luck that the woman who was The One for him was related to the most hated vampire hunter of all time. Talk about a royal snafu. Was this fate's way of paying him back for all the bad things he'd done after his transition?

There was a darkness in a corner of his soul that never went away. He wasn't even sure he still had a soul. He liked to think so. But maybe his soul had disintegrated when Mitch had turned him. Or maybe it had died even before that, during those tormented weeks on Iwo Jima.

Other troops had survived. They hadn't resorted to the violence he had. Of course, they hadn't been bitten and drained of their blood before being forced to drink vampire blood from the wrist of the sire who'd changed him.

Why him? Mitch had never been real clear on that. Lynch had said that Alex wasn't as special as he thought. Did Lynch somehow know what that secret was? Was there something in The Executioner's journal that explained everything?

Keira seemed certain that her grandfather truly was dead. Alex wasn't so sure.

He had to get that journal. Glancing over at the bed, he saw that Keira had already fallen asleep. He tried to reach into her mind while she was dozing. He'd tried before at the loft without success. But she trusted him more now than she had then.

Her thoughts were jumbled, but they were all images of them having sex on the skydeck. He leaned closer and noticed the slight smile on her lips. Avoiding temptation, he whispered in her ear. "Where is your grandfather's journal?"

She shook her head, almost clocking him in the process.

"It's okay," he soothed her. "You're safe. We need the journal. Where is it?"

He saw an image of downtown Chicago. The Water Tower, one of the few buildings left standing downtown after the Great Chicago Fire. Could she have hidden it there? Why? The iconic landmark was hardly a safe depository for something as valuable and irreplaceable as the journal.

Unless her grandfather told her to take it there for some reason? Why? Was there some sort of portal there dating back to the fire that only The Executioner knew about?

Shit. If that was the case, how the hell was Alex supposed to retrieve it? What if the journal was returned to her grandfather back in 1871? Was it locked in some weird time–space continuum like you saw in science-fiction movies? He was certainly no expert on that stuff.

Starting a turf war between the Gold Coast vamps and Vamptown would be a smart move on The Executioner's part. But why had the blood thefts started after his death? Maybe so no one would suspect him.

Had Keira been sent to Alex so he could protect her? He had no doubt that she was not part of whatever plan her grandfather may have devised to destroy vampires. But that didn't mean she wasn't being used as The Executioner's unwitting pawn in this mess.

She moaned in her sleep, reminding him of the noises she'd made the night before on the skydeck when he'd kissed her. Despite knowing what he was, she hadn't shown any fear of their joining. Sure, she'd asked questions, but that was part of her natural curiosity.

She'd told him he was incredible. He doubted she'd

think so if she knew he'd just been sneaking into her mind while she was asleep. She'd kick his ass for sure. Which was one of the reasons he couldn't let her know what he'd been up to.

"Why is no one here to report in on the status of the search for Sanchez?" Lynch demanded, speaking into his cell phone. "I was supposed to get an update five minutes ago."

"Everyone is out in the field," Lynch's second in command said. Lynch no longer bothered assigning him a name or title.

"Well, get them out of the damn field. At least one of them. And send them to me with an update."

"Our team is two members short."

"I know. Move some fledglings up."

"They aren't ready yet."

"They're ready when I say they are ready."

"Yes, master."

"Good help is so hard to find these days," Lynch said. "That doesn't mean I won't have you all replaced." He'd already tried doing so with demon mercenaries, but that hadn't worked out as he'd hoped. They were too hard to control. And control was something critical to the continued success of the Gold Coast clan. Control and obedience. "Do you understand?"

"Yes, master."

His plan was brilliant even if he did say so himself. Overall, things were progressing as he'd hoped. Except for Sanchez. Oh, the vampire cop had fled Vamptown as he'd expected. But Lynch hadn't anticipated that it would take so long to catch him.

He'd tapped into the police department records to get information on the cases Sanchez covered and had sent his vamps to those locations. He'd even tried to capture Sanchez's vamp cop partner, Craig, again without success. Then he'd tried to get Craig's vampire wife, again without success. They'd both gone into hiding, the cowards.

Lynch could feel his aggravation rising. He should have just grabbed The Executioner's granddaughter when he'd first seen her at the police station. And he would have had he known her true identity at that time.

Taking a deep breath, he reminded himself that they were getting closer to resolving the problematic issues. He would win in the end. He always did.

Keira was dreaming that she was in a very tall, very old building looking for someplace safe to hide. She was in danger. She wanted to run but couldn't. She felt frozen in place. Unable to escape.

"Wake up, Keira. You're okay." Her eyes flew open and she blinked at Alex.

"You're okay," he repeated. "But the bedspread isn't." He pointed to a still-smoking burn hole the size of a silver dollar. "You just blasted it."

"That's not good."

"It's better than blasting the skydeck last night," he pointed out. "Listen, we need to retrieve your grandfather's journal. We can't wait any longer. There could be something in it that will help us track down whoever is behind the blood thefts."

"I won't tell you where I stashed it." She put her fingers over his mouth when he would have protested. "But I will show you."

"Let's go."

"I guess I have to tell you where we are heading," she said. "I haven't done that yet, right?" She rubbed her forehead in confusion. "Did I talk in my sleep or something?"

"Yes."

"So where is it?"

"The Water Tower."

She nodded. "The historical building, not Water Tower Place."

"Why there?"

"My grandfather said to put it there."

"So he could retrieve it?"

"You think he's still alive."

"I think it's a strange place to stash it unless . . ."

"Unless?"

"Unless it's a portal of some kind," Alex said.

"A portal? To where?"

"I don't know, but I aim on finding out. Let's go."

"Wait. Do you have any clean clothes in that duffel bag of yours?"

He handed her a black T-shirt. She peeled off the Chicago T-shirt and put on the black one, which was almost equally large. She tied a knot in the bottom hem and made it as normal-looking as possible.

"Okay, I'm ready," she said.

Alex disabled the security cameras along the way as they exited the hotel. Putting his arms around her, he moved at the vampire freaky-fast speed of his to the Water Tower building on Michigan Avenue, known around the world as the Magnificent Mile.

The Gothic Revival building looked like a mini castle surrounded by towering modern skyscrapers. "The yellow Joliet limestone blocks made me think it was built out of shortbread," Keira said. "The towers were originally intended to hide the tall standing pipes. The building was built two years before the fire and was meant to pump drinking water from Lake Michigan."

"Let me guess," Alex teased her. "You wrote a story about it?"

"Yes, but actually my first visit here was with my Girl Scout troop when I was a kid. I thought it was a magical castle."

Once they were inside, he looked at the visitors with disapproval. "I wasn't expecting a crowd."

"It's not a crowd. It's just a few people. Come on." She took him by the hand. She paused at the display of before-and-after photos from the Chicago Fire before moving on to a deserted far corner of the building.

"It's this way." Keira's evil eye ring felt warm on her finger and glowed in the sunlight streaming through one of the high windows. Putting her hand on the wall, she said, "It should be in a hidden cavity right here."

And then she was gone.

Chapter Eighteen

Keira looked around in alarm. What the hell had just happened?

She was standing outside the Water Tower, but it looked very different. There was nothing but smoldering ruins around it. No ritzy Water Tower Place shopping center. No skyscrapers. No car traffic on Michigan Avenue.

Someone was holding her hand. "Grandpa?" she whispered. "Is that you?"

He nodded.

"What's going on?"

"We need to talk."

She reached out to touch him. He stood before her just as he had in the photo in the newspaper with that white streak in his hair. He didn't look like he had the last time she'd seem him alive. Then he'd looked to be a spry sixty-year-old who was really seventy. Now he looked to be in his mid-thirties or -forties. And his clothes were period pieces out of a museum. "Are you real?"

"Yes."

"Where am I?"

"You're in Chicago in 1871."

"How . . . ?" She was too stunned to finish the question.

"The portal. You came through the portal."

"You *yanked* me through the portal."

"I did," he admitted.

"Why?"

"Like I said, we need to talk."

"You couldn't talk to me in current times?"

"No."

"Why are you hiding out here? Why did you fake your death?"

"I didn't fake my death."

"I don't understand."

"I know you don't. We don't have a lot of time."

"Where have I heard that before?" she muttered.

"You need to take the journal back with you."

"That's what I was trying to do when you grabbed me. Aren't you worried you're going to mess up the space–time continuum or something?"

"Not for this short period of time."

"So it's like dropping food on the floor? The five-second rule applies?" Keira could tell by the confused look on his face that he didn't understand what she was saying. No surprise there. She could barely understand what she was saying.

Cupping her face in his big hands, he said, "You have to listen to me."

"Do you realize that people think you're still alive in 2015? Are you? Alive in 2015, I mean."

"Apparently not."

She hadn't thought so, but she still felt a pang of re-gret and loss. More than a pang really. Ever since she'd found his journal in that safe-deposit box she'd been hit with one thing after another, without time to recover from any of the wild discoveries she'd made. "Why did you bring me here?"

"There are things you need to know."

Her emotions boiled over. "You think? Like the fact that you're a vampire hunter? How did that happen?"

"I come from a long line of vampire hunters. My father trained me."

"So you went into the family business? Is that why you brought me here? To initiate me into the business? Because I won't do it," she said emphatically.

"Only males in my bloodline are able to be hunters."

She thought that was totally chauvinistic, but since she didn't want the job anyway there was no point in going into that. "Did your mother approve of your line of work?"

"What kind of question is that?"

"My kind of question. I'd appreciate it if you answered it."

"My mother never expressed her opinion of such things. It wouldn't have been proper."

"By all means, let's be proper," she said.

"I didn't expect you to be so . . ."

"Pissed off?"

He gave her a look of deep disapproval that had her squirming before remembering she was twenty-eight years old and had a damn good reason for being pissed off. Just because her time-traveling, vampire hunting grandfather had given her his classic reprimanding frown was no reason to back down. She'd had enough on her plate grieving her mother's death without all this other shit going on.

Her anger took her by surprise and sent a flaring

ember glowing at her feet. Okay, she could not be blasting here or she'd start another Chicago Fire. She had to
calm down.

She took a deep breath. "Tell me about my ring. It's
what got me through the portal, right?"

He nodded.

"You said you got it in Turkey."

"I did. About thirty years ago."

"Thirty years from when? From the nineteenth
century or the twentieth or twenty-first?" she asked.

"The ring is what allowed you to be transported
through the portal."

"I sure hope it allows me to be transported back to
my own time."

"It does."

"What else does the ring do? Is it the reason I blasted
a hole in that tunnel?"

"What tunnel?"

"Never mind. What else does the ring do?"

"It provides you with some protection."

"Some protection against what?"

"Evil," he said.

"By evil do you mean vampires? Because all vampires are not evil."

"You are wrong."

"No, *you* are wrong. But there's no changing the past."

"It's your future I'm worried about. It's in jeopardy."

"In what way?"

"From vampires."

"How do you know this?"

"I know."

"Did you read the journal?"

He nodded.

"Then you know what your own future holds," she said. "Isn't that against some rule of the universe?"

"Perhaps."

"I don't understand."

"The vampires want this journal."

"What does that have to do with you knowing your own future? By the way, I'm assuming that if you change the future, then I won't have been born." She paused as a flare of panic hit her. "Is that why I'm here? Because I wasn't born? I don't exist in my own time anymore?"

"Stay calm. I'm not going to change anything." Having said that, he opened the journal and tore out half a dozen pages.

"What are you doing?"

"Protecting you." Without future ado, he lit a match and set the pages on fire.

"Stop!" she cried out.

But it was too late. The pages went up in flames. The air was already still thick with the smell of smoky ruins surrounding them.

"Why did you do that?" she demanded.

"I told you."

"What was on those pages?"

"I did what I had to."

"That isn't an answer."

"It's the only one you'll get from me on this matter," he said.

"Was it the pages in some sort of old language?" She could tell by the look on his face that her hunch was accurate. "I'm right."

"I'm not discussing it any further."

"Maybe you already have changed the future by burning those pages."

"I just made sure they didn't fall into the wrong hands."

"Meaning vampire hands. Why did you leave the journal to me in the first place?"

"So you would know the truth."

"Why did you send me to see Alex when he was next on your vampire hit list? I didn't see anything about your reasons for that in the journal."

"It was written in the old language."

"In the pages you just burned?" She looked at the charred remains at her feet in dismay. "You destroyed information about Alex and me? I don't understand any of this!"

"I'm not explaining it very well, I fear."

"You've got that right," she muttered.

"Those pages contained ancient legends."

"About Alex?" She frowned. "But he didn't become a vampire until the Second World War."

"The legends foretold someone to come."

"You mean that Alex was destined from ancient times to be a vampire?"

Her grandfather nodded.

"How ancient are we talking about here?" she asked,

"The Crusades."

"Whoa." She tried to wrap her mind around that. "What about me? Why do I feel this strong connection to Alex? And don't tell me it's just sex."

Her grandfather looked like he'd just swallowed a frog.

"Sorry," she said. "I forgot who I was talking to for a moment there. You looked older when I knew you."

"There is a legendary connection referred to as The Longing in your case and The One in his."

"By connection do you mean we're meant to be to-gether?"

Her grandfather nodded.

Keira had sensed as much. "Is that why you wanted to kill him?"

"That decision was made by future me. I can only assume I was concerned for your safety."

"Yet you sent me to him."

"Something must have happened to change things."

"The blood thefts?"

"I don't know the answers."

"Did you die of natural causes or did a vampire kill you?"

"Again, that's the future. I have no knowledge of that."

"What about your past? Can you tell me about that?"

"You are a tenacious one, aren't you? You must have gotten that from me. I was never going to marry or have children. I didn't want to pass this burden on to another."

"Burden?"

"Being a vampire hunter."

"Can you teach me how to blast?" she said.

"Blast?"

"You know what I mean. You used blasting to hunt vampires."

"You want to become a hunter?" he said.

"No. I want to be able to protect myself."

"There isn't time. You have to go back or the portal will close."

"Then why did you pull me back here?"

"I confess I wanted to see you to talk to you, my own flesh and blood." His voice was gruff. "I never thought that day would come again. I never thought that I'd have a family. Not when I was doing what I was doing."

"I heard you were married before."

He nodded. "Before I became a hunter. Everything changed after that."

"Why didn't you stop?"

"It was my mission in life."

"Why couldn't Mom and I have been your mission in life?" she asked unsteadily.

"You were." He brushed his hand across her cheek as he had many times over the years.

"But hunting vampires was more important."

"More urgent. When Almina, my first wife, died from a vampire attack, I knew I had to follow the path of a hunter and do it better than it had ever been done before. I never planned to marry again . . . but I did."

"What about these blood thefts? Did you plan those?"

"No. I did not."

"How can I believe you? Why should I believe you?"

"I've never lied to you."

"Your whole life was a lie."

"No. What I did was not share certain information with you for your own good."

"You said you were an accountant."

"I was an accountant. An accountant who also hunts and kills vampires. I left that part out."

"Lies by omission are still lies."

"If only life were that simple," he said.

It took Alex five minutes to evacuate the Water Tower building. It was the longest five minutes of his afterlife.

Even moving at vamp speed, it was difficult to reach all the visitors. There weren't a lot, but they were all over. Too bad he didn't have the ability to do a mass compulsion. He could have sent them all out of the building in seconds.

The worst was the Girl Scout troop that had just entered. Seeing them reminded him of Keira telling him about her first visit here as a Girl Scout. "I thought it was a magical castle," she'd said.

He compelled the troop leader first. "The girls are in danger. Get them all out of here immediately. Head out in an orderly way."

The woman obeyed without causing a stampede.

"Are we going over to Water Tower Place to shop now?" one scout eagerly asked.

"Your eyes are glowing," one astute scout with her hair in braids told him before he compelled her to forget.

Of course there were security cameras, but he disabled them with a mass surge of energy. Security would merely see images from earlier in the day.

All the while he told himself that Keira was okay. The connection between them was so powerful that he'd know if she was dead. So she must be okay. It had to be her grandfather who grabbed her. The bastard.

But what if that wasn't the case? What if someone else had grabbed her? What if Lynch had taken her somehow? How would the Gold Coast leader know their location? Alex had taken great pains to make sure they weren't followed.

No, it had to be her grandfather. He was the one who had told her to stash the journal here. Was it possible that he was still alive and had somehow grabbed her in some sort of hidden passageway?

If that was the case, her claustrophobia would make her panic as she had in the Vamptown tunnels. Alex hated to think of her that way. He also prayed that she wouldn't try to blast her way out, because the Water Tower wasn't as sturdy as the Vamptown tunnels and any secret passageway could collapse. Yeah, the place had survived the Chicago Fire, but it might not be able to survive a supernatural blast from the granddaughter of a legendary vampire hunter.

Alex frantically ran his hands over the wall looking for some device that would trigger the passageway or the portal. He had to use caution that his strength didn't knock the wall down or he'd never get her back. No matter how carefully he looked, he didn't see anything out of the ordinary. There was no hint of anything magical.

"Come back to me, Keira!" Alex shouted before whispering raggedly, "You have to come back to me."

"I have to go back," Keira told her grandfather. For a second there, she could have sworn that she heard Alex's voice calling to her.

"I know."

She couldn't resist asking, "What do you know about my future?"

"More than I can tell you," her grandfather said.

"That's not real helpful. You know something about my future yet you can't tell me about your future, about how you died. Why is that?"

"I don't make the rules," he said. "I just have to abide by them." He paused a moment before adding, "I will say this . . . you'll do well in the end."

"In the end?" she repeated. "What does that mean? The end, as in right before I die?"

"Don't talk that way."

"It's hard not to." She took a deep breath. "Will I see you again?"

He shook his head regretfully.

Two tears rolled down her cheeks. Damn, she'd been doing so well up until then. "I didn't get to say good-bye to you before you died. I wanted you . . ." Her breath caught. "I wanted you to know how much I love you."

"I love you, too. Remember that and think of me when you look at your ring."

"What about my tattoo? It's changing."

"That's as it should be. It's a sign of your future."

"A future you can't tell me about."

"That's right."

"No, it's not right. None of this is right. You dying. Mom dying. Me being alone."

"You have Alex."

"And you're okay with that?"

"It's out of my hands."

"Whose hands is it in, then? No, wait. You can't tell me, right?"

"Right."

She'd been holding on to his left hand all this time. He held his journal in his right hand. When he opened it, she realized what he was doing. "Stop!"

Alex knew time was running out. Sooner or later the security crew would notice something off with their footage. And while he'd barred the entrance door, newcomers he hadn't compelled were bound to think that something was wrong. If he flashed his badge, he might gain some time, but that would mean leaving his post at the wall where Keira had left him. He wasn't willing to do that.

Leaving was too much like giving up, and that was not an option. He'd tried everything he could think of, from pressing his mirroring tattoo against the wall to compulsion. Nothing worked. Logically he knew he couldn't compel inanimate objects, but he was desperate.

Checking his watch, he realized she'd only been gone fifteen minutes. It seemed like forever. His gut told him that her ability to return if there was a portal would be limited.

He had no experience with time-travel issues. What if she was stuck in some other time forever? What if she couldn't come back?

His blood froze. The thought of never seeing Keira again left him bereft. He refused to accept such a possibility. No way.

Yes, Alex was persona non grata in Vamptown right now, but he was just about to contact Craig or Damon or Zoe anyway when he got the feeling that something was about to happen. There was a change in the energy around the wall.

Then Keira appeared as suddenly as she had disappeared.

Chapter Nineteen

Alex hauled Keira into his arms and hugged her so tightly she almost couldn't breathe. Not that she was complaining. In fact, she was hugging him just as tightly.

"Where did you go?" His voice was gruff.

"Back in time."

He didn't seem surprised by her answer. "Your grandfather?"

She nodded.

"Let's get out of here." He reset the Water Tower entrance and security cameras before whisking her back to their hotel room at the Palmer House. "Are you okay?" he asked her.

"I am now. That was quite a trip. My grandfather pulled me back in time to a few days after the Chicago Fire."

"Why?"

"He wanted to talk to me. It was my 1871 grandfather, if that makes sense. He was younger than when I knew him."

"You're sure it was him?"

"Definitely."

"You've got the journal?"

"He burned it."

Alex cursed loudly and vehemently.

"But he didn't burn all of it." She held it out. "Only some of the pages. He was going to burn more but I stopped him."

"Why did he do that?"

"They were the pages in some ancient language I didn't understand."

"Great. Just great."

"Most of the journal is still intact," she said.

"Tell me everything."

"We were standing near the Water Tower but it was right after the Chicago Fire. Well, not instantly after. Maybe a couple of days after. I'm not positive. There were no remaining flare-ups but the air still reeked of smoke."

"What did he want?"

"Like I said, he wanted to talk to me."

"About what?" Alex said.

"He wanted to meet his own flesh and blood. That's what he said."

"How did he know about you?"

"I'm not sure. He'd read the journal so he knew what happens to him in the future. He knew he would marry a second time and have a child and grandchild." She rubbed her forehead. "I'm still trying to make sense of it. Which came first, the chicken or the egg? Did he read the journal back in time and then arrange for me to stash it in the hidden portal a few days ago? I don't know the logistics of how it worked out."

"So you didn't know the hiding place was a portal that would take you back in time?"

"Absolutely not."

"Yet another thing your grandfather kept from you."

"I know. I confronted him about his not telling me he was a vampire hunter. He said he was trying to protect me by keeping it from me."

"What else did he say?"

"I asked him if he was behind the blood thefts or if he played any part in a plan regarding them. He said no very emphatically. I also asked him why you were on the top of his hit list."

"What was his answer to that?"

"He said that was the original plan but indicated it had changed. He wouldn't go into details, though."

"Of course he didn't."

"He said he doesn't make the rules. He just has to abide by them." Seeing the strange look on Alex's face, she said, "What's wrong?"

"My sire Mitch used to tell me that."

"Do you think there's a connection?"

"I have no way of knowing."

"It was so strange to see a younger version of my grandfather. Strange and very emotional. I never got to say good-bye to him before he died. I told you that.

"So you said your good-byes?"

She nodded. "He told me I'd do well in the end but he couldn't be more specific than that." She paused as her stomach growled. "Travel these days is hard but time traveling is even harder. I'm starving." She reached for the room service menu near the phone. "I'm thinking of having a burger." She looked at him. "What about you? Have you, umm . . . eaten lately?"

"They don't have blood on the menu," he noted drily.

"I realize that. So what do you do in that case?"

"I order out."

"From the funeral home in Vamptown?"

"Why are you so interested?"

"Because I'm a report—"

"Yeah, I've heard it before," he interrupted her. "You're a reporter. Your job is to ask questions. That's also my job. It's what I do as a police detective. What else did your grandfather say to you?"

"I did ask him about my tattoo changing."

"And?"

"And he didn't seem surprised. He said that's as it should be and that it was a sign of my future, but he wouldn't tell me any more than that. Wait, he did mention something about a legend dating back to the Crusades."

"The Crusades?"

"That doesn't ring a bell for you?"

"Should it?"

"He seemed to think it was tied to you."

"I didn't become a vampire until the Second World War."

"I know that. He used the term *The One*. Does that sound familiar? Have you heard it before?"

Alex got a strange look on his face. "Yes."

"So you know what he was talking about?"

"I might."

"What does it mean?"

"That a woman would come into my life and change it forever . . . for better or for worse."

"So you're saying I've changed your life for the worse?"

"No."

"What does sex have to do with it? Did having sex

with me tie into the legend somehow? I'm just asking because this is your legend, not mine," she said, not caring if she sounded snarky. She'd just taken a trip to 1871. She was allowed to be snarky.

"Meaning?"

"Meaning it's not a legend about reporters. It's a vampire legend."

"Because we for sure don't have enough vampire legends already," he said.

"Hey, if you're going to be pissy about it I'm not going to tell you. I was just curious, though, as to why the reference is The One regarding you and not me. He said it was part of your destiny."

"And yours."

"Yes, but mine is known as The Longing. Which sounds kind of wimpy to me."

"There's nothing wimpy about any of this."

"Why are there two different terms for what from all I can discern is basically the same thing—a reference to the connection between us?"

"I don't know. Does it describe how you feel about me?"

"At times, yes," she muttered.

"Which times specifically?"

She could have said, *Like right now.* But instead she grabbed the TV remote with more than a hint of desperation and turned on the local news. "Here we are at the Taste of Chicago where the crowds are enjoying everything from pierogi to pizza to these hefty turkey drumsticks." The reporter waved one in the air. "Come on down to enjoy the fun. And while you're here, do something good by stopping by the Red Cross station and donating blood."

"That's it," Alex said. "That's the site of the next blood theft."

"I trust you have better news for me this time?" Lynch told the vampire who nervously entered his office.

"Yes, master."

"Excellent. You have Sanchez and the hunter's grand-daughter in custody? Why didn't you bring them with you?"

"We don't exactly have them in custody."

"I'm disappointed to hear that." Lynch reached for the knife he kept on his desk at all times now.

"Wait, master! I know where they will be within the next hour."

"And how do you know that?"

"Because we have set up a sting operation to capture them."

"I want the hunter's granddaughter the most. If in doubt, grab her. We can control Sanchez once we have her. He put his own life at risk by taking off from Vamp-town with her, which means he clearly has feelings for her. Always a mistake. Feelings lead to weakness and weakness leads to . . . ?" Lynch paused, looking at the other vampire expectantly.

"Death," the vampire replied.

"Correct. What is your name, by the way? We've had such a turnover here lately that it's hard keeping track of everyone's identity."

"I'm Seymour."

"Tell me more about this sting idea of yours. It is your idea, right?"

"Yes, master."

"You're the first one who has mentioned the concept

of a plan, so I'm glad to hear you have some initiative. It's tiring having to do everything myself."

"I understand, master. Sanchez will bring the hunter's granddaughter to the Taste of Chicago."

"Why would he do that? It's not like he can enjoy the food there. Yes, I realize she can, but I don't know that she is going to be interested in doing such a touristy thing when they are in danger and on the run. They do know they are in danger and on the run, right?"

"Yes, master."

"What about their whereabouts earlier today? Do you have any idea where they've been hiding out?"

"No, master. We picked them up briefly on one of our vamp cams but then they were gone."

"What use are those cameras if we can't track our enemies?" Lynch pounded his fist on his desk, which made the knife resting there jump a few inches in the air. "Who was in charge of that project?"

"You killed him yesterday."

"Good riddance." Lynch leaned back in his ergonomically designed top-end office chair. "Go on."

"We'll have Keira by this evening."

"We'd better," Lynch said. "Or more heads will roll."

"You are not coming with me," Alex said as he strapped on more weapons. He already had several daggers on his person along with several specialty handguns.

"I'm safer with you than I am without you," she pointed out.

Alex wasn't sure about that but she appeared to be, which should make him feel better that she was no longer trying to escape from him. Her reference to The Longing she experienced had made him hot and hard but there was no time for sex. His gut told him that the blood heist today would be a major one and that this was his chance to catch the thieves red-handed.

"Admission to the Taste is free," she reminded him. "There will be a lot of people there."

"So?"

"So you need me to keep an eye out."

"An eye out for what?"

"Vampires," she said.

"Right. Because you have a secret way of identifying them."

"No."

"Well, I do," Alex said.

"It's the glowing eyes and the bloody fangs, huh?"

"Very funny."

"We're in this together. Besides, what would I do if vamps show up here and try to get in? You said those fledging mercenaries don't need permission to enter."

"You should be safe here."

"I should be, but can you guarantee that?"

"No."

"So I'm coming with you. Now tell me the plan."

"There is no plan," he said.

"You're a cop. Of course there's a plan. You just don't want to tell it to me."

"Correct."

"Why not? Maybe I can help. Did you ever consider that?"

"Not really."

"Well, consider it now."

"I'll be checking out the area surrounding the blood drive station."

"And what will I be doing?"

"Staying by my side and staying quiet."

"That doesn't really work for me, but setting that aside for the moment . . . what happens if you find vampires in the area?"

"They can be in the area as long as they aren't stealing blood."

"What happens if they do steal blood?"

"I arrest them."

She raised an eyebrow? "Really? That's it?"

"No, that's not it."

"What if they resist arrest? What if there are a gang of them and only one of you?"

"This is a surveillance mission only."

"So we let them get away with the blood?"

"There are other ways of stopping them."

"Like?"

"Like instantly sending video to Neville in Vamptown."

"Vamptown where the inhabitants want to kill me."

"Not all the inhabitants. Damon, Nick, and Ronan can be here in a millisecond along with reinforcements."

"You can't have a vampire fight in the middle of the Taste of Chicago."

"It's the first day of the event."

"So that makes it okay to have a battle?" she said.

"No. It means there will be more blood collected as time goes on. More thefts."

"Or maybe your gut is wrong and no one will try to steal any blood at all."

"Possibly but not likely."

She lifted the hem of the black T-shirt he'd lent her from his bag and sniffed it before making a face. "This smells like smoke from the Chicago Fire. Do you have another one?"

"No."

"Come take a shower with me."

"What?"

"You heard me. Take a shower with me. A really fast one so I can wash the smoke off."

"You need me with you to do that?"

She gave him a long look before murmuring, "There may be places I can't reach."

She blinked and he was nude. "Wow, that was fast," she said.

Another blink and she was nude. "Very efficient," she said approvingly. "Just so you know, we are not having sex in the shower."

"Of course we are. It's going to be fast and hard."

"Freaky-fast vampire sex?"

"Yep."

"Okay then."

He turned the water on and then turned her on. He was right. It was fast and hard. It was also sleek and sensual. There was no time to focus on how good he felt as he slid inside of her because her orgasm hit full force, her vagina clenching as he drove into her again and again, creating waves of such incredibly intense pleasure that she thought she'd die . . . but what a way to go.

Screaming his name, she collapsed against him. Scooping her in his arms, he carried her from the shower to the bedroom, where he set her on the bed.

Her body still hummed with tiny aftershocks.

"Are you okay?" he said.

"OMG," she said, still breathless from the entire erotic experience.

He handed her a towel. "I ordered fresh clothes for you from one of the shops downstairs."

Looking in the bag, she found a pair of navy-blue

running shorts, a Chicago Bears T-shirt, and a pair of sunglasses that would cover half her face. She especially welcomed the clean underwear.

By the time she looked up, Alex was already dressed all in black, pants and a T-shirt that hugged his chest the way she wanted to.

"If you keep looking at me that way, we'll never leave this hotel room," he said huskily.

While that sounded very appealing, Keira knew they were on a mission. They needed to solve this issue of the blood thefts and clear her name. She dressed quickly, not as fast as him, but fast enough.

"Okay, let's go."

They joined the crowd in Grant Park at the Taste of Chicago beyond the entrance gate. "I don't want them searching me," he said.

Right. Because he was armed. "So this isn't just a surveillance mission. You are expecting trouble?"

"I always expect trouble," he replied.

The festival was filled with families, women pushing strollers, and teenagers flocking in groups. A dad holding his little girl in pigtails in his arms as she licked an ice cream cone made Keira smile. Her feelings were somewhat bittersweet. She'd never known her father. He'd died when she was a baby. Her grandfather had been the one to hold her and give her ice cream. And now he was gone as well.

She deliberately pushed those thoughts away and focused on her surroundings. People lined up in front of the most popular booths. The smell of various foods, from pizza to those huge turkey drumsticks, made her mouth water and reminded her that she never had ordered anything from room service back at the hotel.

"I'm starving," she told Alex.

"You can eat later. I'm sensing something . . . Don't let go of my hand." He tightened his hold on her fingers.

"Okay."

They walked on, heading toward the Red Cross station. Out of the corner of her eye, she saw someone. Was that Benji? And Liz? When she turned to get a better look and her hand inadvertently slipped from his.

An instant later she was gone. Alex stared in dismay at the card that floated to the pavement, marked with the crest of Lynch.

If you want her back, bring me the journal.

Chapter Twenty

Keira was in a cage . . . and she wasn't alone. She also wasn't wearing her own clothing but a skimpy sparkly bikini worthy of a Vegas showgirl instead. A second ago she'd been at the Taste of Chicago with Alex. What the hell had just happened? "This can't get any creepier."

"You're wrong. It gets much creepier," a woman with red hair said from the other side of the cage. Like Keira, she was wearing a bikini decorated with a colorful array of crystals. But she had had a chain around her ankle, limiting her movements.

The cage was in the center of an ornately decorated room with French decor and gilded fixtures. Large darkly tinted windows displayed the city's skyline. So they were still in Chicago. That was something.

"I'm not supposed to be here. Uh, where is here?" Keira asked.

"Lynch's Petting Zoo."

Okay, that didn't sound good. Keira knew Lynch was head of the Gold Coast vampire clan and no friend of Vamptown. Why had he grabbed her and why had he stuck her in a cage?

"Who are you?" she asked the other woman. Voicing her questions prevented the panic inside from bubbling out of control. Yes, there were spaces between the bars of the cage, but the bottom line was that she was still trapped and captured liked an animal.

"I'm Fiona."

"Why are you here?"

"Because I'm a witch."

"A witch who has lost her powers," Lynch said as he entered the room.

"I didn't lose them," Fiona said. "They were stolen from me."

Keira had never heard a vampire tsk before, but Lynch was doing a good job of it. "It's all a matter of semantics, isn't it?" Turning to face Keira, he said, "Welcome, my dear. I'm so happy you've joined my menagerie."

"I haven't joined anything. I was taken against my will," Keira said.

Lynch waved his perfectly manicured hand in the air. "Semantics, semantics. I must say that having a vampire hunter's granddaughter in my collection is quite a coup. And not just any vampire hunter, but The Executioner no less. Quite impressive indeed."

"So you're behind the blood thefts," Keira said as if she already knew that was a fact. Not that she did, but she liked the confident way she spoke. Her gut told her this was the enemy responsible for more trouble than she realized.

"Naturally."

"Why? It's not like you're trying to cure cancer or something."

"Actually that's exactly what it is," he said.

His comment momentarily threw her. Was it possible that she'd somehow misjudged him?

Probably not. He had her locked up in a cage after all.

"I find it hard to believe that your goal is to cure cancer," she said.

He planted his hand over his perfectly tailored Italian suit's lapel. "I am wounded, but you are right. That isn't the goal. Increasing the wealth of the Gold Coast vamps is my goal. Always has been and always will be."

"So why are you stealing blood?" she demanded. "To sell it at a higher price on the vampire black market? To deplete the supply so that the demand can't keep up?"

"My, my, my. You do have an active imagination." Lynch smiled at her, his teeth brilliant white against his tanned face. No sign of fangs, but his congeniality dripped with evil intent. "I like that in my pets."

She refused to focus on what being his pet might involve and stayed on topic. "Am I right?"

"No. I told you the truth when I talked about curing cancer and other deadly human diseases. Vampires are immune to those diseases. Our blood has special antibodies that are super powerful. But humans can't tolerate unadulterated vampire blood. It either turns them into vampires or kills them. It has to be mixed with human blood. The trick is in the details. Getting that ratio of human to vampire blood just right requires a lot of human blood. I certainly wasn't going to risk depleting our own food supply from our regular locations so I outsourced it."

"Stole it."

"There you go again. Semantics."

"People need that blood."

"And they shall get it. Actually they'll get an even better blood. For a price," Lynch said.

"What do you mean?"

"We've just recently gotten the mix right and are ready to offer our product to those able to afford it. What is the going price for life these days? It depends on the bidder. There are sick billionaires all over the world who are vying for the cure in an extremely elite high-end auction as we speak.

"You see, it's brilliant economics. Just like making the pitiful vampires in Vamptown think you were to blame for vampire deaths was a brilliant strategy of mine. They panicked and you hit the road."

"But one of the vampires killed was with your clan. You killed a member of your own clan?"

Lynch nodded. "Indeed. I've done it several times and I'd do it again. Right, Seymour?" he added to the vampire standing near the door.

"Yes, master."

"Why do they put up with it?" Keira said.

"Because I'm their master," Lynch said. "This isn't a freaking democracy like Vamptown."

As long as she kept asking questions, she was able to keep the panic at bay. "How did you become their master?"

"I sired them."

"Vampires can't kill the one who sired them?"

"Not in my case, no. A specialty of mine. Something else I've perfected. By adding a certain blend of chemicals and an otherwise deadly poison to my blood, I was able to make it happen. Another goal I've attained. Right, Seymour?"

"Right, master."

"You won't get away with this," Keira said.

"Of course I will. I already have. It's not like your grandfather can rescue you. He's dead."

"Is he?" Keira knew he was, but perhaps she could

use the fact that some vampires still thought he was alive as a way to keep Lynch at bay. If Pat from Vamptown thought so, maybe Lynch would as well.

"Oh, he's dead," Lynch said. "No doubt about that. I killed him myself. Gave him a poison that made it look like a brain aneurysm. I was an alchemist at one point in my long afterlife and then more recently a chemist with several degrees. I'm quite good at such things if I do say so myself. Being the modest sort that I am, I didn't brag about besting the legendary vampire hunter. I could have done so. But I needed that journal of his. It has information about vampire blood that I would find most useful in my various endeavors. I compelled your mother to tell me where it was, but she didn't have any idea. I suspected your grandfather had stashed it somewhere, but I didn't know where. I lost patience two months ago and had her killed. Made it look like a car accident."

Keira crumpled. Her poor mother. She'd had no idea what was going on. Had no idea that she was part of a vampire-hunting family. Had no idea of the dangers that entailed. Keira closed her eyes and saw her mother's smiling face and longed to be held in her arms and told everything would be okay the way her mom did whenever Keira had nightmares as a kid.

Her grief was as fresh now as it had been the moment she'd learned of her mother's death two months ago. It was all-consuming, stealing the breath from Keira's body. Tears ran down her face.

"Come now, don't be so dramatic," Lynch chastised Keira. "I expected better of you. No one likes a crybaby."

She wanted to be distant and emotionless but she was no good at it. Not anymore. Not now.

"Master, you're needed," Seymour said.

"Duty calls." Lynch's voice radiated civil-coated evil. "I'll be back, my pets."

Alex called the number on the card. "What do you want?" Alex growled.

"You know what I want. The Executioner's journal."

"Kidnapping humans is illegal according to our co-existence treaty."

"You kidnapped her first," Lynch said. "I just rescued her from your evil clutches."

"I'm sure she doesn't see it that way."

"I really don't care how she sees it. She's in my evil clutches now, Detective. Deal with it," Lynch said.

"Oh I intend to deal with it."

"I'm glad to hear that. So you'll be bringing me the journal. Excellent."

"Where is she?"

Lynch sighed. "I suppose this is where you demand proof of life?"

"I suppose it is." Alex couldn't afford to show how terrified he was. Not at this point. He'd let his actions speak for themselves when he was face-to-face with Lynch.

"I'm sending you a link to a live video feed now," Lynch said.

Alex almost lost it when he saw Keira crumpled inside a cage. "What the hell?"

"She's fine. She just got a little emotional when I told her that I killed her grandfather and her mother. Humans get so hysterical about these things."

Alex felt his fangs emerging and his vision going red as the screen on his smartphone went black.

"There. You've had your proof of life," Lynch said.

"Now bring me the journal or my latest pet won't be staying alive much longer."

Fiona put her hand on Keira's back. "Lynch's goal is to terrorize and traumatize."

Keira sat up. "He succeeded."

"Don't let him."

"He killed my family."

"He killed mine as well. Don't show fear, you can't let him win." Fiona helped Keira stand.

"How can you sound so calm?"

"I've had time to practice."

"Are we being watched?"

"No doubt."

"How long have you been held here?" Keira said.

"Too long."

"Days? Weeks? Months?"

"I've lost track."

Their conversation stopped as Lynch strolled back into the room with utter confidence. He held a vial of blood between his fingertips, turning it slowly as if admiring a fine wine.

"It doesn't take much to do the job," he said.

"What job is that?" she countered, straightening her shoulders. This was all a game to him. She wasn't going to play the victim. Fiona was right. They couldn't let him win.

"Weren't you listening before?" Lynch said. "This is überblood, which can cure any human disease. Doesn't matter what it is. The bidding has begun and we are fast approaching the billion-dollar range. That's billion with a *B*."

Lynch paused to gaze directly at Keira. Her ears

started ringing and then she heard the loud *SShhhhhish* sound that cable TV makes when it goes out before posting the INTERRUPTION TO YOUR SERVICE notice. Her thought processes felt momentarily interrupted before the noise stopped as suddenly as it had started.

Lynch's perfectly trimmed eyebrows lifted. "I'd heard a rumor that you couldn't be compelled but I didn't think that applied to *my* compelling you. No problem. I love setting new goals. I'll be able to compel you eventually."

"Never."

"Never say never, especially to a vampire," Lynch said. "You'll see. You'll have a long time, a longer-than-usual lifetime, to enjoy being my pet."

"What do you mean 'longer-than-usual lifetime'?"

"That's for me to know and you to find out," Lynch said in a mocking singsong voice.

Infuriated, she shot back, "What are we? Twelve?"

He smiled. "You have such a delightful sense of humor. I shall have to eradicate that, of course. As for my own sense of humor, I delighted in hacking the Vamptown security system to make them think that they were being invaded. Child's play but worth a momentary laugh."

Tapping into her inner reporter, Keira said, "Is that the only vial of your specialty blood?"

"Of course not. We have half a dozen more."

"And you are auctioning them all off?"

"Why the interest? Were you thinking of using it for your little buddy . . . what is his name again? Oh yes, Benji."

"Would it cure him?"

"Of course it would. But you couldn't afford the price of even a tiny drop from this vial. And you'd need the entire vial. Unless you've got a billion dollars stashed that I don't know about."

"No." She kept her face impassive, but the knowledge that the blood could help Benji renewed her courage.

"No." He glanced at his watch before pointing to the two women Seymour brought into the room. "I get really light-headed around three o'clock if I don't have a snack."

"Type O Negative or A Positive," Seymour said. "Which would you prefer, master?"

Keira could tell by the blank look on the women's faces that they had been compelled.

"I do believe I'm feeling positive," Lynch said.

Seymour handed over one of the women, who didn't seem to have any bite marks on her neck as yet.

Keira turned away. She couldn't watch. She could hear the sucking sounds as Lynch took his fill. When that noise stopped she turned to see him wipe his bloody mouth with a monogrammed linen handkerchief.

"I'm a vampire. This is what we do," Lynch told Keira. "So get that look off your face. It will be Happy Hour soon and I'll feed again."

"My blood is toxic."

"So is the witch's," Lynch said. "For now. I'm working on a cure for that. With my talent in the biochemical arena, I'm certain that neutralizing your blood toxicity won't take me very long. Not that I'd kill you." He reached through the bars of her cage to stroke her face but she jerked away. "I look forward to having you as my pretty pet."

It was as if the proverbial elephant in the room were sitting on her chest. What exactly did being Lynch's pet mean? Nothing good, she was sure.

She needed to focus. Alex would find her. She had to have confidence in that. He'd find her and he'd free her.

She deliberately hadn't mentioned his name to Lynch. Not that Lynch had mentioned Alex's name to her, either.

"Was that really Benji that I saw at the Taste of Chicago?" she asked him.

"Of course not. It was a hologram. Another project we've been having fun with. Really, the Gold Coast vamps are the fun clan. Those Vamptowners are a bunch of mollycoddlers."

She should never have let go of Alex's hand. She hadn't done so on purpose. Her hand had slipped from his. If she saw him again . . . *when* she saw him again, she'd never let him go. Not a realistic vow, perhaps. But here she was, locked in a cage with a malevolent vampire talking about having her as his pet. A vampire who had killed her family.

Her earlier grief was replaced with anger. She wondered if it was enough to blast her out of the cage. She had a feeling it wasn't. What was missing?

The panic. That was what she needed to combine with her fury. It shouldn't be hard to conjure up.

"I want out of this cage," she growled.

"Too bad, pet. That won't be happening anytime soon. But do feel free to interview me if you like." When she remained quiet, he said, "Then I'll interview you. Do you consider yourself to be a brave shoot-from-the-hip kind of girl?" Lynch mocked her.

"No. I consider myself to be a pissed and panicked blast-from-the-hip kind of woman." And with that Keira shot out her hands as her fury and fear flooded every cell in her body.

Chapter Twenty-One

Keira blasted through the bars of the cage and jumped out. Her hatred for Lynch was like a venom shooting through her. She wanted to obliterate him. But before she could do so, Alex appeared out of nowhere.

Lynch was stunned—by her blast or by Alex, she wasn't sure. Lynch didn't have time to speak or call for help because Alex moved in a blur of speed, grabbing Lynch's knife from the top of the desk and sticking it into the evil vampire's heart.

Sparks flew into the air, instantly turning into flames that enveloped Lynch. A flash like lightning filled the room, displaying him as a burning inferno that turned into a smoky pillar of stone before disintegrating into a pile of ash. The flames were gone as quickly as they appeared.

"What just happened?" Keira whispered.

"He's gone, burning in hell right now," Alex said.

"You should have let me kill him," Keira said.

"You wouldn't have been able to deal with the guilt," Alex said.

"And you can?"

"Yes."

"Why? Because you're a vampire? I come from a long line of vampire killers. That SOB killed my family. Maybe I'd be fine."

"And maybe you wouldn't," he said before enveloping her in his arms.

"How did you get in here?" Keira said unsteadily.

"I was cloaked. I wasn't sure if it would work on the Gold Coast vamps, but it did. I tweaked it some."

"Good job," Fiona said. "Do you think you could cut me loose from these chains?"

"This is Fiona," Keira said. "She's a witch and she's coming with us."

"Okay." Alex broke the chains and set her free.

"Don't argue with me, okay?" Keira said.

"Okay."

"She's coming with us."

"Yeah, I got that," Alex said.

"No argument," Keira said.

"No argument," he agreed.

"Why are you being so nice?"

"Because you've had enough stress for one day." He removed his shirt and wrapped it around her.

"What are you doing?" she said unsteadily.

"Covering you up. Is that okay?" He gently stroked her hair.

"Yeah, that's fine. Thanks."

"So you're a blaster, Keira," Fiona said. "I didn't know they really existed."

"We've got to get out of here," Alex said. "I only had enough psychic energy to cloak to get in here."

"Then how do we get out?" Keira asked.

"I called in reinforcements," he said.

As if on cue, the windows shattered and two people entered the room. Well, probably not people since they flew in. One was male and one female. Vampires most likely. Both were dressed entirely in black except for the red cowboy boots the woman had on.

"Got your message, Alex," the male vampire with light-brown hair and blue eyes said in a charming voice with a slight British accent. "Simon Howell at your service, miss."

The woman with long blond hair said, "Fiona is that you? What are you doing in that bikini?"

Fiona looked at the woman as if unable to believe her eyes. "Pru? Pru Daniels?"

"Let's talk later," Alex said. "I just killed the head of the Gold Coast clan and I'm not sure how the rest of his vampires are going to feel about that."

"Relieved," Fiona muttered.

"Isn't he the one who hired those demon mercenaries at the Christmas fair downtown the last time we were in Chicago?" Pru asked.

"Yes," Simon said.

The door burst open. Keira was expecting to see Seymour and a band of Gold Coast vampires. Instead something even worse flew into the room.

"Demon mercenaries!" Simon shouted, sounding pleased to Keira's incredulous ears.

Fiona put an arm around Keira and rushed her into a far corner. "Best to stay out of their way," Fiona said.

"I should help," Keira said.

"You are helping by not distracting them," Fiona said. "Trust me, they've got this."

"Catch," Simon told Alex as he tossed him a specialized blade he'd taken from his boot.

Alex deftly grabbed the weapon midair and sliced a demon with it. The evil entity disintegrated. Simon reached for a demon dagger in his other boot just in time to stab it into the malevolent eye of the demon about to rip him to shreds. Poof. Another pile of dust.

Keira had never seen anything like the battle she was witnessing. The fight she'd seen Alex have with that vampire at the love hotel was nothing compared with the mayhem in the room. The battle was occurring so fast it became a blur of good versus evil with Keira unable to tell which side was winning.

"Simon is the best Demon Hunter around," Fiona reassured her.

"And I'm the best witch around," Pru said as she kicked a demon, who went tumbling horned head over clawed heels before disintegrating. "With the best damn boots spelled to be a weapon."

"You're only the best witch because my powers were stolen," Fiona shot back with a grin.

"I thought we weren't supposed to distract them," Keira said.

"Right," Fiona acknowledged. "My bad."

Talk about bad, the smell was putrid, forcing Keira to put her hand to her nose.

"It's the demon mercenaries," Fiona explained. "And the demon dust."

A moment later it was over. Simon and Alex stood surrounded by piles of demon dust.

Simon grinned. "I love a successful demon demolition at the end of the day. Do your thing, Pru, before they regurgitate from those piles of dust into more powerful demons."

Pru held her hands out, palms down, and began speaking.

Demons in dust
Do what you must
To disappear
As if you were never here.

Just like that, the piles of demon dust disappeared. So did the awful stench.

"Let's go," Alex said.

"Wait." Keira rushed to Lynch's desk and the vial of blood in the container there. "Okay, now we can go."

"I'll take Fiona," Pru said. "You take the lovebirds," she told Simon.

Keira didn't have time to worry if she would freak out at flying because the airborne transport was done quickly. Once they were on street level, Alex took her in his arms and moved with his customary vamp super speed. She pressed her cheek against his bare chest. She was still wearing the shirt he'd tenderly wrapped around her.

They all ended up back at the Palmer House in Alex and Keira's room.

"First things first," Pru said. She turned to Fiona. "Let's get you dressed. Lavender is your favorite color, right?"

Fiona nodded.

A moment later the sequined bikini was gone and replaced with black yoga pants with a trendy lavender design down the leg that picked up the lavender T-shirt.

"I'll have what she's having," Keira said. "Or can you only do that for fellow witches?"

"I can do it for you," Pru said. "Same outfit?"

"Sure. Why not?"

"Because then we'll look like twins," Fiona said.

"You have red hair and I don't," Keira said.

"No worries. I'll make yours a lovely turquoise color instead of lavender," Pru said.

Keira handed Alex his shirt back. "Okay, I'm ready."

Her bikini, like Fiona's, was replaced with the new clothing. "Thanks," she told Pru. "We took off in a hurry with only the clothes on our backs at the time so I didn't have anything clean to change into."

"No problem."

"That was fun," Simon said. "What else do you have planned for our amusement and amazement on our visit to Chicago? While I'm asking questions . . . what made you kill the head of your rival clan, Alex? And why didn't you ask for help from Damon? Granted, I sired him and have more experience, but he's a damn good fighter."

"Because he thought Keira was behind the blood thefts."

"Why would he think that?" Simon asked.

"Because my grandfather is . . . was a vampire hunter called The Executioner," Keira said.

"Right. Why don't you start at the beginning?" Simon sat on the couch and made himself comfortable.

"It started with the blood thefts," she said.

"No," Alex corrected her. "It started with your grandfather's journal. She marched into the police station and confronted me, referring to my vampire heritage."

"A dangerous move for a human to make," Pru noted. "She is a human, right?"

"She's a blaster," Fiona said. "She can blast her way out of a cage."

"A blaster?" Pru didn't look convinced. "I thought they didn't exist outside urban legends."

"I saw it myself," Fiona said.

"Show me," Pru said.

"I can't do it on demand," Keira said. "And I'm not

about to trash our hotel room. I'm not some rock star from the 1980s."

Simon clapped his hands to get their attention. "Ladies, if we could get back to the basics here."

"Good luck with that," Alex said, sitting down on a chair and throwing one leg over the arm.

"Where is my grandfather's journal?" Keira abruptly asked.

"In a safe place," Alex said.

"Were you going to hand it over to Lynch? That's what he wanted, right?"

"It's what he wanted, yes."

"So were you going to do that?"

"To save your life, he for sure would have done that, right?" Fiona interceded.

Alex paused.

Fiona gaped at him. "You wouldn't turn over a stupid journal for the woman you love? What kind of vampire are you?"

"A smart one," Alex shot back. "Handing over the journal wouldn't have saved Keira."

"And it's not just a stupid journal," Keira said, jumping to his defense. "There is some sensitive material in there."

"Yeah, I heard Lynch talking about the vampire blood info," Fiona said. "I still think it sucks that Alex wouldn't—"

Keira interrupted her. "Alex always has a plan. And he never said he wouldn't turn over the journal if needed." He'd also never said he loved Keira, but there was no point going into that at the moment. He'd told her she was The One for him. That was good enough for now. "But he's right. Lynch wouldn't have released me."

"I know." Fiona sighed.

"How did he capture you, Fiona?" Pru asked. "Did he get you when he got Keira?"

"No, I was there much longer," Fiona said quietly. "But that's another story. Let's get back to Keira and Alex's story. So you went to the police station to confront Alex because he was a vampire."

"No," Keira said. "I confronted him because he was a vampire who wasn't doing enough to solve the blood thefts."

"I ended up having to rescue her from fledgling vampires sent to her apartment to grab her," Alex said.

"Alex grabbed me instead," Keira said.

"I kept her safe," he corrected her,

"You can't argue with that," Simon said.

"She can try," Alex said with a challenging grin.

Keira tossed a small throw pillow from the couch at him. He instantly caught it with one hand, his grin widening.

"Good catch," she said.

"Yes, I am," he agreed.

"Get a room," Simon said with a roll of his eyes.

"We've got one," Alex retorted. "But it is rather crowded at the moment."

"I'm still trying to get a clear picture of what's going on here." Simon impatiently ran his hand through his thick hair. "The blood thefts brought you two together. I'm assuming Lynch was behind the thefts?"

Keira nodded. "He was working on a project to blend vampire blood with human blood to auction to the highest bidder in order to save the lives of the richest terminally ill people in the world. Vampires are immune to human diseases like cancer."

"I heard rumors about an auction but I didn't think it

was real," Simon said. "That's the vial of blood you grabbed before we left?"

Keira nodded.

"The Gold Coast crew is going to want that back," Simon predicted.

"When Lynch took Keira, he broke the truce between our clans. That means we have the right to spoils of war," Alex said.

"Wait a second. Does that mean that you and the Gold Coast vampires are at war?" Keira didn't like the sound of that.

"Why are we having this discussion in a hotel room and not in Vamptown?" Simon demanded.

"Because the Vamptown clan thinks that I'm a vampire hunter like my grandfather," Keira said.

"Because you're a blaster?"

"No, they were okay about me blasting a hole in their tunnel walls." Keira clapped a hand to her mouth. "Was that a secret? The tunnels, I mean? Is Simon a member of the Vamptown clan?"

"I'm an honorary member of sorts," Simon replied.

"Simon was turned in the time of King Arthur," Pru said proudly.

Simon tugged Pru onto his lap. "And this gorgeous witch is from Morgan le Fay's bloodline. A volatile combination."

"If you go back that far then maybe you can help us with something," Keira said. "My grandfather told me that there's a link between Alex and the Crusades. Do you know anything about that?"

Simon nodded. "I do. But Alex has to ask me. I can only answer questions from him directly."

"Why?" Keira demanded.

"I don't make the rules—" Simon began.

"You just obey them," Keira and Alex said in unison.

"I was turned on Iwo Jima," Alex said. "That's a battle in the Pacific during World War Two."

"I may have been turned many centuries ago, but I am aware of current events. Well, relatively current compared with the Battle of Camlann back in Merlin's day. Never mind." Alex waved his hand. "Go on."

"What's the connection between me and the Crusades?" Alex asked bluntly.

"Your mother's bloodline goes back to Spain and the Moors."

"Is that why I was turned against my will?" Alex asked.

Simon nodded. "You were destined to become a vampire with a unique skill set."

"Like cloaking?" Keira asked. "Sorry. I'm a reporter. I instinctively ask questions."

"Like cloaking?" Alex asked. Smiling at Keira, he added, "I'm a police detective. I instinctively ask questions, too."

"Yes, like cloaking," Simon replied.

"Why wasn't I told about any of this earlier?"

"You didn't ask."

"Ask him about the legend," Keira said.

"What do you know about that?" Alex asked Simon.

"You both have The Longing. It affects you both—a longing for each other and for the truth. Each is The One for the other."

"That's so romantic," Pru said.

Simon shrugged. "I'm just stating facts."

"My sire Mitch died under mysterious circumstances," Alex said. "What do you know about that?"

"He wasn't killed by The Executioner," Simon replied.

Keira heaved a sigh of relief. She didn't recall reading about Mitch in her grandfather's journal, but there had been so much to process that it might not have registered.

"Mitch had his own personal demons, and one of those killed him," Simon said.

"You mean demons like we saw today?" Keira asked.

"No, those were demon mercenaries," Simon said. Looking directly at Alex, he added, "There was nothing you could have done. It was part of Mitch's destiny."

"What about my destiny?" Alex asked quietly.

Simon's answer wasn't clear-cut. "It will be what you make it."

"I meant to ask you earlier how you knew how to kill Lynch the way you did," Keira asked Alex.

"Your grandfather's journal said that the usual means of destroying Lynch wouldn't work. It had to be done using his own knife; doing so would ensure he went up in flames."

"Fire does seem to be a recurring theme with us, doesn't it," she said.

Alex nodded. "We should get back to Vamptown."

"If you're not going to use the room, Pru and I will stay here," Simon declared.

"With Fiona," Pru reminded him.

"I don't want to be a third wheel," Fiona said.

"Nonsense, Fiona. You can fill me in on what's been going on with you," Pru said. "Simon will want to hear about it as well, right?"

"I would be royally pissed to miss out on such an event," Simon noted with a grin.

"Ready?" Alex asked Keira.

She nodded. She clutched his shoulders as he lifted her in his arms. All too soon, they were back in the loft. Alex released her so she could carefully set the vial of blood on the end table of her re-created living room furniture.

"I knew you'd be back. Welcome home!" Bruce greeted them before plunging a wooden stake through Alex's chest.

Chapter Twenty-Two

Keira screamed as Alex collapsed. "What the hell?!" She rushed to Alex's side and knelt beside him. "Why did you do that? You killed him!"

"No, I didn't," Bruce said. "He just can't move at the moment."

"Why? If you're angry with me, hurt me, not him."

"You're not the one in trouble. He is." Bruce pointed to Alex. "My instructions are to keep him here so the Vamptown Council can vote on his punishment. Pat was so upset when you disappeared last time. I don't want him stressed out like that again. I love that guy. I'm referring to Pat, not Alex."

Keira remained on her knees beside Alex, clutching his hand, which was frozen in place. "What can I do?" He couldn't answer her.

"You can't do anything," Pat said as he entered the loft along with a throng of vampires. Some she recognized, like Doc Boomer, Tanya, and Damon. Others she didn't.

"Why are you doing this?" she demanded.

"Alex broke one of Vamptown's covenant rules," Damon said. "He disobeyed orders and took off with you."

"So you stake him as punishment?"

"Punishment is death, not staking," Damon said.

Keira couldn't believe what she was hearing. After all they'd been through with Lynch, now this? Hell no.

She was a blaster. She should be able to do something. But her blasting out of the cage at Lynch's had depleted her energy. So she'd stall until she could recharge her abilities. Even if she barely knew how to use them, there was no way she was letting anyone kill Alex.

"You're telling me you punish disobedience?" she said. "So you are just like Lynch. A despot dictator."

"We are nothing like Lynch. Our rules are intended to protect our community. If humans found out about vampires, they would either hunt and kill us or try to use our immortality for torture and research," Damon said.

"That's already happening. You already have humans—Sierra and Daniella—who know about vampires. And Lynch was already doing research using a vampire's immortality."

"You have to understand—" Pat began.

Keira interrupted. "Unstake him," she told Damon. Damon who had been sired by Simon, who had just saved Alex and Keira. "Simon says unstake him."

"Simon says?" Damon scoffed. "If you think this is some kind of childish game—"

Again she interrupted. "I was referring to Simon Howell. Your sire. He just saved Alex and me. Well, he helped us escape from the mercenary demons that the Gold Coast vampires unleashed on us."

Damon frowned. "Simon is here? In Chicago?"

Keira nodded. "So unstake Alex."

"First I have to read the charges against him," Pat said. "Alex Sanchez, you're being charged with breaking your vampire oath to Vamptown. Do you understand this charge as I have described it?"

"How's he supposed to answer that when you've paralyzed him?" Keira demanded.

"He's able to transmit his thoughts to me," Pat said with a slight grimace.

Good. Keira hoped Alex was letting them know exactly what he thought of them. Judging from the look on Pat's face, Alex was transmitting his anger in spades.

"How dare you ambush him like this," Keira growled. "Where is your loyalty?"

"Where is his loyalty?" Pat countered.

"He was protecting me. You wanted to harm me."

"We didn't *want* to," Bruce corrected her.

Keira put her other hand on Alex's chest, careful to avoid the wooden stake. "He's not breathing!"

"That's part of being staked," Doc Boomer said. "It is normal."

"Normal? None of this is normal," Keira said fiercely. "You were all wrong thinking I had anything to do with those vampire deaths. Lynch was behind them. He played you. He knew you'd fall for it. He also hacked into your system and set off those false invasion attacks. Lynch wanted me out of Vamptown and he got his wish. Had I stayed he would have continued his offensive against you. So in reality, Alex actually was protecting Vamptown by taking me away. By the way, Alex killed Lynch, who was behind all the blood thefts. You should be thanking him, not staking him!"

"What did I miss?" Nick said as he strolled into the loft.

"Who are you?" Keira demanded.

"Nick St. George."

"You're Daniella's boyfriend. Does she know what you're doing here? I doubt she would approve," Keira said.

"We had to stake Alex because he took off last time," Bruce explained.

Keira kept rubbing Alex's hand as if she could somehow soothe him out of his paralysis.

"I'd like to say a few words in Alex's defense," Doc Boomer said. "As Keira pointed out, by taking her out of Vamptown, he removed the target from our back and put it on his. Early on we suspected the Gold Coast vamps were behind the blood thefts, yet we readily went along with the possibility that Keira was to blame for those two vampire deaths."

"Craig will speak up for Alex." Keira looked around. "Where is he?"

"He and Bunny weren't allowed to participate as they aren't objective observers," Doc Boomer said.

"Or business owners," Tanya said. "They are employees."

Keira wasn't about to reveal that Craig had helped them by showing up on the boat on the Fourth of July. If they knew, they might stake him too. She didn't need more trouble. She had to keep her focus on Alex.

"How exactly did he break his vampire oath?" Keira demanded.

"He took off with you," Pat said.

"I explained that," Keira said.

"He put your well-being above that of Vamptown," Tanya said with a flick of her hair.

"We don't make the rules. We just have to obey them," Bruce said.

"If you don't make the rules then who does?" Keira countered.

"Generations of vampire councils," Pat said.

"Are you a do-nothing council?" Keira demanded.

"No." Pat sounded offended.

"Then do something," Keira said. "Damon, you would have gone after Zoe to save her. Nick, I don't know you very well, but I know you'd have taken Daniella to safety. And Bruce, you would have protected Pat, right?"

Bruce nodded sheepishly.

Sierra and a man entered the already crowded loft. "This is Ronan," Sierra said. "We heard what you were saying."

"I would have done the same thing as Alex," Ronan said, putting his arm around Sierra.

"Which is why you can't vote," Tanya said.

"He would be saving me," Sierra pointed out. "Me, your favorite author of all time."

There was a moment of silence. Then Tanya said, "Good point. I move we change the law and exonerate Alex. All in favor say Aye."

There were several moments of silence. It seemed like five minutes or more to Keira but it probably wasn't that long. She wasn't checking her watch, she was checking Alex. He still wasn't breathing or moving, and his hand was becoming increasingly cold.

"I suppose upon further consideration the law could use some tweaking," Pat said. "Aye."

A chorus of Ayes followed.

"All against say Nay," Tanya continued.

No one spoke.

"The motion passes," Pat said. "Alex is exonerated of the charges against him."

They'd sure changed their minds in a hurry, but Keira wasn't about to argue. Maybe her passionate defense was so effective that the Vamptown Council had no choice but to change course. She didn't care. The bottom line was that Alex was exonerated.

She eyed the stake in his chest nervously. Was he in pain? Would pulling the stake out hurt? It couldn't be pleasant.

"Release him," Keira said.

Doc Boomer bent over and grabbed hold of the stake, removing it in one smooth move.

Alex gasped and sat up. The bloody hole in his chest rapidly healed, but the anger remained in the accusatory glare he leveled at his fellow vampires.

Keira squeezed his hand. "Did you hear any of that?"

"I heard it all," Alex growled before standing.

"I'm sorry," she whispered.

"You've got nothing to be sorry about. The same isn't true for the rest of you."

"We were just following protocol—" Pat began.

"Protocol, my ass," Alex interrupted. "I've proven my loyalty to this community time and again over the past ten years. When you have trouble, I make it go away. I anticipate trouble before you even know about it. I have dedicated myself to Vamptown's well-being and this is the thanks I get for it. Screw it. Screw all of you."

"They did exonerate you in the end," Keira pointed out.

"Only because Sierra is Tanya's favorite author," Alex shot back, looking more disgruntled now than seriously pissed off.

"I don't think that's the only reason," Keira said. "I think they realized they'd do the same thing themselves if they'd been in the same situation. Right?"

"Correct," Nick said.

Damon shrugged and then nodded.

Bruce nodded emphatically.

"You couldn't have reached that decision before you staked me?" Alex demanded.

"I'm so sorry," Bruce said. "I panicked. I didn't know how else to make sure you stayed where you were."

"It's not that we don't appreciate your years of service," Nick told Alex.

"Then what is it?"

"An overabundance of caution," Nick quietly replied.

"Caution or paranoia?" Alex retorted.

"Perhaps a blend of both," Nick said.

"You hurt him," Keira said. "Don't do it again."

"Staking doesn't actually hurt that much," Alex admitted. "Bruce did a good job with the insertion and Doc Boomer did a smooth extraction."

"Well, goody for them," Keira said, "but let's not do it again, okay, people? I mean, okay, vampires?"

She took their grunts and grumbles as a yes. "Good. Now if you don't mind, Alex and I would like to be alone."

"I'm going to need a full report on the Lynch incident," Damon said.

"You can wait," Keira said.

"You've got an hour," Damon said.

"Or two," Alex said, snaring Keira in his arms. "Everybody out."

The vampires exited as quickly as they'd entered. Sierra was the last one out, since she wasn't a vampire. She paused to give Keira a big grin. "Welcome home. I think you'll do just fine here in Vamptown."

When she left, Keira asked Alex, "Do you think I'll do just fine here in Vamptown?"

"I do. If you want to stay. You're not my captive anymore." He released her. "You are free to go if that's what you want."

"You're what I want." She ran her fingers up his chest and started unbuttoning his shirt. "I do want to point out that this loft and the funeral home basement are the only areas of Vamptown that I've seen."

"I could give you a tour if you'd like," he murmured. "The tree-lined street with Doc Boomer's Happy Times Dental Clinic . . ."

"Happy Times? Really?"

"Really. Then there's Tanya's Tanning next to Pat's Tats."

"Since I have no desire for either a fake tan or real tattoos, I think I can pass on those two establishments."

"There's also Heavenly Cupcakes," Alex said.

"Now, that is a place I want to visit."

"Right now?"

"No, not right now. Where are you going?" she asked as he moved away from her toward the large table near the kitchen.

"Here." He handed her cell phone back to her. "Proof that I'm giving you your freedom. I'm trusting that you're not going to call the press and tell them vampires do exist."

"I am the press. And no, I don't plan on doing that. Your secret is safe with me. Besides, Sierra told me that even if I wanted to reveal something, it wouldn't work. But that's beside the point since I won't say anything." She looked at the screen. "The battery is probably dead." He handed her the charger.

The minute she plugged it in, the ringer gave a specialized ringtone. It was the emergency ringtone from her best friend Liz. "Hello?"

"We're at the hospital in intensive care. Benji has taken a turn for the worse. Keira . . ." Liz's voice cracked. "They're saying he won't make it through the night."

Chapter Twenty-Three

"I'm on my way," Keira said.

"On your way where?" Alex said.

"It's Benji. They're saying he might not live through the night. I have to get to the hospital."

"It could be a trap," Alex told Keira.

"Lynch is dead."

"But rest of the Gold Coast clan isn't. You never told me why you let go of my hand at the Taste of Chicago."

"It wasn't a conscious thing. I just thought I saw Benji, so I paused for a second."

"That's all it took. They used Benji once to get to you. Who's to say they won't do it again?" Alex said.

"You."

"I couldn't stop them last time." His voice reflected his anguish about that.

A knock on the door interrupted them. It was Neville. "I just wanted to let you know that I'm sorry I couldn't make the meeting and that I've just now turned off the security surveillance video in the loft we installed while you were gone."

An instant later Nick, Damon, Bruce, and Pat were all standing behind Neville.

"You're not alone," Nick stated.

"I was about to tell him that," Neville said, lifting his tablet to show them what looked like the inside of a hospital. "I confirmed it. Your godson is indeed in trouble."

"But just in case the Gold Coast vamps are using the situation to hurt you, we've decided that we're coming with you," Nick said.

"You'll just draw attention to yourselves."

"Please," Tanya said as she joined them. "We know how to stay under the radar."

"I just need to be with Benji and Liz," Keira said.

"We'll make sure you're safe while doing that."

"Wait. I need this." She rushed to the end table and carefully took the blood vial, putting it in a padded case she kept in her purse.

Alex put his arm around her, and an instant later they were inside Benji's room in the intensive care unit. "You're even faster than you were before," she whispered.

Alex nodded.

Liz sat in a chair beside Benji's hospital bed, with her head down, bent over their joined hands.

"I'm here," Keira told her, squeezing her shoulder in empathic commiseration.

Liz lifted her head in surprise. "How did you get here so fast? Never mind. I'm just glad you made it."

"How is he?"

"A little worse than before. The doctors say there's no hope."

"Doctors can be wrong," Keira said.

"He's slipped into a coma."

Keira wiped away the tears at the sight of all the tubes connected to her godson. Machines were beeping, recording Benji's heart rate and other vitals.

"Who is he?" Liz asked, tilting her head toward Alex.

"Alex is a close friend. He helped me get here."

"Thanks for bringing her," Liz said.

"The others are outside," Alex whispered for Keira's benefit.

To her surprise, Doc Boomer entered the room wearing a medical coat indicating he was on staff here at the hospital. "I spoke with Benji's doctor. Time is quickly running out. If we're going to do this, we need to do it now."

"Do what?" Liz asked. "What are you talking about?"

"Liz, if there was an experimental drug that could cure Benji, would you be willing to try it?" Keira said.

"I tried to get him into a clinical trial study but since his disease is so specialized, it filled up quickly and he didn't get it."

"So you would be open to trying something new?"

Liz stroked Benji's hand. "Is it safe?"

Keira nodded and removed the vial from her purse. "I believe so."

Benji's heart rate slowed dramatically and then stopped.

"Do it," Keira told Doc Boomer.

The vampire took the vial from her and used a large syringe to transfer it from the vial to Benji's IV. His actions were a blur.

Keira started praying as alarms went off. "The others will keep the rest of the staff out of the room," Alex told her.

"How long will it take?"

Doc Boomer pointed to the display indicating Benji's heart rate returning to normal. A few seconds later, he opened his eyes and spoke.

"I'm hungry," he said.

Keira panicked, wondering if little Benji was hungry for blood.

"I want a burger," Benji said.

As if reading her thoughts, Doc Boomer said, "He's still human through and through."

"Of course he's human," Liz said.

Doc looked at her. "You'll forget I was ever here. You'll forget I did anything with your son's IV. You're going to believe his recovery was a natural occurrence."

Keira could tell by the blank look on Liz's face that she was being compelled. With a nod in their direction, Doc Boomer took his leave.

"The hospital staff on duty responsible for Benji's care is being compelled as well. I'm going to stay but be cloaked so your friends can't see me," Alex said.

"Are you a wizard like Harry Potter?" Benji said, his eyes as wide as saucers.

"Something like that," Alex said with a grin before gently compelling Benji as well.

Liz came back from her state to stare at Benji in delighted amazement. Moments later nurses and doctors filled the room.

Keira sat beside Liz as the medical staff thoroughly checked Benji out.

"He's turned the corner and is going to be okay," the doctor finally declared. "I can't explain it."

"I don't need explanations," Liz said, going to stand at Benji's bedside to hold his hand. "I just need to know he's safe."

Keira stayed most of the night, hoping her presence

was a reassurance to her best friend and godson. Occasionally she'd feel a brush of invisible fingers over her cheek, as a reminder that Alex was still there, watching her back.

That's when she knew she loved him. The knowledge didn't come as a shocking revelation. It came with the powerful certainty of the sunrise visible outside the window. She'd been moving to this point since she'd leaned over his desk and confronted him. Yes, her attraction to him and her longing for him were intense, but they weren't as soul-stirring as this realization of love for him.

He was a vampire. She was the granddaughter of a vampire hunter. Yet they were destined to be together. She felt it in her bones. She also felt exhaustion from the demands of the past twenty-four hours.

"Go home," Liz told her. "We'll be okay here now. Thanks so much for coming."

"Always," Keira said. "Whenever you need me."

"You're going to make me cry," Liz said with a sniff.

"You do and it'll make me cry," Keira replied.

"Crying is for losers," Benji said. "And I still want a hamburger."

Back at the loft, Keira was all set to collapse onto her couch when Alex checked his phone. "I have to go."

"Police business?"

"Gold Coast vampire business. Seymour wants to talk on neutral ground."

"You mean like on the boat?"

"No, the Palmer House hotel room. That text was from Simon. Seymour is there waiting for me."

"I should go with you. What?" she said when he gave her a look. "I can't be worried about you?"

"Yes, you can be worried."

"I'm a blaster," she reminded him.

"Who doesn't know how to control your talents yet."

"Not my blaster talents, perhaps, but I've got other talents that might surprise you, mister." She grabbed hold of his shirt and pulled him closer to kiss him the way he'd taught her, adding new moves of her own and nearly blasting his self-control. "Don't be gone long."

"I won't," he promised.

An instant later he was gone.

"This better not take long," Alex said as he entered the hotel room where Simon and Seymour were waiting for him. Looking around, he asked, "Where are Pru and Fiona?"

"Shopping on the Mag Mile," Simon said. "Which normally means Magnificent Mile, I'm told, but given the fact that they are both witches it could mean the Magic Mile in their case."

Alex didn't like the sound of that. "They're not going to practice witchcraft in public, are they?"

"Fiona had her powers stolen," Simon reminded him. "And Pru knows better than to allow her magic to be seen by humans. They will no doubt max out a credit card and return laden with shopping bags."

"So the three of us are the only ones here?"

"That's correct," Simon said.

"I wanted to speak to you about the blood issue," Seymour said. "After consulting with the other members of our clan, we took a vote and decided the risk of going through with the auction was too big, so we canceled it at the last minute. Billionaires would want more blood and they would hire chemists who would discover the vampire link eventually. It is in the best interest of us all that humans don't know of our existence."

"Agreed."

"I am aware of what occurred last night at the hospital regarding the vial of blood that the hunter's granddaughter took from Lynch's desk."

"We compelled every human involved to cover the fact that vampire blood was involved in his recovery," Alex said.

"I contacted Doc Boomer with the details about infusing the blood into the IV in order to maximize its effect."

"That was generous of you. Why? What's in it for you?"

"That vial was restitution. But don't consider coming back to take more," Seymour warned him.

"As long as you keep it off the market and don't try to make more, we could live with that," Alex said.

"Understood."

"What I can't live with is anyone messing with Keira in the future."

"Also understood," Seymour said. "We couldn't kill Lynch because he sired us. He got rid of those he didn't sire. He got rid of some he did sire. Our numbers are temporarily depleted, but we have some vamps transferring from our London location here to Chicago. In the meantime, I've been elected the interim head of the clan."

"As long as they comply with the terms we've set here today," Alex said.

"I know a few of those coming in from London," Simon said. "They'll comply."

"They'd better." Alex had his cop face on as well as his vampire glare. "Are we done here?"

Seymour nodded.

Alex looked at a new text on his phone from Nick. "Then I'm gone."

He made one stop on his way to Nick's office in the back of the All Nighter Bar and Grill. He spoke into the hidden voice recognition security box. "To the Vamp Cave."

The hidden entrance immediately opened. Nick, Damon, and Ronan were all waiting for him in the underground room that was the security center for Vamptown.

"Do you have it with you?" Nick asked.

Alex nodded.

"Follow me."

Alex looked around. "Where's Neville?" The computer nerd was usually seated in his chair in front of the various surveillance screens, his fingers flying over the keyboards of his high-tech computer.

"He doesn't need to know about this," Nick said. "No one else does."

Alex eyed them warily. "You're not planning on staking me again, are you?"

"No. That was a mistake," Nick admitted. "I apologize for that error."

"Apology accepted," Alex said. "Where are we going?" he asked as Nick used an eye scanner to enter another area located below the underground room.

"To the safe room," Nick replied.

It didn't seem large enough to be called a room and it didn't have a safe, it had the kind of vault you'd find in a Swiss bank.

"I didn't know this was here," Alex said.

"We're the only ones who do," Damon said. "The secret remains with us."

Nick activated another eye scan, which opened the vault.

Alex reached under his shirt and pulled out The Executioner's journal he'd retrieved.

"Shouldn't we read it first?" Damon said.

"I read it before saving Keira," Alex said. "That's how I knew how to defeat Lynch."

"There could be more useful information in there," Damon said.

"And harmful information about vampires and our blood," Alex said. "We can't afford to let this get into the wrong hands. By the way, I just met with Seymour, and the Gold Coast vamps have voted to halt the auction of the überblood they created."

"Wait, the Gold Coast vampires voted?" Nick said in amazement.

Alex nodded. "I know. Times are changing."

"For the better, I hope." Ronan spoke for the first time.

Alex set the journal inside. He'd stashed it on the boat, cloaking it, while he'd gone to rescue Keira.

Nick quickly closed the vault. "Don't tell Daniella about this or she'll want to stash her secret recipe for red velvet cupcakes in here."

"And Zoe would want to put the secret recipe for her Revive citrus soap in there," Damon said.

"Sierra would want to put the latest draft of her book in there," Ronan said.

"What would Keira want to put in here?" Nick asked Alex.

"The journal," Alex replied.

"What do you think the men are up to?" Daniella asked as she, Zoe, Sierra and Keira sat around the sofa and chairs in the loft.

"No good, most likely," Sierra said.

"I don't know. I think they've done a lot of good things," Keira said.

"That's because you're an optimist," Daniella said as she handed Keira a red velvet mini cupcake.

"I'm a realist," Keira said.

"A realist who is going to live a long time," Zoe said.

"I love Alex," Keira quietly admitted.

"Of course you do," Zoe said, patting her on the shoulder. "What's not to love about him?"

"The fact that he's a vampire," Keira said.

"And you're the granddaughter of a hunter destined to fall for him and no one else. It's so romantic. Not as romantic as Damon and me," Zoe added with a grin.

"Not as romantic as Ronan and me," Sierra stated emphatically.

"Nick and I have you all beat," Daniella said. "No contest."

"It takes a special woman to love a vampire," Sierra said.

"Or a special witch," Zoe said.

"Right." Sierra agreed. "Or a special witch."

"Alex hasn't said he loves me," Keira admitted.

"He will. I've seen the way he looks at you. He tells you with his eyes," Zoe said. "Have you told him how you feel about him?"

"No, but I plan to as soon as he comes back."

"I'm back," Alex said as he suddenly appeared.

He wasn't alone. Nick, Damon, and Ronan were with him.

"What's wrong?" Keira immediately asked.

"We've been apart from the women we love for too long," Nick said as he pulled Daniella into his arms and kissed the cream cheese frosting from her lips before zooming off with her.

"Ditto," Damon said, tugging Zoe into his arms and taking off with her.

Ronan grinned and pulled Sierra to her feet before picking her up and disappearing with her.

"How do they not run into one another when they are all moving so fast?" Keira asked.

"I'll ask the questions for now," Alex said before taking her in his arms and peeling her clothes from her.

She blinked at him. "Talk about fast."

"I intend to go slow from here on out." Picking her up, he carried her to the huge bed in the other side of the loft . . . the bed she'd eyed from the moment he'd brought her here. Lowering her onto the black satin comforter, he hovered over her, propped up on one muscular arm, while using his free hand to caress her from shoulder to thigh.

"Is this good for you?" he murmured.

"Mmmm."

He paused to rub his thumb over her left nipple. "Better?"

She arched her back as pleasure coursed through her. "Yes."

He trailed his fingers lower to the juncture of her thighs. "Even better?"

"Oh yes, yes!"

Her orgasm seized hold as her entire being pulsated.

"Want more?"

"Yes!" she gasped, reaching for him.

He thrust into her with one smooth move that had her vagina clutching him. She hung on to his shoulders and wrapped her legs around his hips as she soared to new heights of ecstasy.

Alex came a short time later, stiffening in her arms before collapsing on top of her. A moment later he rolled so she was spread atop him.

"Good?" he murmured.

"I'm at a loss for words," she whispered.

She felt his chuckle. "That's a first," he said.

Resting her cheek on his bare chest, she said the words she'd been feeling. "I love you."

There was no reply. Keira didn't need the words in that moment. She wanted them but she didn't need them because Alex threaded his fingers through her hair with tender gentleness. "You're The One for me." His voice was husky. "The only one for me."

Keira fell asleep knowing that she was with the only one for her.

One month later...

"Keira, you're crying," Alex said in alarm as he walked into the loft after work.

"It's my birthday."

"I know. Do you always cry on your birthday?"

"My mom got me a present," she said unsteadily.

"What? How is that possible?"

"She arranged it ahead of time," Keira said. "I just got the email about it today."

Alex wiped the tears from her cheeks with the ball of his thumb. "You should have called me. I would have come home to be with you."

"It's the photographs. Here look." She showed him her laptop screen.

"Is that you?"

Keira nodded. "It's me eating my first chocolate cookie. I was just a toddler. These are the family photos I lost in the photo album in my apartment fire. My mom scanned them all before she was killed and had them stored in the cloud." Her tears fell again as she showed Alex the email from her mom that the cloud company had sent along with the link.

> *Surprise! I scanned these photos while you were out of town speaking at that conference up in Madison. I still prefer the real thing, but I think you'll like these and be impressed with your mom's tech savvy! Love you, honey.*
>
> *Happy birthday,*
> *Mom*

Alex took Keira in his arms. "I'm so sorry Lynch took your mom from you. Her and your grandfather."

"My grandfather sent me to you because he knew and finally accepted that we were meant to be together."

Alex tightened his hold on her. "Meant to be together forever."

"Do I have forever?"

"As you know, I asked Simon to do some research into that and he got back to me today. It appears that because of your blaster skills and our bonding that you will live as long as I do."

Keira hugged him fiercely. "That's all I want."

"Really?" he teased her. "Because I had the feeling that you might also want some red velvet cupcakes from Heavenly Cupcakes."

"Daniella is bringing a cake for the party later this evening." Keira had protested that she didn't need a party but everyone had been adamant—especially Bruce, who had put together a theme. He'd pushed for a circus theme but when that hadn't flown he'd gone with typewriters and writing. Keira had already met Liz and Benji for lunch at Keira and Benji's favorite hamburger place. He'd completely recovered and was doing great.

The party tonight comprised Vamptown residents, including Fiona, who'd moved into the vampire neighborhood.

"I know Daniella is bringing a cake," Alex said. "But she grabbed me on my way in and asked me to give you this." He released her and handed her a cardboard cupcake carrier box. Inside was a cupcake charm bracelet and a small card that said, *Welcome to the family.*

Beside that was a mini cupcake and a birthday cake candle. *Make a special wish just for you,* Daniella wrote. *There will be more candles on the cake, but this is to get you started.*

Keira stuck the pink birthday candle into the cupcake's cheesecake frosting.

"Don't use your blaster skills to light that," Alex said. "Or it could end up scorched all over the wall."

"Hah. Ye of little faith." She waved her index finger over the candle and lit it without incident.

Alex was impressed. "You've been practicing."

"I have," she said.

He nodded toward the cupcake. "Make a wish."

She did before blowing out the candle.

"I know better than to ask what you wished for," Alex said.

"If I tell you, it might not come true," Keira said.

"Is there some rule against showing me?"

"No rule against that," she said with a grin.

He checked his watch. "We've got a good two hours before the party starts."

"We're going to have an *awesome* two hours," she corrected him. "And the party starts now—just you and me."

"Open your present from me first," he said.

"Gladly." She reached for the zipper on his pants.

His laugh was part sexy growl and part appreciative approval. "Hold on."

"I'm trying to," she said, stroking him through the material.

"And I'm trying to give you this." He handed her a small box.

"What is it?"

"Open it and find out."

She did and gasped. "It's beautiful."

"It's a pendant to match your evil eye ring."

She removed it from the box. "Put it on me."

Lifting her hair out of his way, he slid the necklace around her neck and clasped it. Then he added a specialty vamp stroke of his tongue on her nape. "I love you," he murmured against her skin, saying the words for the first time.

Keira moaned her pleasure. This was what she'd wished for—an eternity of Alex's love. She felt it in his touch and his caresses. She was enough of a realist to know that there could be challenging times ahead, but she was enough of a romantic to know that with Alex at her side she could do anything . . . and that she would.

Don't miss the Entity novels by Cat Devon!

The Entity Within
Sleeping with the Entity
Love Your Entity

Available from St. Martin's Paperbacks